CHAPTER 1

IT HAPPENED

I t happened much faster than the movies depicted. They came and they conquered. There was no hero to save us. We were powerless against them.

There was nowhere to hide. They knew where to find us. All of us. My whole world—our whole world—now gone.

And none of it mattered to them.

It was early evening when they came. The three of us were together, as always: Mom, Matthew, and me. Our family routine—the two of them watching television as I drew absentmindedly in my journal in our living room—was one of the things I counted on to calm me. By then, Dad had moved on with his new family.

As the day wound to an end and the sun began to set, I looked up from my journal to catch the orange and red-tinged sky shine brilliantly over the shrubbed hill behind our house. A small breeze came through the open window, not strong enough to cool the stuffy room. My blank stare out the window was broken by my lab pup, Thor, trying to curl up on my lap. I ruffled his big yellow head, wondering why he was so smothering.

Thor was still settling when the ceiling lights began to flicker.

We all looked up and then at one another. My little brother just shrugged his shoulders.

"That's strange," Mom said, standing up from her chair and moving toward the light switch to investigate.

I began to slightly worry, just as I always did. Sensing my uneasiness, my pup leaned against me, placing his furry paw on my lap and panting in my face.

"Thor, your breath is awful." I pushed him away gently, wondering why his puppy training didn't stop his clinginess.

"Talking to your dog again, Lauren?" Matthew snickered, smiling at me through his wispy blond bangs. My brother delighted in teasing me whenever he got the chance. His charm worked on others, but not on me. When I glared at him, he quickly turned back to the safety of the TV, just as it blinked into perpetual refresh mode.

"Ugh," Mom sighed in frustration.

With the lights still flickering and the TV out, I began to feel as unsettled as Thor did. I reached for my phone beside me on the couch, almost involuntarily. It was still playing the video I'd forgotten to close out.

Nothing can be wrong if my phone still works, I thought. *Right?*

"Another rolling blackout," Mom said, her tone irked. "It must be this awful heat surging the 'brilliant' new systems . . . *again*."

"Maybe," I mumbled, only halfway listening as I fumbled with the phone. Like the TV, it was now frozen.

L. GALUPPO

ECO REIGN

WARNING: THE BARRIERS BURN

RIVER GROVE
BOOKS

Published by River Grove Books
Austin, TX
www.rivergrovebooks.com

Distributed by River Grove Books

Design and composition by Greenleaf Book Group
Cover design by Greenleaf Book Group

Publisher's Cataloging-in-Publication data is available.

Print ISBN: 978-1-63299-952-8

eBook ISBN: 978-1-63299-953-5

First Edition

"They should never have changed everything," Mom fumed, about to go on her typical rant about unnecessary upgrades to the power grid. But I sensed that there was more to what was going on than a blackout. I couldn't shake the pressing feeling that something was just not right.

A cool burst of air blew through the open window, smacking me in the face. *That's it*, I thought. It was the message I needed to venture outside on my own and find out what the hell was going on.

"Guys, you gotta come see this!" I yelled from outside the front door. "Mom, this is no rolling blackout." And this had nothing to do with the climate change Mom didn't believe in, either. Despite my concern with the crazy, fast-moving storm approaching—nothing like I had seen before—I still delighted in proving my mom wrong on those rare occasions that I could.

Mom and Matthew rushed outside to join me just as strong winds closed in around us. Matthew pointed into the distance, where blackened clouds swiftly swallowed the sky's vanishing colors, leaving only a faint glimmer from the setting sun. From our yard, we could see below us just outside of town, the clouds growing thicker as the storm came closer.

"It *is* a rather bizarre weather disturbance," Mom admitted, staring at the ominous clouds.

My brother shrugged again.

Barreling toward us was a twisting tempest as thick as a mountain, which continued to expand at an alarming rate.

"Are those . . . cyclones?" Matthew asked in disbelief.

"This is California. We don't get cyclones." I stated the obvious, having nothing else to say.

"Mom," I squeaked out, grabbing her hand, hoping to trigger a stronger reaction. I tried my best to pull back from the swirling, dark thoughts of last month's attack to convince myself that my growing distress was irrational.

She squeezed my hand back. "You'll be okay, Lauren. Just breathe."

Thor rushed to my side, sensing my trouble from afar, and I stroked his soft, delicate ears, seeking comfort. With Mom on one side and my puppy on the other, my breathing tempered a bit.

"*They* don't seem bothered by it," my brother calmly noted, pointing down the hillside toward town. He shrugged yet again as his hair blew furiously from side to side. "Maybe this is just . . . nothing?" he added. I was dumbfounded by his lack of awareness, while at the same time amazed by his ability to shrug off any worry of any kind. It was easy to forget that most other kids—almost everyone, really—didn't share my discernment for danger.

Maybe he was right this time. After all, traffic continued to crawl leisurely through town as people went about their business, seemingly unaware of the changing sky above them. But when I looked up at the sky, feeling the deep intensity in the air, I knew.

None of this was okay.

"What are they all doing?" I groused. "Can't they see what's going on?"

Just as Mom registered my alarm and looked at me, the winds abruptly faded. The dark clouds parted, revealing the most beautiful light within. Awed, even my puppy wagged his tail. I sensed an unexpected calm from that glowing light.

Suddenly, just as unexpectedly, the dark clouds engulfed the sky again, blotting out the remaining sunlight. Shards of lightning cracked in the air. Thunder boomed. In each flash of light, I could see my mom's face, worried at last. I hadn't seen that look since the day a month ago, when she found me at school, holding Matthew's bleeding, unconscious head in my lap.

As terrible as that day was, I had a feeling that this was even worse.

My worry grew the moment Thor whimpered, as if in pain. Seconds later, we grabbed at our ears, frantically trying to keep out the piercing, high-pitched hum my pup had heard first. In the shadows next to me, Matthew was trying to shake the pain away.

As quickly as it had all started, it stopped. No more thunder. No more clouds. No more piercing hum. And no lights shining anywhere. None could be seen in our house, nor from the town below. It looked like midnight, even though the sun had been setting merely a moment ago.

Our world was dark and silent.

All that we relied on to survive no longer worked.

All that we knew had become powerless.

Even my phone was dead—I checked.

The disturbing darkness of it all was palpable. Even Matthew could not deny it now.

My hands dropped to my sides, and I reached for Thor.

While my brother and I remained motionless—bewildered by it all—Mom reacted, wrapping her arms around us and propelling us through the silent and dark obscurity to our house. Her hand, which grasped my shoulder, was shaking. The only sounds we heard were our footsteps, and beside me, Thor's panting.

When another burst of light exploded high above our heads, Mom forced us through the door, calling out, "My God!" Her panic was unmistakable.

Peering out through the open door, I saw something, almost invisible, reach across the sky, slowly closing in and swallowing up the world around us: a magnificent, dazzling, purple-pixelated dome. It would soon cover everything in sight, from horizon to horizon.

The dome became our only light.

"What's wrong with your mouth?" Matthew blurted out, pulling away from Mom as she slammed the door behind us. Her teeth glowed creepily like she was under a blacklight. She put her hand over her face, patting it to discover what Matthew had seen. I spun Matthew toward me to inspect—his glowed too. Reaching toward me, he held up a strand of my blond hair, displaying its own sickly sheen. Even the white bonsai tree on his shirt he still had on since karate class gleamed unnaturally.

Mom swore under her breath, and her eyes widened in the purple light. "They're going to be looking for everyone." Panic had seeped into her voice. "We need to hide."

"*They* . . . ?" Matthew and I asked in unison.

I shot a look at Matthew.

"We have no underground shelter, no basement," she continued. "We need to leave the house." As she spoke, I couldn't help but stare at her glowing teeth.

"The caves!" Matthew shouted. "We can hide in there."

"Yes," Mom responded, trying to calm the panic in her voice as she weighed our options. "Grab what you can. Water, food, extra clothes. Quickly, and put something dark on." We scattered, each darting to our own bedroom, guided by the only light from the glowing dome.

I looked around my room, unsure about what to take. Everything was my treasured possession, and all in meticulous order. I didn't want to leave any of it.

"Hurry!" Mom shouted from down the hall.

I hurried to go and grabbed my backpack, shoving in any dark clothes I could find, before struggling into a dark hoodie. Turning to go, I noticed the stuffed kitty on my bed. I'd had it since I was a baby—it went on all our family vacations with me. I shoved it in too and left.

I ran to the kitchen with Thor by my side and threw a few protein bars into my pack along with my drawing journal and pens. I grabbed Thor's leash for the trip . . . or whatever this was.

Mom stopped packing her supplies, just as I opened Thor's food bin. "Lauren, no."

"What?" I said, dropping the lid to the bin.

"We can't risk him barking." She grabbed the leash and unhooked it from Thor's collar. "He stays." Unaware, Thor excitedly wagged his tail as my mom filled his bowl with food.

"Mom, how can you even suggest that?" I cried, wrapping my arms around Thor's neck.

Mom was unmoved. "He stays here, inside, so he can't follow us."

"I can't believe this. You—"

"We'll be back for him, Lauren, I promise." She patted my back, then pushed me gently toward the front door. "*Matthew*."

My brother came rushing toward us, kitchen knives in hand. "I can create a weapon system to protect us. We'll fight back," Matthew declared, not even knowing what we'd be fighting.

Mom disarmed him and handed each of us a dark scarf. "Wrap your hair and face in these." As she wrapped hers, she explained, "They'll keep our blond from glowing."

Before I could say another goodbye to Thor, Mom pushed us out the front door and slammed it shut.

But I couldn't move another step.

The dome had grown.

It was everywhere, all around us, engulfing the whole town and even beyond. Its purple glow showcased the chaos it wrought—the honking, the screaming, the utter panic. Desperate and uncertain, people were trying to flee. Some ran aimlessly through the streets. Others had tried to get away in their cars and were now trapped in bumper-to-bumper traffic. Quickly realizing they were going nowhere fast, drivers had deserted their cars and further obstructed the way out of town. Trying to clear the way, some slammed their own vehicles into the abandoned cars. Some drove into streetlights and signs, while others steered onto the sidewalks, careening past the terrified pedestrians.

Stunned, the three of us watched from the safety of the hillside, away from the heavy despair overtaking the town. I felt the desperation as people struggled toward safety, trying to get somewhere, anywhere—yet all going nowhere.

Until the calmness set in.

Starting from the outskirts of town, the chaos began subsiding and quiet fell—the honking, the crying, the screaming—bit by bit, but not because the threat had stopped. The dome was still there, pulsing purple. The people, however, were not.

Right before our eyes, people were simply disappearing. It was as though they were being plucked from existence, one by one, mysteriously collected from where they once stood—from the sidewalks, from the car. A swift disappearance, as if they never even existed.

Just gone.

"Lauren, the caves. We have to go." Mom's voice came to me as a faint echo, which often happened when I was scared—but never in my life had I been *this* scared. I remained paralyzed, watching it all unfold. All I could do to respond was point down the hill.

The sounds of panic were muffled, with only a few stragglers continuing to flee, seeking safety. That was the most chilling part. They didn't even realize what was about to happen to them, seemingly unaware of the disappearances of the people behind them.

I heard Thor whining and scratching from the other side of the door. My heart ached. Mom had promised we would be back for him, but I was not entirely sure it was a promise she would be able to keep.

"Please," Mom begged, pulling at me, "we *have* to *go*!"

"I—I don't know how to move. I don't know . . ." My voice trailed off. My legs were uncontrollably shaking, just like that day I dragged Matthew, bleeding, off the school bus. "Look at everyone, Mom. They're . . . *disappearing*."

She grabbed my face and turned it away from the nightmare advancing below. "*Lauren*."

"What's she doing?" Matthew shouted. "She's gotta move."

At the sound of his voice, I somehow managed to unfreeze, and together we began running up the steep hill behind our house. Matthew had been clever to think of the caves—a spot he and his crew explored almost daily.

"Go, go faster." Mom whispered from behind us, breathless.

We ran until my throat tightened, and my lungs burned. Whenever I began to slow, Mom pushed against my back to help me keep going. As sharp pains dug into my side, I pleaded, "Can we rest for just a second?"

She held her finger to her mouth and then pointed to a large bush. We scrambled over to hide behind it, trying to catch our breath and assess our whereabouts.

Matthew, barely needing the break, peered around the bush. "There. We're close."

The caves were in sight.

I should have felt relief, but instead I was concerned with what had happened in town—what had happened to all those people we knew.

Matthew must have read my thoughts. "It's so quiet," he said. As our heavy breathing subsided, it was downright silent. And not because we were so high up in the hills, away from it all. No, it was quiet because they were gone. All of them.

Mom whispered, "We're close now. Don't look back. We've got to keep going." We couldn't help it—we were kids. We looked down the hill, especially after she told us not to.

She grabbed our shoulders, lifting us off the ground. "*Run!*"

Matthew was up first, and then somehow, I was running again. A burst of strength and energy propelled me toward the caves, despite an almost vertical climb to reach them. I had no other choice but to scramble ever upward.

We have a chance, I thought, focusing my eyes on the caves above. *We're going to make it.* Deep in my heart, I knew we were going to make it—together, the three of us, just as we always had. I felt relief, even excitement.

Until . . . I tripped. I was so tired. Already, I pushed myself more than I ever thought possible, and even more after that.

It was Matthew who lifted me up this time. Mom had fallen behind. As Matthew and I fumbled in my attempt to recover, Mom caught up to us and lifted me from the other side. We all pushed on, together.

"We're here," Matthew whispered. The entrance to the caves was right before us.

Mom raised her finger to her mouth, motioning for us to be quiet just as the barking reached our ears.

Looking down, I saw Thor's glowing fur in the distance as he sped toward us, barking as loud as he could, letting me know he was there for me. I didn't even have the time to worry about what Mom was going to do with him when a thunderous, unearthly growl unleashed above our heads.

"Hold on to me," Mom screamed as she rose inexplicably into the air.

Matthew grabbed at the space where she had just been, and I tried reaching for the rocks, but we were being sucked upward too, off the ground, toward the obscure and terrifying unknown. The force was too strong to stop.

Mom grappled at the air below her, violently grabbing for the two of us, resolute on keeping us together. Her nails dug into my side just as Thor's barking, far below, faded. I could only hope she had Matthew in her grip, too.

My last memory of that moment was of me being sucked into a darkness and the air being squeezed out of my lungs, while I realized that there was no guarantee we would have been safe in those caves anyhow.

Everything around me turned black.

We were taken.

CHAPTER 2

CONTAINMENT

Am I dead?

That was my first thought when my eyes wouldn't open and my body couldn't move. The only proof of life—my life—was the movement of my eyes underneath my incapacitated eyelids. I noticed the sound of breathing with the air moving in and out of my nose.

I was not dead after all.

But where was I?

Although I could sense the cold against my skin, I couldn't lift a finger. My hands rested on the cement beneath me—a floor. I was inside . . . somewhere, lying on the ground. One thing was for sure: I was no longer on that mountain, climbing toward the caves.

The ability to move returned slowly. My bottom lip shifted from side to side, a movement patterned after my eyes. Although I managed a small peek through my left eye, the brightness of the room prevented me from seeing any details. By the time I could shift my head away from the blinding shine, my right eye had popped open. Still, the rest of my body decided not to awaken.

With only my eyes adjusted and neck working, I looked upward toward the ceilings that rose conspicuously above me. The walls were exceptionally tall and rounded like a dome at the top. Sunlight poured through the windows, which sat high atop the colossal steel domelike structure—too high for me to see what was outside. It was no longer nighttime. How long had I been unconscious?

My pinky finger finally stirred. With each effort, I continued to will the rest of my body to wake up. Soon I could move a little more, wiggling all my fingers and then my toes, until at last movement flowed throughout my body.

After I struggled to sit up, I began patting my pant legs down. This became a familiar comfort for me after the bus attack, which recently had happened. I just could not believe something bad was happening to me again.

I was in a massive room, a structure that looked oddly familiar. Strangely, I was surrounded by a sea of unconscious people, with only a few others sitting up like me. It did not take too long before others began their journey in moving their body parts while they stirred awake.

"Thank God," I breathed, finding Mom and Matthew beside me, still unconscious.

"Mom, Matthew." I nudged them to wake.

They didn't move.

"Get up," I whispered, and I bumped them harder.

They did not stir, not even a little.

Panicking, I pushed harder, rocking their motionless bodies.

"Wake up!" I hollered, without caring about any of the others around us.

Matthew jumped to his feet, with his fists closed in front of his chest, ready for a fight. Mom abruptly sat upright. Saying nothing, she grabbed Matthew's arm and pulled him back down to the cement floor beside us. She rolled us both into her arms and held us tight. Judging by the death grip she had on us, I suspected that she intended to never let us go.

"Look at all these people," she finally said, releasing her grip around us just slightly. Our heads swiveled in unison, taking it all in.

I had nothing to say, no words to describe the improbability of what I was seeing—not only the lifeless-looking people covering almost every inch of the floor, but also more unconscious people every few seconds filling what little empty space was left around us. Every time a new body appeared near us, crowding the area even more, I flinched. Mom patted my shoulder and then stood up, lifting Matthew and me along with her.

"A body better not land right on us," Matthew blurted out.

As more people stirred awake, some began shouting out names of those I could only assume were their family, friends, and loved ones. The shouting became louder and louder as the voices competed with one another to be heard. The littlest of voices, barely heard, just calling out "Mom" and "Dad." Some of the youngest ones just stood in place, crying, and I felt their paralyzing fear. Had Matthew and Mom not been beside me, I would have been just as terrified. I wanted to go to these children and tell them everything would be okay, but I didn't—mostly because I did not even know if that was true.

Increasing panic set in as the people began to actively search around the structure calling out names, looking for anyone they knew, pushing their way through the masses, and tripping over those who were still unconscious on the ground. If Mom had not held us together as we were suctioned off the mountain's ground, it could have been me in here alone, panicked, calling out to no avail, just as others around me were doing. We were together—I suppose we were the lucky ones.

"People have just been . . . appearing," I overheard a woman sitting next to Mom say. She was shorter than me and rounded at the waist, wearing a flowery, flowing shirtdress. The gray strands running through her light brown hair made me think she was older than my mom. She seemed dazed but managed a little smile when the man next to her squeezed her hand. "Just . . . out of thin air."

I leaned in to eavesdrop.

"What the—" Matthew shouted, bumping my shoulder and almost clipping my face as he recoiled from a person who had just appeared behind him, immobile like the rest.

I shoved him off me. "*Shh*," I admonished, pointing at Mom. I wanted to listen.

"Watch this," Matthew said, looking down at the new arrival. Before I could stop him, he nudged a limp arm with his foot and laughed.

I couldn't believe he would be enjoying this moment. We had no idea what was going on. All around us, people were just appearing and were alone. Plus, I hated it when he included me when he misbehaved. Mom always ended up more disappointed with me. "You're the older one," she would say. "You should know better." Meanwhile, Matthew always seemed to get out of trouble.

The person on the floor then stirred. Matthew dropped the arm, and it fell back down abruptly, followed by a moan. We both turned quickly away, trying to hide our involvement.

"You shouldn't have done that," I lectured him under my breath, hoping Mom didn't notice. I knew if she asked what he was doing,

I would be the one to give us up. I was never good at keeping things from her, and she used that to her advantage.

Mom saw none of this, luckily. Her attention was on the man and the woman next to us, whose hands were still joined tightly.

"We saw you three come in together, holding on to each other," the woman was saying. She watched the man with admiration on her face. "Pat and I didn't land together, but somehow he found me."

The man nodded, and his almond-shaped eyes softened with affection. "Followed the love in your voice, Cecie," he said quietly. The two of them smiled warmly at each other.

"That's very sweet," Mom said to my surprise. She had never been sentimental—too bitter from the divorce for any of that. "I'm Joliet, but people call me Jules. This is Lauren and Matthew."

"Your children. Are they twins?" Cecie asked.

Once the woman mentioned us, I nudged Matthew to stop tormenting the unconscious lying beside us. Mom looked over to find us both suspiciously still.

"Oh, no, they're different ages. Eleven—well, almost twelve now—and fourteen," Mom explained, turning back to Cecie. It never made sense to me when people asked that question, and this was not the first time it was asked. Sure, Matthew and I looked a lot alike—and a lot like our mom, with blond hair, green eyes, and fair skin that bronzed in the summer. But I was taller than my brother and clearly older. Then again, I often found that not much of what people said was all that sensible.

"Do you know what's going on? Or what we're doing here?" Mom continued.

Cecie shook her head. "No one seems to know. We're all just . . . waiting."

"For what?" Mom asked.

Cecie shrugged and said, "To leave."

"Some people are saying the government brought us here to protect us," Pat interjected, his tone urgent. "Maybe some sort of invasion from the Russians, or China?"

Cecie's admiring expression at her husband quickly faded into a rigid glare. "We really don't know if any of that's true," she replied through pursed lips. "No one knows."

I didn't even try to hide my contempt. This woman seemed to know nothing, yet she was trying to quiet her husband, who was at least looking for an explanation. People were still just appearing out of nowhere, but why? No one had any answers. Worse, no one was asking the obvious question.

"Why don't we just *leave*?" I asked, pushing Mom aside so I could respond to Cecie's conscious avoidance. "Walk out? You know, through the exit?"

Cecie stared at me, as if offended that a mere child would challenge her. "Sweetie," she said, which I sensed was not meant to be endearing, "there are massive doors at the back of this thing, but no one can open them. There's no exit, nowhere to go."

"We're trapped," Pat added.

My shoulders sank. It was not the answer I wanted to hear. Worse, I had no way to know if she was right because there were no doors near us. I hugged myself, seeking comfort.

Just like Cecie said, we waited.

As more and more people mysteriously appeared, I suddenly knew how the factory-raised chickens felt, the ones Mrs. Pickering had told our science class about a month ago, the day before our field trip to the sustainable farm.

Every detail of that class came rushing back to me, as if I was sitting in her classroom that day. The voices, the inflections, the time, date, and every detail of the persons around me—I remembered it all . . . as I always do.

In my mind, I could hear her voice, "Okay, class, what'd y'all do over the weekend to make the world a better place than how you found it?" Every Monday morning, Mrs. Pickering started class this way. "Anyone?"

And groans from the class always followed. But never from me, nor from the smartest kid in our school, Milo. Milo came from a privileged family, I recalled, with parents who were well educated and connected. They lived in a gated community and were members of the country club. "The best money could buy," was his parents' favorite saying, he explained, with a sense of shame.

"I found a baby bird and put it back in its nest," Paula from class said one day.

"Next time, you may just want to observe it, as it might just fly away." Mrs. Pickering had an answer for everything, it seemed.

"I threw my trash in the garbage and not on the ground," Bodie said and laughed, while his football buddies chuckled along.

After pausing, Mrs. Pickering supportively replied, "Good work, Bodie, but try picking up someone else's trash and throw that away too. That's how you'll help the environment even more. Anyone else?"

"I got my mom to buy cage-free eggs," Liza responded.

"That's great. Though the better option is organic, free-range eggs. You'd think the 'cage-free' chickens are free to roam, but really, they're kept in a large steel containment, with hardly any windows and big fans that just spread the putrid smell around. It's still unsanitary corporate poultry factory farming." The chickens didn't live "free," she explained—they merely existed, packed and stepping on each other, pecking at anything on the ground, including the poop.

"Gross," Bodie blurted out.

Fascinated by the topic, I had raised my hand. "Did you know nineteen billion chickens inhabit the Earth? And 1.4 billion cows?

The environmental effects of the livestock industry—" Sharing random facts was normal for me. Mom called me a walking encyclopedia because of it—though not everyone enjoyed this ability of mine.

Bodie had groaned loudly. "Here she goes again. Does she always have to—"

"I might add, Mrs. Pickering, that our laws are failing the animals and livestock," interjected Milo, while the class groaned even louder.

"*Shh*," Mrs. Pickering called out. "Milo, go on."

"Well, they give us life by feeding us. The least we can do is give them a decent life beforehand," he continued. "But even more significant, feeding the billions of animals held as livestock means destroying habitats around the world, which has, in turn, caused and continues to cause extinction events to the wild animals."

While most were rolling their eyes, I soaked it all in. Mrs. Pickering and Milo both smiled at me, while I nodded in agreement. I was glad not to be the only one concerned about the terrible conditions facing animals on Earth.

Reliving this moment in class and about the chickens made me realize our conditions in this holding area were not much of an improvement. I felt just like them, trapped and cramped in a steel container . . . seemingly doomed.

I snapped out of it and turned back to Matthew. I was no longer interested in hearing the adults' conversation, which provided no answers anyway. He was still nudging the new arrivals around, enjoying it more than he should be. And I watched longer than I should have.

"Matthew, how's your head?" Mom pulled him close, inspecting the shaved area through its growth patches. Matthew was still recovering after the bus attack. "I should've asked you much sooner."

"I'm okay, Mom." He pulled away.

"Are either of you sore?" Mom asked, turning to me after Matthew resisted. "My entire body aches."

I rubbed my arms and then my legs, squeezing to test how tender they were after being inexplicably plucked from where I last stood on Earth before being dropped in—wherever we were. "Now that you mention it, I do kinda hurt," I replied.

"You two need to get some rest," Mom suggested rather strongly.

"I'm not sore or tired," Matthew insisted, sounding impatient. "We should go look around. Try to get out of here."

I felt the same as he did. I wanted to get out, or at least try to get back home and to Thor.

"Matthew, while you were tormenting those unconscious, I was asking around about how to get out. The doors can't open." Mom paused, waiting for Matthew to apologize. He looked a bit startled that she knew what he had done to those people, but he didn't deny it. I was startled too—by her tempered manner, especially after Matthew had just raised his voice to her. Her response would have been far different had we been at home.

She took a deep breath and continued. "There's nowhere to go."

"If the doors won't open," he persisted, "why can't we try to find an opening somewhere else?"

Mom shook her head. "For all we know, we may be let out of here soon," she answered. "Let's rest for now and see how this plays out."

We stayed in the same spot where we landed, claiming it as our own. Mom shifted us into a small circle, facing inward after a couple of the newest arrivals fell too close to us.

"This place looks familiar," Matthew said, as if reading my mind. His neck strained as he looked up toward the high ceiling. "Are we in the hangars outside of town?"

"I think you're right," I replied. "I learned about these in Mr. Prat's history class in the fourth grade. Five minutes before the bell rang to let us out for spring break that year, he showed us photographs depicting how massive these are; he explained that they housed blimps during World War II. Seventeen stories high and more than one thousand feet long. This place totally matches the pictures."

I pointed to the wall and traced it with my finger to the ceiling. "See the rounded walls? It forms a colossal-size cement tube." From where we sat, however, I could not see the front to confirm if the doors were oddly square shaped like the ones in the pictures.

"Yup, Mr. Prat's class." Matthew nodded. "I came here on a field trip. Mom, remember? You came with us."

Mom did not respond while she continued to assess our surroundings. She was unusually quiet.

"Mom?" I prodded to see if we were right.

"I think you kids could be onto something," Mom responded finally. "There's four of them at the old, abandoned military base. These structures were deteriorating after they stopped the funding, but they were just too big and expensive to bring down. Look over there."

She pointed to some scaffolding against the walls. "That's probably left over from attempts to repair this place. People are trying to climb it, but it looks seriously unsteady."

"What are we doing in here?" I whispered. They both ignored me.

"The ceilings open up—that's how they got the blimps inside," Matthew said, apparently becoming a self-appointed expert on the matter. "Like ten of them can fit in here at the same time. Blimps are *huge*."

"If there are three other hangars, I wonder if people are in the others," Mom said slowly. "Keep an eye out for your father. He could be here somewhere."

It was strange to hear her worry, after all these years, about where my dad might be. Matthew and I lived with our mom after he left when I was five years old. Even though I thought she was still pretty, she never dated again after he left. Her life was all about Matthew and me.

Mom carried all the burdens of our little family ever since dad left. She did everything for us. My father didn't help with anything, not even rent—and she reminded us about it constantly. She would always say none of it was our fault, but she kinda made it feel like it was. She was just tired, I suppose. At least that was how she explained it.

Although Matthew and I were closer than most siblings, going through all of it together, we still had our fair share of bickering. Mom would try to get us to stop fighting by reminding us that we'd only have each other one day when she would be gone. Although it made me sad thinking she would be gone one day, it never worked. When we did go at it, Matthew rarely escaped unscathed. But he was scrappy and usually retaliated with a punch or two. He was too scrawny for it to actually hurt me.

Given what we were facing, I guess Mom realized we would want to know where Dad was, or if he was safe. I hadn't even thought about him until she mentioned it, but now I worried about where he might be.

Matthew stood up. "Anthony Tomasso!" he yelled. "Tony Tomasso! Tony Tomas—Dad!" I stood up and called out too. Our shouts were lost among all the others. We moved to step away, hoping to look deeper into the crowd, but Mom pulled us back down.

"We are *not* separating," she commanded, squeezing our wrists just enough for us to know she really meant it. "Just because we know where we are and that we aren't too far from home, it still doesn't explain *why* we're here. Or how we got here." She made it clear she was to be strictly obeyed on this one. "We're going to sit here for now until we get some answers."

Other people around us had begun to sit and rest in small groups, just as we had done. I sensed that being transported here and the fear of what would happen next had started taking its toll on us all.

With nothing to do, I finally laid my head on my mom's lap and closed my eyes, while I listened to the names called out over the crowd. As time passed, the calls became less frequent, and an eerie quiet fell.

CHAPTER 3

NOT ALONE

Thunderous booms startled me from sleep.

I sat up straight and dug my hands into Mom's leg. She jumped—probably awakening in shock, just as I had. The sounds of the bombs triggered all my fears, and the memories of the attack came rushing back.

"Mom, it's a bomb!" screamed Matthew, scrambling to his feet. "We're being bombed!"

Hundreds of faces turned to look at my brother. People mumbled and shifted in their seats, alarmed, as if Matthew was some sort of authority instead of just someone who had played too many video games.

His reaction surprised me. He hardly flinched when the storm first happened before we were taken. Yet as the explosions roared on, he seemed very worried. I squeezed Mom's leg again.

Mom pulled Matthew down to the floor. "You're scaring people. Do you want to create hysteria?" she scolded. "Listen, the sounds are far away from here, almost as if it's in town. I don't think they'd collect us in here, just to bomb us."

Once again, I wondered: *They . . . ?*

Matthew nodded somberly before settling back down next to us.

"Just stay close." Mom wrapped her arms around us, forming a huddle, and began humming her favorite song from church as if to drown out the terrifying booms. Whenever she tried to comfort us, she hummed this song. I grabbed her hand, never wanting to let go.

We sat huddled together in a tight circle, flinching with every thundering boom. We stayed like that for what seemed like for hours.

The booming sounds faded off into the distance just as the sunlight shining through the windows was replaced with darkness. The hangar was lit only by a bizarre, unsettling purplish glow. At first, I thought it was emergency lighting from when the military occupied the hangar, but then I realized it was the same purple radiance that had descended on our town after the violent storm, upending my life and dropping us in this hangar. The darkness, the sinister glow, the groans of the people around me, the faded sounds of the bombs—each provocation made things worse, and I could not sleep.

Eventually the threatening sounds ended, Mom's grip eased, and Matthew's shoulders lowered. He shook his arms to force feeling back into them. I stretched out to release the tension of clenching together for far too long.

While I doubted that anything survived the bombings given the intensity and duration of them, the structure in which we were being held was left unscathed—for the time being, anyway.

"We survived the night," I announced, pointing upward. The sun peered faintly through the windows above. The people around us looked up, too, to the sliver of sky we could see through the glass panes near the top of the hangar ceiling—a light-pinkish hue.

I pulled my cell phone from my backpack, hoping against hope. Matthew peered eagerly over my shoulder to see . . . nothing. He slumped against me.

I felt isolated, frustrated, and defeated. We were no longer plugged in twenty-four hours a day to the newsfeeds, the constantly streaming videos, the social media gossip.

"The battery would be out at this point anyway," Matthew rationalized. "And even if it did work, who would we call for help?"

"Maybe some people were never captured," I replied indignantly. "And they're out there waiting for the right time to save us. Maybe the president, the military—*whoever*—went to some underground bunker and are plotting our rescue right now."

Mom gave me a tired smile. "That would be an answer to all of our prayers, my love."

As the day went on and the sun shone brighter, the structure grew hotter and hotter.

"Ugh," I moaned, whipping my black sweatshirt over my head and slamming it to the cement floor. The air was thick. And I was just—hot.

Mom took notice of my fitful response and shook her head slightly as if to say *No.*

"It's hot," I complained, feeling sticky, tired, crowded, and wholly unable to suppress my discomfort any longer. And it wasn't just me. Others were fanning themselves, trying to cool down.

◆

While much of the initial commotion had subsided, a few people still searched listlessly for a friendly face, murmuring names, and stepping over those too hot, scared, or confused to move. Most seemed to be in a holding pattern like us, waiting silently to see what would happen next. It seemed obvious that word had spread: There was nowhere to go.

"Mom, I'm thirsty," Matthew grumbled, rolling up his sleeves. We had neither eaten nor drank since our abduction the previous day.

My stomach rumbled. I grabbed at it, trying to hide the sound from Mom. I gave her a hard enough time with my sweatshirt tantrum and thought she did not need my hunger piled on as well. After all, none of this was her fault.

"Here, both of you, come closer. And be very quiet." Mom whispered, pulling her backpack from underneath her. "Don't let anyone see."

My eyes widened as she handed me a juice box and a packet of crackers—snacks I had delighted over in kindergarten. I tried my best to sneak a sip here and there, and pop the cheesy goodness covertly into my mouth.

"I see that," one particularly observant man snarled, pointing a stubby finger at my mouth, while he rushed over.

I stopped chewing and quickly swallowed.

"Please, this is all we have," Mom quietly pleaded. She unzipped the backpack to show him the small pile of snacks, a couple of cracker packets and the protein bars I had snatched from our kitchen. "We can share with you. But we don't have enough for everyone."

The stubby-fingered man tore the bag from her hands.

Mom didn't try to grab it back—she didn't react at all. She just looked frightened.

"It's all we have," I whispered to Matthew. "What do we do?"

Without hesitating, Matthew jumped up and grabbed the backpack, pulling it back from the man, who refused to let it go. While the two of them struggled over the bag, the man's face reddened as he tugged viciously and cursed at Matthew.

That man would not get away with treating my brother that way. I had to do something.

Just as I jumped up, the man dropped the bag. No longer enraged, his face turned white. His feet were no longer touching the ground. His entire body continued to hover surreptitiously above the ground, rising swiftly two feet, then three feet above the floor.

I kicked the backpack over to Mom while the others watched the man spin around in slow circles, his legs kicking out in protest. His flailing about trying to get back to the hangar floor made it clear that his suspension was clearly beyond his control.

"Help me! Help me!" the man cried out. He was now the one pleading with Mom, as he continued to rise above our heads. Out of reach, there was nothing anybody could do to help.

We stood frozen, seeing nothing to explain what was causing it. The crowd grew even quieter, while his penetrating wailing echoed throughout the hangar, reminiscent of those released during a horror movie.

After an immense swooshing sound, the stubby-fingered man was swept furiously upward, speeding toward the top of the hangar. Just before his body was about to slam into the ceiling, he stopped and levitated far above our heads.

Mid-scream, he simply disappeared.

"What the—what just happened?" Matthew stuttered as he pointed slowly toward the ceiling. His mouth was wide open, just like everyone else's around us, including my own. The panic on his face mirrored what I felt on the inside. "What happened to that guy?" he repeated.

"I . . . have . . . no idea," I responded, knowing Matthew really wasn't expecting an answer. But I just didn't know what else to say. Mom did, however.

"We're not alone in this hangar," she uttered with an air of certainty.

Why did she have to say that? It wasn't what I wanted to hear. Couldn't she have just said that this was all a big misunderstanding, that whatever threat had forced us in here was now gone? Or that none of this mattered, that it would all be over soon? All I wanted to hear was that we were going home today.

But we were not going home—that was not what was happening. No doors were opening. No one was leaving. Instead, one of us was violently whisked away, while more unconscious people appeared around us, crowding us more and more. It suddenly occurred to me that things could continue to get much worse for us.

"We need to be *very* careful what we do in here," Mom continued, speaking slowly to Matthew and me. "Be on guard. Stay alert. Show no emotion."

Under these thoughts, my mind raced, just as my chest tightened. I struggled to breathe.

Mom noticed my reaction. She always noticed.

"Look," she said, grasping my arms to stop me from nervously wiping my sweaty palms down my pant legs. "That man, he tried to hurt us. He's gone because of it."

"But . . . what do you mean?" I asked.

"As twisted as it seems, Lauren, this could mean that we'll be safe in here."

Mom was right . . . again. After she pointed this out, it did not take long for a woman to disappear the same way. She was ferociously elevated to the ceiling before abruptly vanishing, while screaming in terror all the way to the top. The rumor was that she tried to take a child from another mother after losing her own in the transport. It spread that she kept murmuring a name and erratically pacing right before she grabbed the child and started to choke it. As the day progressed, more vanishings happened, again and again. They were the opportunists—those who tried to steal from or hurt others.

Oddly enough, although we were still trapped in the hangar, the vanishings gave me a sense of safety. The bad guys were being swept away. The understanding calmed me—a quiet calm I had not felt since before the attack on the school bus. My thoughts were soothed, knowing that my attacker—and anyone like him—would be among them.

Once the sun retreated from the windows, the purple haze filled the hangar again. We settled in for another night, holding each other's hands. Matthew squeezed my hand each time howling screams rang throughout the ceiling. The screams of those vanishing now muted the calls of the names of those missing. I laid my head on my mom's lap while the screams continued into the night.

I was nearly asleep when Mom began rocking and muttering repeatedly, "We'll go home tomorrow."

CHAPTER 4

THE PRISON
AND ITS GUARDS

We had reached day three of captivity.

We were not released, as Mom had hoped we would be. Everything remained the same: No answers. Still crowded. Hungry. Thirsty. Our little rationing of food and water were almost out—sadly, many had arrived with even less. My hair was a tattered mess, my underarms really smelled, and my face was getting oily.

"I'm worried," Mom said, holding up our last water bottle, showing what little was left. I had just swallowed the last bit of protein bar—my food ration for the day. "We only have enough left for a day. Two at most."

I looked at the people around us. They seemed to be fading.

"Some of these people are looking *really* sick," Mom whispered to us. "Many have been without food and water this whole time."

Matthew took this as his cue to recall stories of shipwrecks and plane crashes and the terrible things people were forced to do when they had nothing to eat for days and days.

"Ugh! Matthew, stop." I shook my head.

Matthew gagged. "No one's going to eat me."

"We'll be saved before any of that happens," I blurted out. "Someone will come. They have to." While I projected confidence in saying this, I really had not convinced myself it was true. I just had to believe, as Mom always encouraged us to do.

Fortunately, the hangar's toilets still worked, and using them was the only time we moved from our spot. Cecie and Pat—the couple we first met upon arrival—saved it for us each time, and we did the same for them. We felt a sense of connection with them once we discovered we were from the same town, Willow Park.

On my way back from a trip to the bathroom, I overheard some people debating our situation and suggesting some insane theories, like aliens. But none of us had any idea what was going on—who had brought us here and why.

I replayed in my mind all the details about what had happened. Everything had stopped—a massive blackout. A mysterious dome had appeared out of nowhere. We had been *lifted into the air*, helpless to stop it, and rendered utterly unconscious. And now we were locked up. Only a powerful force could do something like that. And it likely didn't just happen to our town, our state, our country, but around the entire world. What if no one survived beyond those of us held captive?

"Do you think we're all that's left?" I demanded when I returned to our spot. My eyes nearly swelled as I uttered those words. "I mean, left of the country or the world? Are we it?"

"Honey, I wish I knew," Mom responded gently. "Surely out of the whole world, we're not the only ones—"

"There are the three other hangars, at least," Matthew interrupted.

"Maybe there are containers full of people all over the country," Mom continued.

"It's our own government keeping us here to protect us," Matthew said confidently, taking my theory on as his own.

"So we're in the middle of a hostile takeover by some foreign enemy?" I snapped.

"Yeah, that would explain the bombings," Matthew responded, defensively. "Our government brought us here to protect us from the bombs and keep us safe."

I paused, wondering whether to repeat what I just overheard. "You know, some people are saying it's an alien invasion."

Mom raised an eyebrow. That got her attention. "Aliens? You're talking about aliens now?"

"Could it be possible?" Matthew's voice was so innocent sounding that I instantly regretted sharing the rumor. His tone made it obvious that he was searching for Mom's reassurance that we shouldn't even be entertaining such a possibility.

"Well," Mom paused. "Those *brilliant* tech minds have sent out signals for a very long time, trying to make contact. They've spent billions on the program, sending out rovers and space launches, landing operations on any planet thought to be remotely capable of hosting life forms—"

"But nothing's been found." I interjected. "Plus, you don't even like those tech people, Mom."

"It's not that I don't *like* them," Mom articulated. "I just don't *trust* them. But I have to admit, we're better off because of the explorations—everything you kids know and have today is so far advanced than when I grew up. But all this searching for aliens . . . I don't know. Maybe they found them?"

I waved my hands at both of them, shrugging off the ridiculousness of the conversation. I shouldn't have entertained the idea of aliens. Instead, I dug around in my backpack for my journal and my stuffed kitty, knowing that drawing would take my mind off the uncertainty and dread. Plus, sketching was my typical signal of my refusal to engage with them.

Sitting the kitty in my lap, I began to draw the mountains behind our house with Thor, the last time I saw him running toward us near the caves. I thought about what it must have been like for him. We had just . . . vanished.

But I couldn't shake what Mom had said. Despite my protestations, I found my drawings turned into aliens and spacecraft.

My thoughts turned to our government's unrelenting quest to find extraterrestrial life. The powers that be made every accommodation to achieve this questionable goal, sending thousands of people into space in recent years—most of whom had not returned. Their searches escalated after the near collision of a meteor, which had evidence of indeterminate and unexplainable genetic materials on its surface. The government justified it all under the pretense of keeping us safe from an alien invasion. If anything—anything at all—was actually out there, wouldn't they have found it by now?

This was no alien invasion. Matthew was right. Our captivity *had* to be an unexpected ambush by terrorists or a foreign government, prompting our own government to confine us here until it was safe for us to be let out. It had to be that.

I stopped drawing and looked up from my journal. "The government will save us," I insisted, interrupting Matthew and Mom's game of rock, paper, scissors. "That's what they do, isn't it? They don't leave people behind, locked in a hangar. Someone will come."

They just stared at me silently. What could they say? None of us knew what was going on. Three days had passed, and no uniformed soldiers had burst through the doors to save us. Instead, thousands and thousands of people were left packed into these hangars—and maybe many more like them—with no food, no water, no answers, and no way out.

I could hardly ignore the reality of our dreadful existence. On this third day, things had become even worse. The restless still roamed the hangar, crying out for their loved ones, but I no longer saw any reunions. The shrieks still came regularly from those furiously lifted toward the ceiling. People were forced to step over those who were injured, sick, starving, or just too despondent to move. Then there were the bodies of those who, after arriving, never awoke at all.

On top of all of that, now I was worried about someone trying to eat me.

Thanks, Matthew.

———————◆———————

Mom and Cecie did their best to comfort the little ones around us, alone and whimpering for their parents. Most of them were just too soiled, hungry, and inconsolable to make a difference. An undeniable despair was settling in. It took everything for me to believe that we wouldn't just be left here, just to die.

"We need to get up, look around," Mom instructed, wrinkling her nose and sniffing the air. The afternoon heat in the hangar was stifling again. The stench had worsened.

"What do you mean?" I asked. Just yesterday, she told us to stay put because we would be released . . . we'd go home. But the worry on her face had deepened. "Mom?"

She reached out and pulled Matthew and me closer to her. "I fear that no one is coming. We need to look for a way out," she insisted. "We're going to have to figure this out on our own."

Matthew pulled back from her with his shoulders held high. He looked ready, revitalized even. This was what he wanted to do all along. He began nodding his head as if he'd been plotting our escape plan this entire time.

"My vote is the scaffolding. If we can get over there, I can climb up and see what's going on. It's a good vantage point," Matthew said.

I had forgotten all about the scaffolding, but I caught Matthew surveying them on occasion ever since we arrived. Not many people were on them. They looked unsteady and too tall to climb. I thought we would have a harder time getting up on them than Matthew realized, but we had no reason not to try. Staying put had gotten us nowhere so far.

"Okay then," Mom conceded.

I slipped my stuffed kitty and journal back into my backpack. Mom grabbed each of us by the hand, and we started to move.

"Stay close," Mom said, squeezing our hands.

We shuffled in a single-file line through the tightly packed room, with Mom at the front and me bringing up the rear. I looked over my shoulder to find Cecie with a surprised look on her face, motioning me back to our spot. I think she knew we weren't coming back. I shook my head, and she slowly waved goodbye.

We had abandoned our spot, and as others hurried to fill the space, a sense of sadness came over me. Amid all the confusion, that spot was the only "home" I had known for the past few days. But the sadness was much bigger than that. I missed my real home, my puppy, my best friend, Zary. Where was she now? I missed my bed, our evening routine, the view of town from our house—even school. I would gladly go back to being jeered at in the school hallways by the football crowd if it meant leaving this nightmare behind.

I missed all of it.

As my thoughts swirled about home, my hand loosened around Matthew's. As I nearly let go, his hand closed around mine. We couldn't be separated. He knew that.

"Hold tight," Matthew urged. "We're close."

These were the same words he uttered before we nearly reached the caves. It reminded me that we had a goal now: to get to the other side of the hangar and the scaffolding and find our freedom. No more just waiting around, passing the time. I suddenly felt a little better in spite of the dreadful conditions. In the moment, it did not matter whether we would succeed at escaping—we had a purpose.

Open space between the throngs of people—sitting and standing, alive and some, possibly, dead—grew noticeably smaller and tighter to get through as we got closer to the wall and scaffolding. Before we could reach either one, we had to stop. Standing before us with his arms folded was a large man, one of many in what was a human wall. The people closest to the hangar's side had formed a barricade with their bodies, making it clear that no one would be allowed to pass and securing whatever rightful place they believed they had.

We had gotten as close to the scaffolding as we could.

Strange, I thought, eyeing a noticeable distance between this human barrier and the hangar's side. None of them were actually touching it. In their place, I would've been leaning against the hangar wall, sleeping, or resting—that is, if I could have gotten to it. Only now I fully realized the luxury we had having our little spot next to Cecie and Pat, with floor space to sit on.

"We aren't getting by anyone here," Mom said gloomily, turning to head back. "And we can't sleep standing up."

"We don't have our spot anymore," I sighed. "People swarmed in right after we left."

"We'll just have to wait for our chance to move closer," she replied.

For what seemed like for so long, we stood and watched for our opportunity to move.

"We can't just give up," Mom announced, intermittently nudging our shoulders to keep us alert.

"Mom, over there. There's a space opening up." Matthew pointed toward a small opening very close to the wall.

"Quick, let's grab it." Mom dragged us ahead, plowing toward the space.

We got it. A new spot. We could finally sit. And we were near the coveted wall. We needed to look for a way to escape. Maybe we would outsmart those who were there before us standing in our way.

"So this is the end of the line," said a young man with tight, curled black hair, who looked like he had been plucked from his college lecture before being dropped in here. He stood next to us, staring at the wall. "There were so many people in the way, I didn't think I could ever get here." He turned to look at us, clearly hoping for conversation. He was trying for lighthearted but failed miserably.

My mom just shrugged and turned away. Cecie and Pat had been helpful, and they were kind enough, but Mom wasn't eager to engage with anyone else or let anyone join our little family. It had been just the three of us since for so long. That didn't faze her then, and it was no different now.

The curly-haired man seemed to be alone—very alone. Once again, I was grateful that the three of us had one another. Without my mother and Matthew, I didn't know how I would get through any of this.

But for this young man, we were the only ones he could share this experience with. I felt compelled to respond and nodded to him.

"I've been wondering if there's a weak spot anywhere in these old walls," he said, "that we can open up for all of us to get through."

Matthew and I watched intently as the man reached out with a shaking hand toward the wall, seemingly ignoring the fact that no one else was touching it. To me, that was a clear red flag to stay away. At first, he poked the wall, then quickly retracted his hand. Nothing happened to him. He next flattened his hand against it, smoothing the wall with his palms. After a minute or two, he looked at us and winked, just as the tip of his pointed finger seemed to disappear into the wall.

He had managed to dig his finger into the side of the hangar and was pulling out old, crumbling cement, holding his finger up to show us—and then looking back at the small hole he had just made.

I gasped. My hand flew to my mouth to hide my excitement, especially after Mom said to show no emotion.

"Hey, look at this hole," the young man said to Matthew. "See how weak this structure is."

Mom watched the man closely, with her eyebrow raised ever so slightly.

"If I dig around more, maybe I can punch through it," he continued, realizing that he had our attention. "Maybe we can make it large enough for someone to get through."

Matthew stepped in for a closer look.

"Whaddaya say?" The man pointed to Matthew and then to the wall. "Game?"

Mom pulled Matthew back by the shoulder and stepped between him and the young, black-haired man, just as another's shrieking ripped across the hangar while the person accelerated to the ceiling.

The young man looked slightly confused and, I sensed, a bit put off. I was troubled that he felt that way and wanted to clarify that it had nothing to do with our noticeable differences.

"No, it's just that my mom—" I wanted to explain that she kept us isolated to protect us, but I couldn't get the words out fast enough.

"We want no part of this dangerous plan," Mom said with a firm stare. "We all just heard that screaming," she uttered under her breath, while she continued to hold my brother back, even as Matthew strained to watch the wall.

Undeterred, the man continued digging as if to convince my mom that his plan would work. More cement dropped to the floor in bigger chunks. Matthew and I beamed at each other. It looked promising, really promising. Not since we arrived had I felt this type of excitement, this glimmer of hope. Was this our chance for escape?

A few minutes more, and the man was able to fit his whole hand into the hole.

Our luck had changed! We came at the right time, finding this man, who was figuring out an escape for us.

Why did no one else try this? We could have been out of here days ago.

Another chilling scream interrupted my thoughts, but it was not from the hangar's ceiling.

The curly-haired man feverishly retracted his hand from the wall as if bitten by a viper. He swiveled toward us, revealing his deep brown skin had turned gray and cracked.

Pieces of his flesh were falling off.

CHAPTER 5

FIRST GLIMPSE

W e watched in horror as within seconds, a ring of a cinder-burn engulfed the man's hand, blazing toward his wrist. His horrifying screams continued as the skin and tissue on his forearm simply melted away, leaving the bones of his fingers visible.

With a terrified look in his eyes, the man moved toward my mom for help. Mom did not budge. No one moved to help him. We were all stunned by the sight.

This had to be another type of punishment, just like the death sentence for the stubby-fingered man after taking our backpack. But this man . . . he had weakened the wall. Tried to escape. That had to be worse than trying to steal our backpack.

The man dropped to his knees in front of Mom, begging and screaming as the burning ring traveled further up his arm, taking with it more flesh. Still my mom hesitated.

I heaved, breathing in the stench of the man's burning flesh. Mom looked at me, and her eyes steeled. She was going to try to help, just as I knew she would. The man was desperate—and alone.

"Give me the backpack!" she yelled, and began rummaging furiously through it, searching for something useful. Our empty water bottles fell to the floor. Only one bottle remained, with the last of our water. She had been saving it for tomorrow.

The man screamed again in pain.

"A shirt. I need a shirt from your bag!" she cried out to Matthew.

My brother just stood there with his mouth open, gagging intermittently.

"Matthew, now!" Mom demanded.

When Matthew finally pulled a shirt from his bag, she yanked it away and doused it, emptying the last of our water on it. Maybe she thought the moisture would offer some reprieve from the burning. Only a little poured out, and I doubted it would help, but there was nothing else she could offer. Stepping closer to the man, she reached toward his arm with the dampened shirt.

She was trembling and then slipped, likely under the fear of reprisal from her helping.

The suffering man hollered again as he watched her fall, his face now covered in tears and snot. He collapsed into a disheveled heap. I was paralyzed, unsure of what to do, but Mom did not give up. She got back on her feet.

Except it was too late—the man's body was plucked from the floor, exactly like the others. Contorting and twisting, he tried to stave off the force pulling him upward. His blistering arm and exposed bones flailed in the air as he struggled desperately to remain in the hangar. We all knew what would happen next, he must have known too.

It was happening right in front of us again.

I convinced myself not to turn away this time. This man's demise had become my puzzle to solve. I had to know: What was happening to those who were abducted, plucked out of thin air? My eyes searched the ceiling, hoping to find a clue.

There it was.

Hovering just between the windows and the ceiling, directly above the flailing man, was a shadowy figure—not a body, but just a floating, black-hooded cloak the size of a small man.

The figure was striking in its darkness, which pulsated in the rhythm of the suffering of the curly-haired man. A tremendous sense of foreboding filled me, and I knew I should look away from this soulless thing.

But I could not pull my eyes away from the darkness diving toward its human victim, while those around me focused on the man's ghastly suffering. Maybe that's why the cloak stopped suddenly, suspended just above the man, as if to delay the abduction. The hood turned slowly in my direction, revealing dim, silvery eyes staring out from the black depths. I held my breath and did not move, as if this would somehow hide me from its gaze.

A strong blast of air threw us all to the hangar floor while the man was whisked to the ceiling and then disappeared.

The others stood up quickly, chattering with each other about what they had seen, but I hardly heard them. I sat motionless, replaying all the dark details in my mind: the hollowed area where a face should've been, the mechanized nature of its silvery glare, the coldness emanating from its cloak, and the obscurity of it all.

What would have happened to Mom had she been able to reach the man and help him? She, too, might have been whisked away.

Matthew leaned down to me. "Did you see that thing?"

I nodded.

We all did.

They had showed themselves to us, allowed us to see them.

After this unveiling, the shadowy creatures never left the hangar ceiling. They continued to hover above waiting to descend upon their next victim—only to leave with a screaming human. It could have been any one of us at any given time. They became our ever-present prison guards. The prisoners—all of us—were incarcerated just for being humans.

———◆———

It was our first look, the first glimpse at our captors. Aside from the hordes of trapped people, these flying creatures were all we had seen since entering the containment. This was our only answer for what was responsible for our captivity. They yanked us from our regular lives, contained us without providing anything for our survival, and left us powerless and vulnerable to their daily abductions, plucking whoever they chose from the hangar floor to meet a mysterious fate.

It was day four, and we would soon be out of food. The water was all gone after Mom tried to help the man by the wall. She knew what this meant—we all did. We may have been kids, but we were not stupid.

As I was finishing my last bite, low growls rumbled overhead, and faint bursts of air breezed through my hair. Although I'd been trying to avoid looking up at the shadowy creatures, I had to find out what was causing the commotion. To my surprise, they were making a panicked escape out the windows. A blistering silvery light burst into the space they left behind. Its placement ensured it was out of our reach. A new feeling suddenly filled the air—a presence of indescribable power. Nothing I had felt ever before.

Has someone finally come to save us? Hopeful expectation surged through me. *This could be it*, I thought, *our release. We could be saved today!* I stood on my tiptoes, delicately clapping my hands in delight. Matthew shot me a disappointed glare, not sharing in my excitement.

A second light, pixelated and hypnotic, seemed to bloom from the darkness above our heads and connect with the original silver light. As a digitalized image grew and formed, gasps rang throughout the hangar. Not a single person looked away.

Matthew whispered in my ear. "What the—?"

"Maybe we'll get some answers finally," Mom whispered, linking her arms with ours and locking us in her firm grip, just like when we were first taken from outside the caves.

A single-word command boomed throughout the hangar in a deep, mechanical voice: "RISE!"

We rose quickly to our feet, as did everyone around us, including those who were too weak to rise on their own being helped by others. No one dared look away or disobey this order. More than just hearing the command, I seemed to *feel* it deep in my body.

Had our captors been a foreign military—the Russians or maybe the Chinese—we would have believed it. Had this been a terrorist attack, we would have believed it. Had this been some type of new technology, or our captivity mandated by some unknown disease, we may have believed it more. Had it been anything else, however unexpected—anything other than what it was—our minds would have been able to process it.

But this thing—the image that appeared before us—defied logic. This was an otherworldly invasion.

CHAPTER 6

OUR CAPTORS

T he pixelated image shimmered to completion above our heads, ominous and surreal: an illuminated, iridescent life-form covered in a white robe with a noticeable golden trim. Transfixed by the magnificence of the shining light, Matthew's round, teary eyes told me he was just as confused as I was in this moment—awestruck and terrified.

Had they arrived without immediately overpowering and imprisoning us, we might have thought they were divinely sent—angelic even. Under other circumstances, the world may have even worshipped them instead of feared them.

The light dimmed slightly, revealing the being's features to be unexpectedly humanistic. Its elongated face looked remarkably similar to ours, with features that were the same—yet different. Everything about it was more pronounced and defined. The jaw was squared and sharply chiseled. The forehead was prominent despite the fact that much of it disappeared under the robe's hood. The cheekbones were high and protruding. Its dark, deep-set eyes were dazzling, larger and more rounded than ours.

In contrast with these larger features, the mouth was small, thin, and pursed. There was not much of a nose—just a long, thin bump with two small openings set below the eyes. The only other body part I could see were clasped hands extending from the robe's sleeves; the skin on its knobby knuckles were a harsh white with an ever-distinct silver hue.

The being spoke:

"We received your messages."

"Your calls for help."

"The signals sent by your kind."

When its hands lifted in the air, the robe slipped down along its sleek, skeletal arms, exposing their strangely long proportions. The glistening white skin caught my eye, but not as much as the lightning-like silver streaks that ran faintly across that skin like veins. This was so lifelike, so present, but it was undoubtably a projected image of whatever it was that had captured us. Even if the image was a true depiction through an implausibly realistic hologram, this creature had to be twice our size.

I buried my face against Mom's shoulder and grabbed her even tighter, almost choking on my fast, shallow breaths. My heart raced with curiosity and fear about what might come next.

The calm, menacing voice from the being went on to explain:

"This planet plays a critical role in the infiniverse. We cannot allow your callous destruction of its resources or its precious animals to continue. Such would cause mass disorder to the rest, causing a ripple effect to our kind and beyond. Should this planet perish, the rest shall crumble."

Was this message an attempt at rationalizing our capture?

Were these creatures claiming that they came to save Earth from *us*?

That was bullshit. My fear instantly turned to muted outrage. All I ever wanted to do was save the environment. Every school project I ever did was about endangered animals, saving the environment, or some combination of the two. I even drove my mom crazy about it. And I was not alone. A whole generation of us was joining the fight to protect the Earth. We were trying to make the world a better place for *everyone*—animals included.

Nothing could justify our treatment, our imprisonment. Nothing could explain the inhumanity we had experienced by their forced captivity. My hand turned into a fist as I resisted shouting out in protest.

"Help us!" someone cried out to the image.

Another person yelled, "We have nothing to eat!"

"Release us, you invaders!" the boldest of them all demanded.

Those poor, brave souls, I thought, expecting the shadow creatures to appear at any second and take them away. But they didn't, and the hologram went on.

"Our universe is a symbiotic life system that is now being threatened by your unrestrained existence. This destruction must come to an end. We will selectively enforce minimization of the use of this planet's resources. For now, your needs will be met."

Before it disappeared in a shimmery flash, the being's last words were: "Vellatros. Keep watch."

No instructions.

No Q&A session.

No talk of our release.

Nothing.

I turned to Mom. "What did it mean about minimizing? Does that mean us? Minimizing *us*?"

Matthew added, "Are the shadow creatures the Vellatros?"

Before Mom could respond, panic broke out all around us. Confusion. Screaming. Commotion. Chaos. Everyone started running.

They were trying to get out.

But why? Nothing had changed—there was no exit, no way out. No one had been able to leave before, and the strange piercing white being had never said that we could do so now. Instead, it had been very clear that we would remain prisoners here, and it even blamed our imprisonment on something we had done to some broader universe of other beings. We could not escape now any more than we could have done before the creature's speech. The panic was utterly pointless.

"Where exactly are these people running to?" I murmured aloud.

I got my answer almost immediately, as throngs of people rushed toward the walls of the hangar, trampling those in their way. Even little children were mowed under the brute strength of the stampeding mob. The very old and ill didn't stand a chance. Once knocked down, they were too weak to get back up.

Mom refused to give in to the hysteria, standing her ground, and we followed her example. But the sheer force of the crowd knocked the three of us to the floor—and tore my arm away from her firm hold.

I reached out to her outstretched hand, struggling to fight the panic. Through racing legs and stumbling feet, I saw Mom still had ahold of Matthew with her other hand.

"Lauren!" she cried out, grabbing one of my arms as Matthew found the other. Staying together was the only important thing.

After yanking me to my feet, Mom maneuvered the three of us to face inward, with our backs to the crowd like a shield. We locked arms and eyes, holding on tightly to one another, swaying back and forth as the hordes pushed and pulled, desperate to reach the hangar walls.

Human callousness was on full display. Our collective behavior proved the being's very point.

Mom and Matthew fell to their knees, and I collapsed to the cement floor along with them. At first it felt like exhaustion, but the way it happened—collectively and suddenly—made me think otherwise. All the chaos around us was immediately quelled. Despite being forced to kneel alongside the other prisoners, I felt a perplexing sense of comfort, as if some invisible force was compelling me to settle even though I was still tense from the being's menacing speech. Whatever the source, it calmed me.

When the purple haze, which signaled evening, fell across the hangar again, I realized the calm plied all of us.

Sleep overtook me.

———◆———

I jolted awake to find myself lying on the same cement floor, my body stiff and my arms straight by my sides. I didn't know how long I was out, but the sleep had been deep, and I awoke nearly forgetting for a second our captivity.

What about Matthew and Mom? I fought back panic, still squinting as I reached out to either side of me. Matthew was lying on my right and Mom on the other side of me. I released a muffled sigh.

But they were stiff, still deeply asleep, as was everyone else around me. I had no doubt that this sleep was ordained by the creature that had visited our hangar. The need to sleep had been beyond my control—beyond everyone's control—just like the collective calm that had overtaken the chaos earlier.

Somehow I fought it off. Why was I the only one awake under this potent light? The purple haze was gone, replaced by an intense light that filled the hangar. I sheltered my eyes with my hands.

Peering upward, I shook my head in disbelief. Could it really be? The hangar roof was *open*. I didn't know why the roof was open, and I didn't care to continue to ask unanswerable questions at this point.

After days of being deprived of both sun and fresh air, I just blinked and blinked, until I could see it clearly. My eyes slowly adjusted, as if suddenly remembering what it was like to experience the direct, natural light. The roof was only partly open, but it was just enough.

I lifted my chin up toward the sky to breathe deeply. The crispness of the morning air was enchanting and in stark contrast to the thick-smelling stench from the ailing captives packed into the hangar.

The sky was streaked pink, dotted with puffs of delicately placed clouds. It was sunrise. The sun's sparkling brilliance washed my ailing body in its warmth, and the open sky gave me a brief sense of freedom.

The feeling was fleeting. I was guilt-ridden that I was the only one able to enjoy this beautiful moment. No one else was awake, not even my mom or my brother, to experience this moment with me. None of the others in the hangar were even aware of the sun touching their deprived skin.

There was something else. Also beautiful in a way, but nonetheless alarming.

Hovering just beyond the hangar's open roof was a rounded edge of a massive sparkling structure, made of what appeared to be glass and steel, with a middle portion that shot straight upward, disappearing behind the gathering clouds.

It looked spherical and unlike any building that I had ever seen before—meticulously clean, alarming in height, and so wide that I couldn't see it all from my vantage point, being many stories below it.

Maybe it was their mothership, given the massive size. This spaceship could have been above our heads with these beings busying themselves, while we've been locked away in this hangar and completely unaware of what was happening in our town . . . in the world. Worse, how long had they been on Earth, plotting and scheming the human abductions, before revealing themselves? A chill ran through my body—not from the cold floor but under the fear of it all.

Most intriguing of all, however, were the clear tubes encircling the vessel like Saturn's rings. My eyes narrowed, attempting to focus on one of the hollow tubes. Something was inside. There it was, with its glistening white robe floating through the ring. It was one of *them* . . . in an alien transport tube.

More of the beings flowed through, looking like they were floating within, just above the tube's flooring, which continually changed colors below them.

These were no holograms like the one that arrived in the hangar yesterday. The ones I watched were real—live beings traveling through a glass corridor on some sort of prismatic moving walkway. More robed beings passed through the tubes—until an unhooded one caught my eye. With its elongated, rounded head exposed, I could see long, straight hair, a vivid white matching the robe and skin, flowing to midway down its back. The only distinction between all the white was the silver hue reflecting from the being's veins and the silvery strands shining through the hair. Pointy ears peeked through the hair ever so elegantly, stretching toward the back of its head. Even from afar, the sheer size of the creature amazed me as much as its unnatural beauty.

As the exposed creatures passed far above my head, time seemed to slow. I captured a mental picture and replayed it over and over, trying to focus on the different characteristics that I could recall. Upon realizing that Matthew was still asleep, missing all of this, I snapped out of my enchantment.

He had been right all along.

Aliens.

CHAPTER 7

SEPARATION

"Look up," I whispered, as I leaned down to Matthew's ear.

No response.

Nudging my brother lightly, I whispered a little louder. "Look up, Matthew."

He startled awake and demanded, too loudly, "What's going on?"

"*Shhh.*" I covered his mouth with my hand and nodded up to the ceiling, prompting him to follow my view.

"Slowly, quietly," I warned him, worried that any abrupt movement might bring the attention of those around us—or worse, those above.

"Whoa," Matthew murmured into my hand.

"Look closely—you can see them moving through the tubes." I lifted my hand from his mouth.

"Holy shit!" he blurted out, lunging into a sitting position, completely ignoring the need to be covert. "The roof is open. And what is—?"

I covered his mouth again and pushed him down hard to the floor. "We can't get caught," I breathed firmly, removing my hand from his mouth. "Don't move." My trembling legs interfered with that plan. I worried that a Vellatros would appear—or worse, one of *them*.

I felt Matthew's leg twitch beside me. He must have had the same fear as I did. *What would they do to us if they knew we were awake and watching them?*

We stayed as still as we could, staring up into the open sky, watching our captors travel above our heads in a spaceship. They passed through tubes circling their mothership, with one set of tubes on the level above moving the aliens in one direction, while the passageway just below it moved the aliens in the opposite way.

The only way to explain it was *surreal . . . unbelievable . . . unimaginable*. But it was our reality.

Together, we took a deep breath and exhaled, just as the roof began to close.

Matthew reached his fingers toward the sky as if to capture a handful of air and save it for later. "It's only been a few days, but I'd forgotten how amazing the sky is," he murmured, "feeling the warm sun and breathing the fresh air."

We both groaned, knowing that our sun and fresh air were being taken away—and we couldn't do anything about it.

"What's going on with you two?" Mom asked in a tired voice as she awakened from her forced sleep. She had missed it.

I pointed toward the sky. "The roof was open," I whispered loudly. "You were sleeping and—"

"Wait," Matthew interrupted. "How were *you* awake?"

"I was forced to sleep, too, at first," I said defensively but then softened my tone, realizing he just wanted answers. "I was in and out of sleep. When I broke through it, I found the roof open . . . and the spaceship."

"Spaceship?" Mom sounded wide awake now.

"It was crazy. And we saw them floating through the rings—the aliens, the Invaders." Matthew's eager voice rose above a hush, seemingly ignoring any concern about being caught awake before any of the others.

"Yes, that's exactly what the guy shouted out earlier. Invaders, that's what they are," I agreed. We finally had a way to explain our captivity—and a word for our captors.

Mom held her finger up to quiet our agitation. But it was too late. Everyone awoke in unison, just as another holographic image materialized above us. This time, the image was fully formed and came to give another lecture.

"You will be marked," the Invader explained bluntly. "Your symbol represents the division to which you are assigned." Then it disappeared.

The announcement was unnerving.

"Marked?"

I wish I had not asked. My upper arm began tingling, just below my shoulder and felt as if something was crawling under my skin. I shoved my hand down my sleeve trying to rub it off. Matthew feverishly scratched at the same spot; he felt it, too. The tingling soon changed to a painful sear. I winced and grasped at my arm. This was no bug. Coiling under my hand was my bubbling and blistering skin—pulsating.

It was Mom's reaction that ruined me. She held her arm as her eyes welled up with tears, silently bearing the pain. Without even muttering a word, her warning was loud and clear: Do not make any unnecessary cries for fear of the Vellatros.

Somehow, our matching affliction made it more tolerable. Mom tilted her head and narrowed her eyes at me, affirming my pain, as we stood there in silence while our flesh singed beneath our hands.

Others were not so silent as they were being marked. Babies' wails echoed throughout the hangar. Young and old alike howled in pain, their screams filling the hangar. No one was spared.

I knew I shouldn't cry. I knew Mom didn't want me to cry. But it was so hard seeing her this way—gripping the same spot on her arm, enduring her own suffering—just as I was.

I had held it together for them for so long—through our imprisonment, the confinement, the rescue that never came, the discovery of aliens—but the howling from the babies in pain just broke me.

Unable to stand it any longer, I burst out crying.

So did Mom, and Matthew followed. I fell into Mom's shoulder, shivering and heaving, stopping only to wipe my spit and tears on her shirt. She didn't care. She let me slobber all over her. She just wrapped her arms around me and held me close. I felt her chest rise and fall under my blubbering face.

I cried until the burning finally stopped.

"I need to see this," Mom said, peeling me off and drying the tears from her face. She pulled Matthew closer to us.

Rolling up my sleeve felt like I was peeling away a crisp bandage from a fresh burn. I traced my fingers over the blistered skin, like I had been branded with some kind of symbol.

Matthew and I held our exposed shoulders together for Mom to inspect.

"Yours match," she said, and pulled her own sleeve from her shoulder. "Mine, too." Our three shoulders brandished identical markings: two vertical, half-circular lines facing each other but not connected, around now a hardened ball of skin.

While I studied my coiled skin, new screams surged throughout the hangar.

Prisoners were pulled and propelled from one another, separated and filtered by an invisible, inexplicable force without a Vellatros in sight. And no one was rising to the ceiling.

"They can't stop it!" Matthew yelled. No matter how hard people flailed, kicked, and tried to hold on to one another, they lost their grip and vanished into the crowd. Mom and child. Husband and wife. Sister, brother, grandparent, friend . . . none of it mattered. They were systematically divided and moved.

From behind me, I heard, "My baby! Take care of my baby!" The torment in the mother's voice was painful to hear. I turned to watch as her baby nearly fell to the ground, while the mother was forcefully moved away. Another woman nearby just barely caught the child, cradling it in her arms. The baby's mother mouthed *thank you*, just before she disappeared through the frenzied crowd.

Across the hangar, a man broke free from the compulsory separation and lunged toward another group, shouting, "Claudia! Claudia!"

"Oh, no," I murmured, grabbing my mouth with my hands.

Mom's eyes widened. "What's wrong?"

I pointed. "Don't you see it? It's blocking them." It was translucent and oscillating, resplendent with an array of dazzling colors running the length and height of the hangar.

Mom shook her head, but Matthew noticed it right away. "He's running right at it, full speed," he called out.

The woman, who I assumed was Claudia, ran toward the translucent barrier. Just as they were about to reunite, the man recoiled, shrieking. He had reached through the light.

"Stop!" he directed the woman, as he held up one of his hands to show her the flesh beginning to melt away, exactly like when the curly-haired man had done after reaching through the wall.

A Vellatros appeared—the first we had seen since the hologram lectured us the previous day.

"Go back!" the man bellowed, just as the Vellatros howled above his head. While he rose to the ceiling, he screeched Claudia's name over and over, until he was . . . gone. The woman collapsed in grief and fear, only to be immediately pulled back to her group by the same invisible force that had initially separated them.

"What is *happening*?" I lamented to Mom and Matthew, who looked just as confused and horrified as I was. Given the terror of the past four days, we should have become accustomed to such cruelty. But we weren't that broken. Not yet.

Then I realized that the three of us hadn't moved. No invisible force had come to tear us apart.

"Look, the same symbol." Matthew pointed to several bare arms around us.

"Ours match," Mom said, nodding. "We may have stayed together because of it." I let out a deep sigh—grateful we were together. After losing everything I had in this world, I would have been unable to bear losing the only thing I really had left: my family.

Not long after the separations occurred, the purple haze eclipsed the remaining sun in the hangar. Another night came, and we hadn't been saved.

In spite of the all-consuming, lingering pain I felt from the brand and the anguish I just witnessed in those separated, a deep sleep began to consume me. My eyes closed as the cries of those that remained, but torn from their own, turned to silence. Sleep had finally brought escape from the screams and cries, even though I believed the young ones might never have stopped.

CHAPTER 8

THE NEW ORDER

On the fifth day, I woke to bright sun peering through the windows and chattering among those around me. Disappointed with myself for not being the first one to wake and missing out on the opened roof, I just lay there on the hard cement floor. There was nothing for me to do anyhow.

"Lauren, come on," Matthew urged, pushing me up. "Look."

I was unwilling to move.

"Beds!"

Not truly believing what Matthew just said, particularly given the impossibility of it, I rose slowly just to indulge him. He was right. Rows of bunk beds, three levels high, had appeared in the hangar while we were asleep. I turned to Matthew, momentarily delighted. Without uttering a word or waiting for Mom's approval, we ran toward the beds.

Matthew jumped to a top bunk, so I dove to the middle one,

slinging my backpack to claim the one below it for Mom. Compared to my bed at home, the bunk was not at all comfortable—the mattress was thin, firm, and dirty, with no blanket or pillow in sight—but anything was better than the cold, hard floor we had been sleeping on. My backpack had hardly served as the softest of pillows either.

I gently ran my fingers over the mattress. "This feels good," I yelled up to Matthew, who was wrestling so much on the top bunk that he shifted the frame back and forth. He couldn't contain his excitement.

Sinking into the mattress, I felt both relief and concern. I closed my eyes and imagined that I was home in my own bed, with Thor beside me, hoping that when I opened them *that* would be my reality, and our alien captors would be just a long nightmare.

No such luck.

Matthew looked down over the edge of his bunk. "No more sleeping on the ground. Right, Mom?"

Mom wandered over, with an eyebrow raised and a crooked smile, while she sat at the end of her bunk. Sensing her disappointment that we remained imprisoned here, I gave her a half-hearted smile in return. Why couldn't she at least be *a little bit* happy about the bed?

Mom bounced a little on the edge. "This will be much better for us." I felt better hearing her strained approval.

From the top bunk, Matthew's stomach grumbled so loud I could hear it. Mom must have heard it, too, because she stood up, placed a hand on my head and raised the other up to Matthew. I knew that touch—it always came when we were hurt, like the time I fell off my bike and after the attack. It was meant to comfort me, but in this case, I knew the consoling touch came because we had nothing left to eat.

"Maybe we should rest for a bit." Mom paused. "It might help with the hunger."

We had just woken up, but Mom was right: We hadn't eaten for two days, and I didn't have much energy left. I pulled my backpack up with my feet to grab my stuffed kitty, which I placed delicately beside me, and rolled up my sweatshirt as a pillow. It felt so good to be off the ground and on the mattress—to have a bit of my own space.

"Matthew, stop moving," I yelled up. Whether he did it for fun or just couldn't settle, he kept shaking the bunk. "Now!" I yelled again, not hiding my frustration.

Mom appeared from below, stepping on my bed to get to Matthew. "There's nothing we can do right now," Mom told him. "Just rest, okay?"

On her way back down, Mom said to me, "Get some rest, honey, and remember, it's hard on all of us. Matthew doesn't need to be yelled at by you."

I closed my eyes and tried to ignore the shaking. Although we had recently awakened, I fell back to sleep, but it was on my own, and it was the soundest sleep I'd had since we were first taken.

With a gentle tug on my shoulder, right at the brand, I was jolted awake. My skin raised slightly as my body shifted, responding to some kind of gravitational force.

"Pack up!" Mom shouted from below. "It's happening again!"

I threw my stuffed kitty and sweatshirt in my bag just as Matthew rolled down from the top bunk, extending his arm toward me. His body was unusually contorted as he twisted my way. This was not of his own doing.

"Grab on," he yelled, grasping for me, for the bed frame, for anything, but it was too late. The unseen force was too strong. He tried reaching back to us but continued to be hauled away.

The tugging at my brand grew stronger, yanking me from the bunk and onto the ground, right behind Matthew. Others around us shifted, too, line by line, powered by some organized force. My concern was overtaken by an extraordinary, unexpected smell in the air: *food*. The food aromas consumed the ever-present foul stench of the hangars. Maybe it was the trauma and my crushing hunger pains that made me believe we actually would be fed.

My stomach grumbled. I closed my eyes, imagining pizza, but I greatly doubted I'd be biting into a cheesy slice.

"Look, there's food!" Matthew called out in excited disbelief, pointing to the area just ahead of us. Rows of tables were arranged for seating like in a school cafeteria, and beyond them was a long countertop—a giant buffet.

The tugging stopped, and the invisible force released my shoulder. I grabbed his hand, and we rushed ahead with a skip in our step along with the rest of the group. But we weren't alone in our feelings of hunger, thirst, and the urgency to survive. We were pushed aside and to the ground by those clamoring to get to the food first.

Mom caught up to us and pulled us aside. "They're like animals. I don't want you to get hurt."

Matthew tried to wrestle out of her grip. "Mom, we need to eat. I'm starving."

"I know how hard it is to wait—believe me, I know," she replied. "Hang on. We'll get there."

"They're going to eat it all, Mom." Matthew pleaded, just as his stomach loudly grumbled while watching the other prisoners gorge on what looked like tofu chunks.

"How do we know it's even safe to eat?" Mom warned. "Let's just watch what happens to everyone else before we rush in. It's not as if these beings—"

"The Invaders," Matthew muttered.

"Yes, the Invaders. It's not as if they're looking out for our best interests here. They've done nothing to earn our trust."

I knew she was right, but it didn't matter. Whatever the other prisoners were eating, I wanted it. Starving was even more painful when you had to watch others eat.

But I appreciated her restraint once several Vellatros began circling above. Most of the disorderly crowd, all too desperate to get to the food, didn't notice their arrival. We cowered as the Vellatros whisked away the worst offenders—those who were violent, tossed others aside in their rush toward the food, or even pushed to the front of the line. The message was clear: Be orderly and civil or be taken. The crowd settled into some semblance of a line, respecting the needs of the younger and more frail people.

When no one dropped dead from eating the food, Mom finally released us. We joined the others at the back of the line, hoping the food wouldn't be gone by the time we got to it. Matthew and I looked down the line, checking over and over how soon we would get to the food, while Mom was away filling up our water bottles at the water fountain that had arrived with the buffet.

When it was finally our turn, the food was bland-looking—chunky, colorless squares like the tofu Mom tried to make us eat once when she went vegan for a week. It wasn't the chocolate I so desperately craved in this moment.

I bristled as Matthew piled up chunk after chunk in his hands, taking bites while still in line. I understood his compulsion—none of us really knew when we would eat again—but Mom and I needed to eat, too.

"Hey, slow down." I yelled. "Leave some for the rest of us."

"Look," he responded, "no matter how much you take, more reappears. It won't run out."

"You don't know that."

But he was right. With each chunk I grabbed, more filled back up. I grabbed as many as I could shove in my backpack and fill my hands with, until Mom handed me a plate she'd just found. *That's right*, I thought, *civility*. It was required to avoid the Vellatros.

Despite the loathsome taste, odd smell, and spongy texture, I savored each bite. After having nothing to eat for nearly two days, I was going to eat *all* that I could. And in a way, sitting down to eat together created a welcome sense of normalcy. Matthew and I looked at each other with stuffed faces.

"Look, Mom, it's like the fake meat you tried to make us eat," Matthew said. He smirked, pretending to spit some out.

I chuckled. It was nice to smile at Matthew's attempt to bring humor to the situation.

"Well . . . I tried my best to make us all healthier." Her weary, overwhelmed tone was hard to ignore. "And look what it got us in the end, huh?"

"Sorry, Mom. We're just trying . . . I don't know, just trying to stay . . ." I was not used to Mom being discouraged. I sensed her tension—she just couldn't hide it any longer. But we were finally eating, and I dared to hope that we had turned a corner.

"I know, honey." She grabbed my hand and patted it. She pulled her hand from mine and rubbed both hands against her face and through her hair. "I just don't have it in me to stay positive right now. I don't want beds and food—I want us to get out of here. We have no answers, and there's no end in sight. None of this makes sense."

I had the same thoughts, but I didn't want to hear it. Talking about it made it all too real for me. Worse, Mom was feeling down, too. She always tried to stay brave and strong for us, and Matthew and I looked to her for all the answers. Since the moment we were taken, she had remained unwavering for us so we wouldn't crumble beneath the weight of this tragedy. Her invisible armor was cracking—a small crack, but a crack nonetheless.

"We can't just continue to go on like this." She winced. "Jesus, what's going to happen to all of us?"

I didn't answer, but I think we all knew the answer to her question. We were not getting out. That I knew for certain, particularly given nothing that had happened thus far remotely suggested we would.

"At least we're still together, unlike those who were separated," Matthew said, gulping his food before shoveling more into his mouth.

I squeezed Mom tight as she had done for me countless times. Just because she was the brave one didn't mean she should go without a hug.

Mom squeezed me back. "Matthew's right. We're together— that's what matters most. I have my babies with me, and we'll figure this out *together*, like we've always done." Her back straightened and she sat upright, wiping her tears away. She looked ready to tackle whatever came next.

◆

I moaned, having eaten until I was bursting. With the food barely edible, I was surprised that I hadn't thrown up yet. We had nothing to do, so we just waited while our food uncomfortably digested.

Eventually the tugging at my shoulder started again, moving us into another area of the hangar where rows of showers and sinks now stood. How or when these had appeared was a mystery, but I'd given up trying to understand any of it—especially at the thought of finally getting clean.

Matthew and I beamed at Mom, nodding our heads to prompt a *yes*. Instead of instructing us to wait or warning us to stay put, she just shrugged and said, "You can go. Just don't drink the water."

I furrowed my brow at her, thinking that was a rather odd directive.

She shrugged. "What? It could make you sick."

Matthew took off and got there first, claiming a shower stall so the three of us could take turns. A line started to form behind him, and I realized there would be little in the way of privacy, but I didn't care. My skin smelled, my hair was greasy, and my filthy clothes clung to me.

Not long after Matthew started his shower, he let out a yelp. The water had stopped—not just in his stall, but for all the other showers at the same time.

"Mom," he called out. "Why is this thing off?"

"Maybe it's on some kind of timer," Mom called back to him. "Try to step out and then step back in." Matthew jumped out and back in . . . soapy. How did he have soap? Matthew tried to sneak in another cycle.

"You're done, Matthew," I demanded. I wanted a wash, no matter how short it would be. "It's my turn."

"Hey, I'm not finished," Matthew grumbled, after I pulled him out half-dressed.

The water was pleasantly lukewarm and came out soapy at first. I reveled in the feeling of it. Washing the dirt off me felt like I was scrubbing away the thick stench and filth that had collected over the past five days. It was almost as if the captivity itself could be washed away.

Before I could finish, the water turned off. I stepped out and back in, as Matthew had done. "Hey, you can't do that." I heard yelled out from the line. "We all need to get clean, here."

I then realized the reason for the short showers. The water was being strictly rationed so we could all get clean. I jumped back in anyway to get in a double wash.

Putting on fresh clothes reminded me, for just a moment, of the feeling I used to get from changing into my pajamas and getting ready for bed. Welcoming, comforting, cozy. I shoved my grimy, crusty clothes into my backpack, never wanting to see them again. But my clothing options were limited, and I knew they'd likely make their way back on me at some point.

Once Mom had finished her shower, we made our way over to the rows of sinks. Unexpectedly, the counter was furnished with toothbrushes and toothpaste. Like the shower stalls and the food, it all just appeared for us when we moved into the specific areas of the hangars. I thought how trivial brushing my teeth was under the circumstances. Did I really need to worry about rotting teeth if we were all going to die soon?

And I found it peculiar that the Invaders seemed to be tending to our essential needs. How did they even know what we needed to survive anyway?

Why did the Invaders suddenly care that we were living creatures who needed to be fed and cleaned? Were they trying to prevent our death or just prolong our harrowing existence? Was this our new normal, or just a ploy before the imminent death they had planned for us?

Mom's hand rested on my shoulder. "Are you okay, honey?" She always seemed to know when I was lost in my thoughts, bordering on panic.

"I don't know, Mom," I replied, trying to keep my voice from shaking. "Are any of us okay in here?" My response seemed to worry her, but she didn't push it. "I'll be all right."

But nothing was okay, and making things better seemed out of our control. Mom, Matthew, and I would have to find a way to live with it.

We had no other option—except maybe death.

Death didn't come, though. Instead, we shuffled our way through the new normal, being tugged by our branded arm through the same rotation—sleep, eat, shower, repeat. The days continued to pass as we succumbed to life in this prison. Our health faded, and with little sunlight or air, we became listless. Keeping track of the days became less of a priority, although there still was one good reason to count: Matthew's twelfth birthday. Mom had already started planning his party before we were taken.

"Five more days until you'll be twelve," I told him during one of our eating rotations. I guessed it was just days away.

"What are you talking about?" Matthew asked, looking less than amused.

"Well, your birthday was coming up before," I had to think of the best way to say "abducted by aliens" without ruining my attempt to make this special for Matthew, "we got here. So let's do a countdown."

"I'd rather celebrate my birthday at home," he bristled. "My wish will be to get out of here."

I didn't let his bitterness stop me. The birthday countdown gave us something to look forward to while we were shuffled into the eating rotation.

On the big day, when we sat down to eat, there were no presents, no pizza, and no friends to celebrate. All we had was the "Happy Birthday" song. As Mom and I began to sing, Matthew's cheeks reddened, and he shook his head *no*, but his smile grew. Mom squeezed him, and we continued singing.

Much to our surprise, people at the nearby tables started singing along, like when we used to celebrate at a restaurant and the wait-staff and other tables joined in. Soon the entire eating area—where we usually ate with our heads down, murmuring occasionally—was singing in unity, with only the names changing during the song. The tradition was familiar for all of us, a reminder of life before the hangar—before what seemed like endless captivity. A few people smiled and embraced, and I pulled Matthew into a big bear hug so he couldn't see my tears.

Although Mom warned us not to show any emotions for fear of the Vellatros, she, too, smiled while her eyes welled up with tears—from what I recognized was joy instead of the usual fear. I felt the collective harmony of that moment within our hangar community all the way to my soul.

CHAPTER 9

AN OPENING

Most days were full of boredom and dread. The only time I could even remember what happiness felt like was early each morning, when I drifted out of the forced sleep and listened to the simple silence—no moaning in pain, no howling from being abducted by a Vellatros, no crying child calling out for their missing mother. No one else was awake.

While still drowsy, I forced myself to picture the most vivid memories from our vacations down to every last detail, from the cold snow in my hand as I rolled a snowball to throw at Matthew to the warm sand under my feet as I ran to the waves. According to Mom, I had a photographic memory passed down from my grandfather—and I was grateful for it now.

One early morning during this twilight period, I spotted an unfamiliar sliver of light shining from the far end of the hangar, near the floor. I peered at the light, realizing that it came from a small opening near the massive hangar doors. My stomach fluttered with nervousness, since the doors had been sealed shut for nearly three weeks. No hint of light had ever shone through them and not even a finger could be wedged into them.

Is this real? It seemed highly improbable.

I had to go inspect.

Before I could change my mind, I jumped down from my bunk—chest tight, heart pounding—intending to tiptoe away from the other sleepers. Before I could take another step, the hangar suddenly shook with a deep rumble. The massive doors were opening.

The thundering sound woke everyone in the hangar. My chance to share this amazing discovery with just Matthew and Mom was lost. People sat up, looking stunned after abruptly awakening from their forced slumber . . . until the sliver of light, growing wider, caught their eyes.

"The doors are opening!" someone shouted.

Hysterical excitement rang throughout the hangar from the prisoners who, longing for escape, leapt from their bunks. Without a care for those in their path, people ran and stumbled toward the hangar doors, seemingly unafraid of the Vellatros.

Has the time finally come? I stood frozen with hopeful anticipation that I would be home today.

Matthew jumped to the floor next to me, preparing to rush toward the doors along with the crowd, but Mom pulled us back, preventing us from partaking in the hysteria, and pointed frantically in the opposite direction. I should have expected this from her by now. But with an opening to escape, I thought maybe this time would be different.

She wanted us to head for the scaffolding, despite the fact that she previously forbade us once we realized that the Vellatros seemed particularly fond of taking the humans who had tried to climb it.

"But the Vellatros," I shouted over the screams of the running crowd we pushed past to get to the wall. I hadn't moved that fast since the day of the invasion.

"Climb up! Do it *now!*" I heard the panic in her voice as she yelled.

The rushing crowd, in its desperate attempt to escape, had grown into a stampede. All three of us reached for the lowest beam of the scaffolding and wrapped our legs around it just before the hordes engulfed us. The beam was shaking and swaying, and I wasn't sure my arms had the strength to pull me up. Above me, Matthew offered his hand to help.

"Go help Mom first," I yelled. They both came back, pulling me up by my shirt, and we climbed to the next level, ten feet above the floor. A few other prisoners with the same idea were clustered around us.

From above, I watched the mob clawing and pounding at the enormous hangar doors. Inch by inch, the doors moved, but only slowly under the weight of the cold, cemented enormous doors. Those in front, up against the doors, pushed their arms through the gap as if they were waving to people outside to save them or reaching toward safety. Those at the back were pushing to get to the front, lashing out at anyone who got in their way, stepping over those who fell to the ground—all of them vying to be the first to escape.

Slowly, the doors opened a little wider and more arms reached through to wave out. It was excruciatingly slow and drawn out—the agonizing anticipation to escape.

"Someone small," came a faint voice from the front. "We need someone small to get out!"

A little boy, probably not more than four years old, was plucked from the ground and lifted in the air, kicking and screaming as he was carried over the crowd.

Reaching backward, the boy called out, "Mama! Mama!"

A woman's voice wailed in response, and her arms thrashed above her head to get her son. "My boy!" she cried, trying to push through the crowd. No one would step aside to let her through. Instead, they all joined in on passing the little one above their heads to the front—the equivalent of a human sacrifice.

"What are you doing with my boy?"

The desperate prisoners brought him to the ground and tried squeezing him through the opening, but he wasn't small enough.

"Stop! You're hurting me!" The boy howled. They tried again, squeezing him harder and shoving his head through the small opening, ignoring his heartrending pleas.

He popped out.

The boy just stood there, his eyes wide, too young to know what was expected of him.

"Run. Run away." someone screamed, flapping their arms to prod him along.

Another yelled, "Go get help. You're out! Get help."

By then, so much time had passed inside the hangar that it was the only safe place the boy knew. He was not going to move—even I knew that—and I couldn't blame him. At least in the hangar, we knew what to fear. Alone with the unknown, I wasn't too sure I'd move either.

He didn't run. He didn't get help.

Tears streamed down his face as he cried, "Mama, mama."

Once the boy's mother forced her way to the front, he slipped back inside to get to her. She scooped him up and disappeared into the crowd away from the doors.

Amid similar shouts—"Grab another!" and "Try again"—the opening continued to widen. The shouts faded when the doors had opened just enough for a few of the thinnest, sickly looking adults to push through. Unlike the little boy, the adults disappeared almost immediately from my view. I imagined that once they touched the outside ground, they just started running as fast and as far as they could, regardless of their fragility.

The doors opened even more. Those waiting impatiently at the front were able to slide through—but if they were too big or too slow, they were pulled back to make way for those who could. A wave of screaming followed as the opening became wide enough for two people at a time to pass, and then three and four. The gap became wide enough for me to watch, even from afar, them fleeing in all directions. But my attention was no longer on the escapees.

Off in the distance, past the dirt flatlands right outside the hangar doors, was a lush, extraordinary world. The world as I had known it did not remotely compare to the amazing beauty just outside the hangar doors. While we had been held captive, Earth blossomed and had been reborn.

CHAPTER 10

FRESH AIR

Could it be real? Or were we on another planet, transported while we slept? This couldn't possibly be just outside the hangars near our town. Either way, I took in a deep breath of the crisp, fresh air that filled the hangar, reaching all the way to the scaffoldings on which we still stood.

Although we had no real answers about our captivity, none of that mattered anymore. The hangar doors were wide open, and people were pouring out. The Invaders were finally letting us go. As long as this *was* Earth, I could get home, find Thor, and go back to normal. We could get our *lives* back.

The occupation was over. Maybe the Invaders would leave our planet alone, forever. Maybe they were done with whatever they needed to do. Maybe they were already gone. After all, no Vellatros had punished us for climbing the scaffolding or abducted the other prisoners for escaping through the doors.

We have learned our lesson, I thought. *We will finally make changes—we understand better now. The Earth has flourished, and we will take care of it now. They can leave.*

Matthew and I started climbing down from the scaffolding. We wanted out, too.

"No," Mom commanded, wagging a finger back and forth. "You two stay put. We aren't going anywhere just yet."

"Mom, we'll be trapped in here if we don't leave now," Matthew pleaded.

I joined in. "What if this is our only chance to escape?"

Mom raised her eyebrow, looking at us without a single blink. "Do you really think it would be this easy? That they'd just open the doors, and we'd be free to run home and start all over again? Just hold tight. There's something else going on here."

"That's what you thought about the food, and we didn't die," Matthew jeered.

I just stared at him, disappointed. Being testy with Mom was unusual for my brother.

Before she could respond, we heard bloodcurdling screams from outside the hangar. Through the opened doors, I saw hundreds of people who had left, hunched over and fallen to their knees, writhing in pain. Their skin peeled and their hair incinerated.

Then I saw it. Out there, just before the tree line, the sunlight reflected a translucent, oscillating multicolored barrier—some sort of electrical force field like the one used in the hangar during the initial separations.

How had they not seen it? "Look out!" I wanted to shout. "Look for the iridescence." The poor souls wouldn't have heard me anyway. I wasn't close enough, thanks to Mom, while we safely watched the carnage unfold from inside the hangar.

By running frantically to escape from the hangar, they had pitched themselves onto this dangerous barrier. The barrier responded differently this time. Instead of burning whatever body part touched it first, it sucked people into the force field and held them there while the burning ravaged their body. They collapsed and rolled out of the barrier, lifeless. Undeterred, some of the prisoners still ran for the barrier, either that desperate to escape or in such denial that they thought it wouldn't happen to them.

All they wanted was their freedom, but instead they were tortured. The sky darkened. A horde of Vellatros swept in as Mom suspected they would, collecting the limp, lifeless bodies of the fallen and lunging at the poor escapees, carrying them away—the punishment for trying to escape. It all seemed like a setup, a trap . . . a lesson. Although the Invaders permitted us to go outside, this wasn't an act of mercy. There were limitations.

After this first wave of humans was sacrificed—both by the barrier and by abduction—the other humans stopped in their tracks, reconsidering escape. I sensed this was exactly what the Invaders had planned, exactly the reaction they wanted—to instill fear to the point of paralysis. These vicious human deaths sent a message to all of us: Obey, or we too would be met with this fate.

Mom was right. Escape wouldn't be that easy. The Invaders were not just going to let us go.

Terrified, I looked at Matthew, whose eyes looked as wide as mine felt.

After all that we'd just witnessed, Mom quietly stated, "We can go have a look now."

Matthew and I exchanged a look. My jaw dropped in disbelief. She offered nothing to console us to counter the carnage that just occurred. That was all she could muster up, even after we just witnessed hundreds of humans get ruthlessly burned and then disappear within seconds. The lack of empathy from my mother was troubling.

We followed Mom in silence toward the open doors, grasping each other's hands, uncertain of what might come next.

Taking that first step past the hangar doors, we were hit with an unexpectedly crisp blast of air. Mom stopped and held her head back, breathing deep and squeezing our hands. After weeks of the thick, stifling air indoors, the three of us relished the fresh, invigorating air filling our noses and lungs. It felt new.

"It smells so clean," I said, delighted.

"I can finally breathe," Matthew added.

"I watched it all, very closely," Mom remarked. "Do you both see where the dirt stops and the growth begins? That's where the barrier lies."

Matthew and I looked to where she pointed.

"Stay away from the growth area," Mom warned. "We're limited to the flatlands, remember this."

I knew she was right, but it was hard to think about anything bad when the air was clean and the sun was bright. I held my hand up to my forehead, squinting as my eyes adjusted to the glare. We'd been deprived of this for so long. We were *outside*. We could see the sun, the sky, the clouds. It was glorious . . . absolutely glorious.

I could see that others felt the same way. The panic and chaos had subsided, replaced by the guilty delight of being outside. Some people just stood and looked toward the sun-kissed sky, while others twirled around and around in giddy disbelief. Being free in those beautiful surroundings, we could almost overlook the fact that we remained captives—and somehow ignored the hundreds of lives lost at the barrier to educate us on the penalty of escape. In stark contrast, there were those still on their knees near the barrier, mourning the loved ones taken by the Vellatros.

As Mom surveyed the area, she crossed her arms, making it clear to Matthew and me that there was no enjoyment in any of this for her.

"If this is still our town, and these are the hangars just outside of it, where is everything?" Matthew asked. "The houses? The stores? I just see trees, bushes. There's nothing out here. What happened?"

I pointed up. "*They* know."

Panic rose within me.

It had arrived from who-knows-where, and now it was hovering not far away. The spacecraft—the spherical vessel that had brought the Invaders to Earth. It appeared to be made of reflective metal and glass, assuming they used the same materials we had on Earth. The reflectiveness prevented any of us from seeing inside—from learning their secrets. Only the surrounding transport tubes revealed what was inside.

With the hangar roof no longer in the way, I saw the vessel more clearly—part of it, anyway. Although the vessel dwarfed the hangar itself, which was already massive in size, the vessel was so wide that I still couldn't see the other end. Its interior tower, which stood in the middle of the vessel, extended so many stories into the sky that I couldn't even count them.

If the vessel's enormity was anything to go by, the Invaders eclipsed our world in all respects—minimizing our existence and capabilities. Unmistakably, we were no longer the superior species on this planet. Unbeknownst to us, we were vulnerable. The Invaders leveraged their enormity and conquered us with ease.

We're doomed.

I tried to remain calm, just as my mother had encouraged me to be under these circumstances . . . actually, under most circumstances.

I took a deep breath, closed my eyes, and told myself that maybe things would be a little bit better now that we were outside of the hangar.

When I opened my eyes, I gazed beyond the wide shadow of the vessel, finding a few birds basking in the sun on a fallen tree trunk nearby, just outside the luminous barrier. One had glistening, snow-white feathers and looked like a tiny angel as it flew away.

For the first time in a long time, I smiled.

Further off in the distance, far beyond where the birds were fluttering, were the three other hangars my mother had mentioned. I squinted, thinking that I'd just seen people milling around the closest hangar to us, maybe even entering them. I wondered if my dad was in one of them. Between us and the other hangars was the barrier, and getting anywhere near it was forbidden. That meant we were kept separate from the others—more controllable that way, I supposed. I doubted Mom would allow us to go that far away to find out, when to her walking out the doors merely ten feet was a concern. Venturing to what looked like a football field away was never going to happen.

"We've got to go explore out here," Matthew announced as if reading my mind. He gazed hopefully in Mom's direction, seeking to preventatively thwart any hesitation on her part.

"Come on, Mom, it's been awful inside," I chimed in. "Let's look around a bit."

"All right, let's explore," Mom agreed. "But stay away from that barrier."

CHAPTER 11

THE GARDEN

Our newly permitted but highly controlled outdoor freedom became part of our daily routine and was worked into our structured rotations, offering a new existence and, in a way, meaning. Inside, we did very little *all the time*. We took care of our basic needs while waiting and hoping for the Invaders to magically leave. There was nowhere to go, nothing to do. But outside, we had room to walk around—run, even—as long as we stayed within the flatlands and never strayed too far in order to return quickly when our brand started tingling.

Their massive vessel was always in the sky above . . . watching.

Because the flatlands mainly consisted of grass patches and dry dirt, with not much else, Matthew and I pushed Mom to walk further away from the hangar each day and in all different directions—except to the barrier, of course. Mom was willing to go along with our adventures, mostly because she preferred venturing far from the other prisoners. We made a game of it; when the doors opened each day to release us into the outdoors, the three of us walked swiftly in the opposite direction of anyone else who tried to follow.

My choice always was to get as close to the barrier as possible to look out upon the luscious growth and changes to the world, which sat just beyond our reach. No more buildings, no more roads, no signs directing us where to go and what to buy. It was all replaced with the tallest and greenest of trees and the thickest of bushes, with the wildflowers growing beneath. Would we ever get to see beyond it?

"Look over here," Matthew called out one day, pointing to an area surrounded by tall reeds.

"Pay attention to the edge . . . and the barrier," Mom warned. This was the first time we ever reached this area, and we were too close to where Mom wanted us to avoid.

Matthew bent down and ran his hand through the sea of grass surrounding the taller stalks. "It's really damp," he noted. "Looks untouched, like no one else has been over here yet."

"Do you think it's safe?" I asked, turning to Mom just as she caught up to us.

Gauging the area in relation to the barrier, Mom replied, "It should be okay since the flatlands extend enough past the stalks. Maybe test it with a rock, just in case."

Matthew grabbed the biggest rock nearby and tossed it hard into the reeds. Nothing sparked or burned. The stalks parted momentarily, exposing a greener area inside.

"Look, there's an old sign," Matthew pointed to the side.

Mom read it aloud:

YOU'LL BE LIKE A WELL-WATERED GARDEN,
LIKE A SPRING WHOSE WATERS NEVER FAIL.

Matthew and I smiled at each other, grabbed hands, and stepped forward.

"Hang on." Mom's arm swung out in front of us, just like she used to do after braking the car too quickly. "I'll go first." We stepped aside allowing Mom to reach a foot through the stalks. She pulled it back quickly. I squeezed Matthew's hand.

She put the same foot back through again, touched it to the ground, and put her weight on it.

Nothing happened.

"It's just a bit mushy," she cautioned, continuing in through the reeds. "It's okay. You two can follow."

I let Matthew go in before me since, after all, it he had found it.

"Oh, cool," Matthew uttered.

"What, what is it?" I yelped, worried that I might be missing something.

Hidden in the middle of the stalks was a garden—untouched and unexploited. "It's ours . . . our own garden," I whispered.

I clutched Matthew's arm as we stood looking at our discovery.

"I remembered reading about this from school," I said. But I refrained from sharing with them that I read it on page forty-six of our history book in the fourth grade. "This was farmland before it became the base, and the military planted a garden during the war since the soil was so good." I noticed Mom's brow lift a little after I mentioned that food once grew here.

"What's in here?" Matthew reached down, parted some green stalks, and pushed off some topsoil to expose a row of orange circles peeking through the soil below. "Carrots." He squealed.

I fell to my knees beside him to clear another patch. "There's some green over here," I called out. "There's red too. Strawberries!" Matthew's favorite. I picked a small one from its stem, remembering the little garden my brother and I had started at home. Like most everything else, despite our enthusiasm, we never saw it through. All that survived at our home garden were the tomato plants, which never seemed to die. But I still loved that garden.

I brushed the dirt off the tiny berry. "Here, Matthew. Try it." In that moment, it seemed like a slice of heaven, even making me forget about the chocolate I craved each day.

Matthew looked at Mom. "Can I?"

"I couldn't keep you from it even if I tried." Mom chuckled. "Go ahead."

I was a bit astonished that Mom gave her approval so easily, especially coming from a mother that made us wash our hands immediately after school, slather on hand sanitizer while out in public, and soak any produce from the grocery store before eating it. Maybe she realized, rightly so, that none of that really mattered anymore.

Matthew popped the strawberry in his mouth and flashed us a big smile. "So good . . . so delicious." I plucked another berry, took a bite, and sighed in delight.

This moment brought me back to a month before we were taken—the dream trip to the sustainable farm with my ninth-grade science class and my best friend, Zary. That farm we visited was everything I imagined. The animals, the garden, the well, the solar. All off grid. All of it made sense. It coexisted without harming anything. Mrs. Pickering, my teacher, pointed to the free-range chickens out of the barn, enjoying the sun, pecking away at the grass.

I remembered grabbing Zary during that field trip, explaining, "I want this!"

"Really? It kinda stinks," Zary had responded. I even remembered her wrinkled nose. I waved her off, not letting her ruin the moment for me.

Reliving it took me back to that feeling—the feeling of seeing my future, knowing what I wanted, and being so excited about it all. Until it was ruined. During the entire bus ride back from the sustainable farm that day, I didn't release my tight grip from that armrest. Not until we parked. It was the first time I was happy to arrive at school . . . ever. The smell on Coach Blaizer's breath that day was unmistakable—it was just like my dad's the morning he left, after he had been drinking all night, again.

"Lauren?" Mom touched my shoulder. Her touch brought me back to the garden. "Where'd you go?"

"The garden of the shackled spirit," I whispered to her.

Mom's eyes coated with tears.

Matthew rolled his eyes and groaned.

Mom had told me about the belief of a shackled spirit, after the school bus attack when I cried about it happening to me. *Lauren, you can't allow this singular, dark event subjugate your spirit with despair—it doesn't define you*, she had cautioned. *Continue to have hope in this world and in your life. Release your spirit . . . to love, to trust, to be free.* I remembered us sitting together beside the bus, just after she found us, and falling into her and closing my eyes. She caressed my hair and hummed her favorite song to comfort me.

And that was what the garden symbolized to me—its hidden life growing within a protective ring of tall reeds, discovered in the midst of tragedy. It continued to grow within, never failing despite its pitiable conditions. I wouldn't let the memory of the attack ruin it for me. This time, I focused on the *positive* of the moment—in the garden—just as Mom had encouraged and the counselor had taught me.

All that day in the garden, we pulled weeds and shifted topsoil until our hands were filthy and our clothes were splattered with dirt. When I caught Mom humming her favorite song, I knew she enjoyed it as much as I did.

"Do you think we could grow our own food here?" I asked her. "Like we did at home?" I hoped that, by keeping this garden, it meant a new way forward for us, and that perhaps life in the containment could become just a little better.

"We can try," Mom responded. "But we need to be cautious about it. No one should see us coming in and out of it, especially not from above."

What a day. I sighed . . . until I felt the tingling on my shoulder, right where I was branded.

"Do you two feel that?" Mom asked, patting her shoulder. "It's time, before we're dragged in."

We had just slipped out of the garden when, out of the corner of my eye, I saw strange movement.

"Matthew," I whispered just as the bush rustled. "Something's out there."

"Where?" Matthew asked, just before a large, golden paw was exposed. "I just saw it." He hunched down, instinctively.

"Stay still," Mom demanded from behind me.

We were exposed out here in the flatlands. There was no cover for us, nowhere to hide, aside from the stalks we had just left behind. Even the garden wouldn't provide much safety.

A snarling mouth appeared from behind the bushes—a cougar, a large one, trailed by two smaller ones. We must've appeared to be easy prey, or maybe a threat to her two cubs.

Ignoring Mom's command, Matthew slowly moved toward me. With each step he took, the cougar slowly stalked. Once he reached for my hand, the cougar leapt straight at us.

Matthew pulled me to him, and we broke into a sprint. Behind us, a sudden yowl shook us to a stop.

"Mom?" Matthew called out.

"I'm here!" Mom panted as she reached us. We'd left her

behind—not thinking, just running. "But you've got to come back and see this."

The cougar paced just outside the barrier, with her cubs wrestling nearby.

"She was stopped by the barrier. See, her fur is singed." Mom explained. "Just as we can't get out, nothing can get in."

"So essentially our prison kept us from being mauled to death," I remarked sarcastically.

Matthew grabbed his arm. "That time was strong." The tingling in our brand turned into a painful singe. We got the message: We had to go.

"We have to get back to the hangar," Mom commanded. "Now."

CHAPTER 12

A SHIFT HAPPENS

That night, I welcomed the sleep rotation. I was exhausted, not only from the frightening experience with the cougar but also from the amazing discovery of the garden. Even before the Invaders had a chance to force us to sleep, I closed my eyes and wanted to drift off, thinking about all the wonderful foods we could grow in the garden.

No matter how hard I tried, though, I couldn't sleep, kept awake by a group of prisoners who had congregated around nearby bunks. Seemingly ignoring the risk of punishment by a Vellatros abduction, they talked in low murmurs, and I couldn't help but eavesdrop.

"They're meeting our basic needs—for now anyway," one man warned. "But we aren't meant to just sit around all day doing nothing. We're becoming complacent."

"We're caged up like animals," another groaned, "and only let outdoors when *they* feel like letting us."

I rolled over and squeezed my eyes shut, hoping they'd stop

talking or, at least, move away. Their talking about our situation wasn't going to change anything.

"You are all correct," I heard a woman's voice saying. "Humans aren't meant to sit still and do nothing. We need purpose and meaning beyond our basic needs. Being held captive doesn't change who we inherently are." She paused. "But be wise. In talking like this, you risk much, with those shadow aliens above."

Clearly, she was the smart one of the group.

The discussion died down after that, but before I could finally sleep, Matthew's face appeared over the side of the bunk. "Hey, did you hear those guys?" he asked.

"*Everyone* heard them," I responded, rolling my eyes.

"Well, they made a good point. I'm tired of being dragged around by my shoulder, going wherever the Invaders want me to go. We need to do something more around here."

"No, we don't," I snarled, still annoyed by the group. "*We* have the *garden*."

Matthew disappeared back up to his bunk, but I heard him murmur, "It's not enough."

Every time the hangar's door opened, the excitement of Matthew and me racing to the garden never faded for me. We went there every day, clearing brush and soil, searching the ground for new vegetables or seeds to plant, examining how much the blossoms and fruit had grown overnight. The garden filled a void. I had work to do, a purpose—that was what those other prisoners were lacking, not us.

After a while, though, Matthew slowed to walk with Mom each day, letting me race to the garden on my own. I realized then it wasn't enough for him.

"I can't just sit around here anymore," he said one day.

I heard the defeat in his voice. "Come on, the garden is great," I protested. "Plus, what else would you be doing?"

Matthew stood up, angrily brushed dirt from his jeans, and poked a finger through the tiny hole starting to tear at the knee. "What happens when they come for us?" he demanded, crossing his arms in frustration. "How are we going to protect ourselves? How am I going to protect the two of you?" He stomped off through the stalks, leaving Mom and me to look at each other in surprise.

"While I was enjoying my fresh carrots, he apparently had other things on his mind," I joked.

"Lauren, be kind to your brother," Mom responded. "This hasn't been easy for anyone. He's only a boy, and even though it's not his job, he seems to have taken on the burden of protecting us."

I don't need his protection, I almost said, but I stopped myself, remembering the bus attack at school. I needed Matthew then, and he *did* protect me. He tried his best to fight the varsity quarterback at my school, ending up with staples in his head for protecting me.

I lowered my head and went back to gardening.

The next day, Matthew stayed outside of the stalks instead of joining us in the garden.

"Is he coming in?" Mom asked me after a while.

I shrugged and turned back to clearing the weeds. I didn't really care what Matthew was up to, especially not after finding a new tomato large enough to eat.

Mom peered out of the stalks and then waved me over. I poked my head out next to Mom. Just a short distance away, out in the open, Matthew appeared to be exercising. He ran in place, did some jumping jacks, grabbed a large rock next to him, and then started all over again. A dust cloud formed around him as he jumped around. It looked like he had created a little routine.

After that day, my brother didn't return to the garden with us—wouldn't even go in. I supposed a twelve-year-old boy was not meant to sit around all day, gardening with his mom and older sister. Instead, he spent his outdoor time exercising—creating new routines and then repeating them over and over.

As we sat down to eat one day, Matthew squeezed in between Mom and me, which was unusual since he liked his own space most of the time. "You two need to keep your muscle strength up," he urged. "You can't just sit around and do nothing all the time."

"Hey, we dig in the garden," I retorted. "It's hard work." Maybe it didn't increase my heart rate, but it was all I had to look forward to each day. I wasn't going to let it go. Besides, I didn't have much more physical or even emotional energy to do anything else than to be in that garden.

But Mom nodded. "I'll join you tomorrow," she said. "I've noticed that a few others have been following you. Lauren, you should come too." From her tone, I gathered that it wasn't optional for me.

"What? No. I'm not giving up my garden," I challenged.

Matthew chuckled. "You're coming."

The next day, before I could dash off to the garden, Mom steered me toward the large rock outcropping that marked Matthew's exercise spot. "Just try it," she pleaded as I tried to wrangle myself from her light grip.

"For a little bit," I grunted. "But then I'm going to the—" I stopped before uttering "the garden" just as a few others filed past us, not wanting to give away my secret. "You know where."

Before I knew it, a small following gathered around Matthew's exercise spot. Where had all the people come from? This was for Matthew?

Standing in front of the rock face, Matthew clapped his hands a few times, and people stood to attention. Younger kids ran up front to be close to him. I crept to the back, not wanting to be caught by Matthew or Mom, or be seen by anyone, when I planned to sneak away to my garden.

"Reach!" Matthew instructed, his arms in the air. "Feel that pull!" Then he demonstrated a squat position. "You can do it! Hold!"

At Matthew's direction the group started doing squats, burpees, jumping jacks, and other exercises with names I didn't know. Most of them seemed to know what to do, as if this was their daily routine. I couldn't believe it. Matthew had formed this exercise group and become its leader, all while I was hidden away in my garden. I was proud of my little brother. His enthusiasm had inspired others.

But to me, the idea of it was rather comical: a bunch of people exercising in the dirt, playing with rocks, while imprisoned by aliens. I nearly laughed out loud during the jumping jacks when I thought about what was really happening.

A few stragglers came to watch and then stayed. After all, what else did any of them have to do? I could barely keep up. I couldn't even do these exercises in P.E. class before our captivity, and that certainly hadn't changed. Plus, I was afraid I looked ridiculous. But I didn't leave. I stayed for my brother.

"Nice job today, everyone," Matthew said at last, offering fist bumps and high fives. Then he turned to us with a disappointed smirk. "What are you two doing . . . *sitting*?"

"Help me up," Mom responded, lifting her hand toward Matthew. "We'll do better tomorrow. I promise."

"Tomorrow?" I huffed. "Not likely. I'll be . . . well, not here."

But the next day, Mom pulled me back. "Matthew is right to be doing this," she puffed as we jogged in place. "It gets us up and moving. He's trying to keep us strong and motivated."

"Maybe," I replied.

I stopped jogging and stole a glance at the vessel, overwhelming and ever present. In the garden, I was always looking down and tended to forget the Invaders were even there. But being in the open flatlands, I felt exposed, helpless even. Everything about us was dwarfed by the Invaders.

"There's nothing we could do to fight them," I murmured, pointing upward for Mom to see. "They're massive."

Mom stopped. "Lauren, you're missing the point." She grabbed at her chest as if that would help her breathe easier. "More people are coming to Matthew each day. It's giving them something they didn't have before."

"Hey, you two in the back!" Matthew called out, flashing a smile. "Try to keep up." Mom and I turned to each other with a shocked look and quickly got back to jogging in place.

We finished . . . finally. Much to my surprise, I felt good—a bit sore, but energized. My mood was lighter, too. I saw people shaking Matthew's hand and thanking him, and it clicked. My brother was giving them the motivation and sense of purpose we all needed.

I wanted to let him know I supported him. "Matthew, that was great."

Mom nodded. "You're really making a difference for all of us. I'm very proud of you, Matthew."

He blushed and stood a little taller. "Just keep coming, okay?"

As he walked behind the rocks, I realized that my brother seemed different now—older and maybe even a little wiser than a typical twelve-year old. Matthew had always had a sensitive side, but now he seemed to be growing and maturing as if years had passed, not just months.

I followed Matthew. Maybe if we talked about it, I could lift some of that burden he took on, as Mom had mentioned.

I found him with something pointed in his hand, striking at a rock. "What're you doing over here?"

"Carving," he explained, holding up a sharp piece of metal.

"Whoa," I responded. It was practically a blade. I bit my underlip. We both knew the risk of what he was doing. "Where'd you get that?"

"Near the scaffolding, just after that guy was taken. Don't tell Mom. We might need it . . . someday."

I realized Mom was right. He really did believe he had to protect us.

"I started sharpening it on this stone a while back, just in case," Matthew continued. "Now I just like carving."

I kneeled to see what he cut into the stone:

UNITED

COURAGE

ST

"When I'm done, it will say *strength*—to keep people's spirits up," he explained. "Kinda like to keep a light going inside, if that makes any sense."

"It does." I touched his shoulder and sat down next to him on the rocky edge. "Look at all that you've done, all these people you're helping. That's all you—no one else."

"Well, we need everyone to be strong, just in case—" He paused. "Lauren, we need to get through this somehow."

I knew if I stayed any longer, I'd miss my afternoon in the garden. But it didn't matter. Matthew had never shared his thoughts like this with me before. It wasn't like I'd reached out to him to ask, though.

Mom always said he had a big heart. My brother was that kid on the soccer field who helped another player up when they fell or cheered the team on even when they were losing. His adorable grin and perfectly placed freckles could make anyone laugh, except for me, of course. But I had never really thought of his compassion as strength—not until the school bus attack . . . and that day by the rock.

Matthew always seemed to find a way to work his charm, even when he was hurting and wooing the nurses at the hospital after the attack. Those memories come rushing back to me in perfect detail.

◆

As Mom and I drove silently to the hospital that day, about a month before we were taken by the Invaders, she squeezed my hand like she never wanted to let me go.

"Matthew saved me." My eyes welled as I spoke those words.

Mom careened into the parking lot when we reached the hospital's emergency room entrance, and she ran inside, pulling me along.

"My young son, he came alone in the ambulance. Has it arrived yet?" Mom blurted out, without allowing the nurses time to answer. "Do you know where he is? Can we see him?"

"We've been waiting for you." One of the nurses responded, finally calming Mom. She walked us through the double doors and down the brightly lit hallways before we stopped at another, more private waiting room. "Please wait here. The doctor will be out to see you soon. He's working to stop the bleeding on your son's head. He'll explain what's going on once he's finished. Please be patient. Just know he's in the best of hands."

The doctors had to shave my little brother's head, exposing the metal staples in it to close the wound. Between that and the machines beeping and tubes disappearing into Matthew's body, I didn't know which was scarier.

Matthew grinned weakly when he saw us at the door, and I instantly regretted all the times I had teased him. After all of our fighting, he still saved me.

Mom rushed to Matthew's side, dropping my hand. "My baby boy," she mouthed. She leaned in, hovering over him. It would have been suffocating for him if he wasn't so hurt.

"Mama, my head hurts." He ran his little hands through his hair, slightly touching the shaved part. "Am I going home?" Though I could see he was trying to be strong, his eyes swelled with tears.

"Soon, baby," Mom assured him. "You were so brave, so strong, both of you kids."

I squeezed in next to her, lightly touching his arm. "Thank you," I whispered to him.

I touched the ground next to Matthew's carvings near his exercise spot. We hadn't been summoned to return to the hangar just yet. "How about you work in *faith over fear* next?" I suggested.

"Ha, you must be kidding me. Have you seen what I have to carve with?" Matthew grinned. "How about I just carve *hope*. For you."

I liked it. "Perfect. That's all that needs to be said."

"And you'll come back to exercise tomorrow?" His expression turned serious.

I nodded and smiled at him.

"Good." Matthew returned to carving. But under his breath, he added, "Next I'm adding in fight training."

Months passed. We lost track.

Matthew's exercise sessions progressed and were much advanced. He implemented sparring techniques in the routine, just as he said he would. We practiced blocking, leg sweeps, and punches. Mom made us take karate lessons after the attack but that seemed like a lifetime ago, and we hadn't learned what Matthew was now teaching. He explained that the advanced techniques just seemed to come to him, in his thoughts, and he couldn't really explain it any better.

The exercise group continued to grow in both size and intensity. Despite lingering in captivity, the people in our group were invigorated by the idea of reclaiming their strength. It was empowering and uplifting, and Matthew had created it all. He began to open each session with an uplifting message that he changed daily and reinforced that we had to stay strong and be ready for whatever may come.

Soon after that, he started calling us all "warriors."

After so much time had passed, one thing had become very clear. Our captivity was not coming to an end. Our daily life remained the same. Inside the hangar, we eagerly waited each day for the doors to open so we could garden, exercise, and really, just breathe. Not much changed for us on the ground.

But in the sky, more Invaders arrived.

Smaller vessels appeared day after day, clustering around the larger vessel that had been there since the beginning. Earth's airspace was being occupied by an entirely new world—*their* world. It seemed that, as their conquest expanded, our existence would remain restricted to the hangars. Meanwhile, our populace continued to be thinned by the Vellatros' abductions.

I figured this was it for us—this would be our day-to-day existence, forever.

I was wrong.

It happened again.

CHAPTER 13

NOTHING STAYS THE SAME

I was startled awake in the morning by that familiar tingling on my shoulder, which quickly turned into a strong tug followed by a surge of pain. With no warning and no control, I was yanked out of my bed, hitting the side of Mom's mattress, shaking the whole bunk as I fell to the floor. I knew what was happening. We'd been through this before. None of us could resist once the tugging of our arms began taking us.

I screamed out, and extended my hand up to Mom, expecting her to grab it and pull me up. But she couldn't reach, just wriggled and grappled with the air as if pinned down against her will by an unseen force.

"I can't move." Matthew yelled from the top bunk. "I can't move!"

I fought against the void that controlled us, grabbing and kicking against . . . nothing that I could even see. I tried with all my might just to move a leg toward them, but the invisible force overpowered me, dragging me in the opposite direction.

"Mom!" I screamed, reaching out to her again, hoping this time she would grab me and keep us together. Tears flooded my eyes; I couldn't shake it. "Momma!"

"Lauren, I'm trying," Mom called out.

"Matthew!" I shrieked, choking on my own spit. I thought I would vomit after that last strong tug that pulled me away further from them.

"Someone, help us!" Mom cried out. "Help my daughter!"

But no one came. Screams filled the hangar as other girls were pulled from their bunks too. We were grabbed without warning. Like me, they kicked and screamed and grabbed at the air, trying desperately not to be dragged away. Everyone else remained in their beds, paralyzed.

We had seen this invisible force move others before, taking them whenever the Invaders chose and wherever they directed—never knowing the end point. It was my turn. My separation was methodical and swift, just like everything else up to this point had been during our captivity.

I flopped to the ground with nothing left in me to fight it, simply powerless. I was pulled along the ground, convulsing and sobbing. Tears and slobber mingled on my face, and I didn't care. I was being torn from my family—the only thing I had left in this world, the only thing that mattered. Other girls continued to scream the whole way, while some, especially the little ones . . . they just huddled up in a ball and cried as they were dragged away.

My bunk was almost out of view. I held out my arm toward Mom and Matthew one last time, as if it were my last chance to hold on to them. It was a pointless gesture.

Just as I lost sight of them, I blacked out.

When I regained consciousness, I bolted upright.

"Ouch!" I winced, rubbing my forehead where I just had hit it. A bunk was above me, along with rows of beds around me, with people sleeping in each one. I looked for Mom and Matthew, but they were nowhere near me.

No Matthew bouncing on his bunk above me. No Mom planning our next move. I'd never been away from her for more than a day, and now my protectors, my support, my everything—they were gone, taken from me.

We were separated.

Around me was all so familiar. The bunk beds, and the same unnerving quietness of the forced sleep that I somehow managed to shake before anyone else. Beyond the bunks were the same cement walls leading up to the same soaring ceiling, with the same line of windows just below the dome. Still, I hadn't grown accustomed to any of it.

I was in a hangar, that was for certain. There was an eating area on the other side of the hangar, but it looked different.

This wasn't the same hangar.

I was wearing a uniform—an olive-green jumpsuit that zipped up the front. Where was my favorite sweatshirt? Where were my backpack, my journal, my stuffed kitty? They were all I had left from home. Would Mom be able to keep them for me? I bit my lip so as not to make a sound, but I couldn't hold back the tears, which fell silently down my cheeks. *Mom.* I didn't know if I would ever see her again, or Matthew.

I was alone.

Wiping my eyes, I peered at the bunks closest to me. There were only girls sleeping in them. Some looked to be around my age or a little older, and others were much younger. No older women. No boys and no men.

No Mom and no Matthew.

Silence remained as the other girls began to wake.

I should have been crying out loud by now. I thought everyone else would be crying too. I *wanted* to cry . . . to yell out to my mom and brother . . . to jump out of the bunk and run back to them. But I was overtaken by a peculiar, involuntary sense of calm and became oddly complacent. Suddenly, I knew. The calm, like the forced sleep, must have come from *them*.

Some of the others stared at me as if I could explain what was happening, being the only one sitting upright and fully awake. I said nothing. I had no answers for them, or even for me, though I wanted to share encouraging words. I shrugged my shoulders instead, just as Matthew would have done before we were taken.

Although no one said a word, I suspected we were all thinking the same thing.

Where are we?

Then the tingling began. I rubbed my shoulder, wishing it would go away. It didn't. The tingling turned into a harsh tug, pulling us all out of our beds in unison. Only a few resisted. I no longer had any fight left in me to even try, and without Mom or Matthew around to get back to, there was no point. My feeling of complacency was all my own, not from the Invaders. I let myself be taken to wherever the Invaders wanted us to go.

As in the other hangar, we were pulled from the bunks to the eating area, and then to our hygiene routine and back to bed. I kept to myself, not talking to anyone else. I followed Mom's early instincts not to interact with others in our captivity. Isolating was meant to protect us from another's punishment and from a capture in the wingspan of the shadow creatures.

What did I have to say to these girls anyway? *I miss my mom and my brother and everything from home, from before the invasion.* Why would they want to hear about that? They were living through the same nightmare. At this point, I didn't have it in me to make any friends, just to lose them at the whim of the Invaders.

Days, possibly weeks even, passed like this, in the same way as before, but this time things were worse. We were deprived of outdoor time. It seemed that the purpose of our existence was merely to stay alive . . . until a familiar boom rang through the hangar.

The doors were *opening*.

I sprinted toward them, pushing aside smaller girls and clawing at the doors, determined to be one of the first to get out. Why be polite anymore? I was on my own and only looking out for me.

Then I remembered the frenzy when the doors had first opened at the other hangar—how Mom held us back and saved us from that massacre. What would we find outside this time? I quickly stepped aside, letting the other girls swarm the space I'd just given up. I even chuckled a bit, being somewhat proud that I had possibly just saved myself from a gruesome death.

As the gap widened, a few of the skinny, younger girls slipped out and ran beyond my view. No cries of pain, no torching of skin, and no shadows darkened the doorway—meaning no Vellatros had appeared. Maybe we really were getting outside the hangar after all. Maybe I'd get to see Mom and Matthew again. I pushed my way to the doors.

I was out.

After I took another step out, I was blasted by crisp, fresh air from which I'd been deprived for too long. I had lost the will to count the number of days that had passed, too numb to care.

Closing my eyes, I turned my face toward the sun, feeling its warmth on my cheeks, and took in another long, deep breath. I felt as though I had been reunited with an old friend—the outside—which was the one thing I had left worth living for. Everything else had been taken away.

I opened my eyes to find the ever-lingering Vellatros swirling around the skies, looking for their next victim.

Then I ran.

In my mind, I was running back to Matthew and Mom, as if they'd been there the whole time, just waiting for me. But as I grew closer to the clump of tall reeds surrounding the garden, I saw that familiar iridescent rainbow crisscross design, this time blocking the garden like a pixelated chain-link fence.

I knew what it was. There was no need to test it with a rock, like Mom had us do before. It was the barrier—the same one that rotted human flesh off the bone.

My knees buckled and I fell, just out of reach of the stalks. I couldn't get to the garden . . . or to my family.

I stayed there on my knees, staring at the stalks that swayed faintly in the light breeze for what felt like hours. I didn't know if the breeze was even real, or if the warmth I felt on my cheeks was from the real sun. I didn't know anything anymore.

When the tingling on my shoulder began—the warning by the Invaders that it was time to return—I didn't move. Just sat staring at the garden, the one I couldn't get to. The tingling turned to tugging—a stronger warning—and I still didn't move. The tugging turned to forceful dragging, pulling me along the rocky ground all through the flatlands. Being one of the last girls to be pulled into the hangar, I felt that I'd managed to resist the Invaders in a way, even though it accomplished nothing. Or so I thought.

Off in the distance was a priceless view I caught just before the doors slammed shut.

It was another hangar—and those doors were just opening.

In my bunk that night, I couldn't stop thinking about the people being released from the other hangar. Were Mom and Matthew among them?

The next day, when we were released to the outside, I stayed beside the barrier with the best view I could get of the other hangar, determined to see the others released . . . to find my family.

I came back to that same spot day after day, refusing to move until I was forcefully dragged along the ground with no choice but to return inside. My pointless attempt to physically resist the invisible force made a bit of a commotion, with my flailing about—enough so a few distant figures outside the other hangar stopped to watch each afternoon.

I even saw some of them point my way.

After a week or so of making a spectacle of myself, I started to lose hope. What was I achieving anyway? I shuffled my way over to my spot, nonetheless. After all, I had nothing else to do but to plop down into the dirt and toss a few pebbles around, just waiting. No one had been released at the other hangar yet. As I searched for more pebbles to throw, I noticed scratches in the dirt on the other side of the barrier. They almost looked like letters.

Careful not to come in contact with the barrier, I sat on my knees for a better look, keeping steady. The scratches *were* letters—a message that read:

> **LAUREN**
>
> **ITS MOM**
>
> **I LOVE YOU**

She had seen me!

I lightly touched the ground in front of me, writing:

MOM IM HERE I MISS YOU

I tried to contain my tears so as not to ruin my message. I missed her; I *so* missed her. I missed her voice, her hugs, her voice of reason—all of it. It was unbearable trying to get through any of this without her or Matthew. I was lost, so lost, and just . . . sad.

The next day, I found a new message: *We'll be together again*

And another one the following day: *I miss you my baby*

The one that hurt the most was when she wrote a simple: *Smile*

It was impossible to smile. Aside from when I saw Mom's messages, I hadn't smiled since being forced to the girls' hangar. Weeks had passed, and in all that time, I hadn't talked to a single person. I felt alone and disconnected. Mom's dirt messages made me realize that I needed someone to talk to. My self-imposed isolation had to end.

My chance came at the next eating rotation, when I decided to join some of the other girls, approaching a group sitting together at the table not far from the food.

"Hi," I said hesitantly. "Can I sit with you?" I felt like I was in second grade, asking to join the popular girls' table. It seemed so inane under the circumstances.

"Sure," one spoke up.

As I quietly released the breath I held back while waiting to see if they'd accept me, I slid in beside her. She seemed safe. Some of the other girls looked my way and surprisingly smiled. I smiled back, but then quickly looked down at my plate. I caught myself patting down my pants for comfort. I wasn't ready to fully engage just yet.

They didn't talk much, just exchanged glances. I got the sense that they were just as overwhelmed as I was.

One of the girls, with long, light brown hair, who looked to be about my age, broke the table's silence. "Did any of you notice yesterday the other hangar was released *before* we were brought back in?"

"I think it's a men's hangar," a girl down the table replied. "I didn't see any girls."

"I tried looking for my dad," said another quietly.

"Did you find him, Mazie?" asked the girl with the brown hair who first spoke.

"No," Mazie replied. She slumped a little in her seat, and I felt sorry for her. "I'm going back—"

I interrupted, "Can I go with you?" I needed her to show me exactly where she saw the boys' hangar.

Mazie looked at the brown-haired girl sitting next to her. The friend shrugged her shoulders and responded, "Sure, I guess." I smiled, and felt a flutter in my stomach, thinking that maybe Matthew would be there.

When it was our time to be released outside, I waited right beside the opened doors. Others passed by me, but none looked my way, keeping their heads down as they shuffled along. I finally spotted Mazie hand in hand with her friend with the long, light brown hair.

"Hi," I called out. "It's me from the table." Just as I waved her over, she pulled the other girl along with her through the group to get to me.

"I'm Mazie," she confirmed, "and this is Shaila."

Shaila gave a small, unenthusiastic wave, trying to avoid an abundance of eye contact.

"I'm Lauren," I answered, but I wasn't really interested in unnecessary formalities. "Can you show me the other hangar now?"

"Um," Mazie responded, turning to Shaila for the answer, just like she did at the dining table. Shaila pulled her aside, and they began whispering.

Being intentionally excluded from their conversation was irritating. Whispers like that were all too familiar to me, particularly after my return to school following the attack on the school bus.

Finally, the two girls stopped whispering and walked past me. "Let's go," Shaila ordered.

They stayed ahead of me, while I followed behind. Though I needed them, I didn't appreciate the strange attitude. Maybe my morose approach at the table wasn't well received by them. I told myself that I needed to do better if I was going to try to be friendly with anyone.

After a few minutes, the other hangar was within sight, which was in the opposite direction of the hangar Mom was in. I had not yet seen this one, but I really didn't look for it. I never expected to leave Mom's hangar, not wanting to miss her messages.

"Just meet me back at our spot after you show her," Shaila directed Mazie, before walking off, not even looking my way to say goodbye. Mazie gave her a quick nod.

"Hey, are you okay?" Mazie asked. I wasn't breathing well and felt a little weak. "You look pale."

"Um." That was my only response. The thought of seeing Matthew again had me anxious and excited—and then there was the fear of *not* seeing him. None of this I was about to share with her, though.

"Well, it's over there." She pointed to the nearby hangar, then left to catch up with Shaila.

When I stepped closer, the hairs on my arms rose and tingling rang through my ears. I knew what that meant. It happened every time I sat too close to the barrier looking for Mom. I learned how to feel the electrical feedback off the barriers. One more step, and the translucent, oscillating barrier shimmered into view, with the hangar in the distance beyond it. I couldn't go any further, couldn't get any closer.

The doors were shut, and the outside area was empty. Mazie and Shaila had already turned to head back toward our hangar. But I sat and waited, scribbling in the dirt, while my mind wandered. If this was an only boys' hangar, as they said, then it was likely I wouldn't find my dad in there.

Though he hadn't lived with us for a long time, I still wondered what happened to him after the invasion. Was he taken by a Vellatros? Was he with his other family? I thought about him and the last time we were together as a family.

✦

After leaving Mom, Dad had his girlfriend and her kids move in. Her kids even took the beds he set up for Matthew and me. We got pushed out. We tried not to let it get to us, but I guess that was why Matthew and I grew so close. I thought about how we shared our allowance money, keeping it in a box at home, under my bed. That's where all eleven- and fourteen-year-olds saved their money, wasn't it?

The day he left our home, Matthew and I found him on the couch, unmoving. I could never forget that smell.

Dad had done this before. He stumbled around, smelled, and yelled at me for my toys being on the ground. Mom explained later that was likely the reason why I kept my room and things in such meticulous order as I got older.

"Just keep getting ready for school," she huffed, bundling us out of the room. "I'll take care of this."

"I can help Daddy," Matthew insisted. He was six years old and as sweet as he'd always been. I wasn't going to help, and I knew enough to stay off to the side of the room so I could avoid Dad's attention when he was like this.

Mom dragged him off the couch, and he landed with a thump.

He jumped to his feet, unsteady. "Why'd you do that?" he yelled. "*You* don't touch me again." He raised his hand to hit her.

That was the last morning we found Dad at the house.

Too much time had passed while I was lost in my memories, and now I worried that I might not see Matthew before being dragged back to my hangar. And I'd strayed too far from my hangar just to try to see him.

I decided to leave a message for Matthew, just as Mom had done for me:

MATTHEW ITS LAUREN
IM

Before I could finish my message, I heard a scraping boom—the familiar sound of the massive doors struggling to open. I jumped to my feet, and watched as the doors opened, little by little. Mazie and Shaila were right. The hangar's occupants were all boys, about the same ages as the girls in my hangar—mostly teenagers and younger boys. No men.

The hangar doors opened wider, and more boys poured out. They seemed to be gathering or circling up for some reason. Fearing that Matthew would blend into the crowd and I'd be unable to see him, I jumped up and down to call attention to myself, shouting, "Matthew! Matthew!"

From the middle of the crowd, a boy looked up. His grin was unmistakable.

I found my brother.

CHAPTER 14

BITTERSWEET REUNION

When I awoke in my bunk the next day, it felt different. I had important things to do.

When the doors opened for outdoor time, I pushed my way through, being one of the first to get out. I ran to the barrier, hoping to find a message from Mom. A new one read: *I so miss you.*

My poor mom, I thought. I had found Matthew, but she was still all alone.

I kneeled down and scribbled a new message in the dirt:

I FOUND MATTHEW

WAIT FOR ME HERE IF YOU CAN

Next to it, I drew an arrow pointing in the direction of the boys' hangar. There was no longer any time to sit and mope by the barrier—I had to get back to my brother. He would be released soon for outdoor time, and I wanted to be there.

The previous afternoon, Matthew had spotted me over the shoulder of another boy.

"Matthew," I called out to him.

Even from afar, I saw him narrow his eyes and shake his head in disbelief. He pushed through the other boys and ran toward the barrier at full speed. An Olympic sprinter could hardly have reached me faster.

And then he was there, right in front of me—almost close enough to touch.

It was hard to say which one of us was more stunned that I'd found him.

The crowd of boys who had surrounded Matthew were still milling about near the hangar with confused looks on their faces. They seemed to be waiting for him.

"Lauren! I can't believe it," Matthew said, wiping his eyes.

Tears fell down my cheeks. I couldn't respond. I couldn't even touch him, separated still by the barrier.

"Can you hear me?" Matthew shouted. I shook my head, frantically.

"I found you. It's really you!" I rubbed my arm over my face to clear off my own tears.

Now he was the one who couldn't respond. His eyes filled with more tears.

"Have you seen Mom?" I sniveled.

He pulled in a deep breath. "No. My hangar is just a bunch of guys."

"I'm in there, and she's in that other one." I pointed to my hangar and then to hers.

"How are you so sure?"

"I get messages in the dirt from her." I explained.

"What?" Matthew asked, looking a bit baffled.

I told him about the messages. "I return to that same spot, day after day, and finally got her attention."

"But you haven't actually talked to her yet?"

I shook my head. "She would have to run out as soon as she's released to find me before I get pulled in. It hasn't worked out yet, and I don't know why."

Matthew nodded somberly. "Our outdoor time used to overlap with theirs. I'm usually busy with drills, but I saw them get released for their outdoor rotation a few times. It seemed like mostly older girls and young women. Babies too."

Babies? "I didn't see any babies."

"Well, my hangar is closer to hers than yours is." Matthew responded. "I'll go over and try to find her."

"You look bigger," I observed.

He perked up. "Lauren, I don't know what it is, but our food has gotten so much better. It actually tastes good—fresh, not like that weird tofu loaf we used to get. I'm stronger . . . taller . . . faster— we're all getting healthier in here. The boys in our hangar . . . Lauren, they follow me." He lowered his voice. "We're training to fight, too."

I nodded slowly to signal that I understood, but the thought of being overheard by *them* still worried me. I changed the subject. "My hangar is only girls. We don't really do much of anything. I just keep to myself and sit by Mom's hangar." I paused. "I miss you and Mom so much."

"Remember my exercises," Matthew urged. "We all need to keep our strength up. If we ever get the chance . . . we need to be strong and prepared. I keep the boys in my containment ready—you need to do the same."

I rubbed my arm. The tingling had started.

It's not enough time. I don't want to leave him.

I didn't want to go back to the lonely girls' hangar. I wanted to stay. I wanted to be back with Mom and him.

"It's started, hasn't it? You're getting pulled back in." Matthew sounded agitated.

I nodded, and then began stumbling as my body jerked toward my hangar. "I'll come back tomorrow to see you," I cried out, trying to keep my balance. I wanted to throw myself to the ground and fight it off to stay with him, but I couldn't. If I had, my whole body would have been cut up by being dragged over the rocks and dirt all the way back to my hangar. I was just too far away, and I knew there was no fighting this invisible overseer anyway.

My brother stood there like an angry statue, with his arms rigid beside him and his fists curled tight. But there was nothing he could do to stop it. I saw his frustration. It was the same enraged look he had on the school bus long ago, just after he got knocked down. I was broken having to leave him again.

Just as I said I would, I came back to wait for him the next day. At the boys' hangar, Matthew was one of the first to push through the doors. I waved, excited to see him. While no tears fell down my cheeks during this visit, my eyes still swelled.

Just like the day before, Matthew wasn't alone. His followers were with him. A few feet from the barrier he stopped and waved his arms behind him. I heard a faint call of "Warriors," and then they all fell in line. He walked the final few steps alone.

"They obey your orders?" I asked, a little shocked.

Matthew nodded sternly. "I need to get back to them soon. I looked for Mom before I went in last night, but I didn't see her."

"I just found you though." I didn't hide my disappointment.

"We train every day," Matthew responded. "Today, and every day, you're going to join us, before you get pulled back in."

I laughed.

Matthew crossed his arms. "You heard me. You need to start with the drills again. You've gotten soft."

"Hey!" I glared at him. In my attempt to explain myself, I vented. "It's not like I can do anything in here."

"You can do it." Matthew asserted. "A little with us today, and then more tomorrow and each day after that. Bring others with you, too."

"You can't be serious about that." I tried to imagine bringing Mazie and Shaila out here to work out. *No way.*

Before I knew it, though, I was following Matthew's instructions—jumping jacks, lunges, push-ups, running in place. He got to me. I couldn't keep up. Matthew's followers didn't take breaks, and their workout was more advanced than before. I was almost glad when the tingling began.

"Look for Mom," I called out. "Find her!"

———◆———

The next day, I woke up with an unfamiliar feeling: happiness. It was slightly tempered by the soreness throughout my body, but I didn't let the thought of Matthew's exercises slow me down. At the slightest opening in the doors, I forced myself through and ran toward my spot near the barrier between my hangar and Mom's. My heart pounded in my chest, and my throat swelled.

She was there. Standing right by the message. Waiting for me.

"Mom . . ." I almost couldn't be heard under the crackle of my shaky voice.

Her hands trembled as they covered her mouth, while tears flooded her eyes. But she didn't call out to me. She was unlike her normal self, so silent. She just held up her hands near the barrier, with her palms facing me.

I trampled over my dirt messages in front of the barrier trying to get to her.

I had found her—finally.

"Lauren." She finally spoke. "It's really you, my baby girl."

Tears rolled down my cheeks. There was no holding them back. I just couldn't bring myself to follow her rule to contain them.

On my side of the barrier, I held up my hands to align with hers. "I got all your messages." I tried clearing my swollen eyes on my shoulder.

"I think of you every day—you and Matthew," she muttered. "My babies. You were taken from me. I never thought we'd be separated. I never thought . . ."

"Mom, I've seen Matthew. He's in the third hang—"

She interrupted, as if I hadn't been saying anything. "Both my babies taken from me," she continued under her breath. "I couldn't stop it—couldn't stop it."

I gulped. "Mom, I'm here now." If only I could hug her.

As if reading my mind, she stretched her arms for a hug toward me, just shy of touching the barrier. Her arm began to tug. She grabbed her shoulder at the same time she dug her heels into the ground, which was a futile attempt to fight the firmer pulls. Harder and harder she was jolted toward her hangar, with her outstretched hand toward me. I couldn't reach her, couldn't touch the barrier.

"Mom, go back. You can't stop it," I yelled. "I'll meet you here tomorrow."

Then she was gone—swallowed into the hangar. The doors slammed shut. I fell to the dirt, with my hand on my trampled, dirty messages.

I softened the dirt in front of me and wrote *I LOVE YOU*.

I wanted her to have it when she came back tomorrow.

I rushed to tell Matthew.

He was there at the barrier already, surrounded by a crowd on his side—and a crowd was growing on mine. A large group of girls had gathered near the barrier, watching the boys. Maybe they were looking for their brothers, too.

I saw Matthew and waved. The girls all turned and looked at me, maybe wondering who I was to know someone as important as Matthew. Once Matthew arrived, I heard some giggles from the group and saw some of them blushing and whispering.

"I saw Mom," I told him, ignoring his new fans.

"You did," Matthew responded, without looking my way. Instead, he flashed a big smile and nodded to the girls. I heard the girls giggle some more.

I was annoyed. "Hey," I snapped.

He looked back at me. "How is she?" Matthew finally engaged.

"To be honest, she seemed a little off."

"What do you mean, off?" Matthew asked.

"She didn't really listen to me or track what I was saying."

"She probably was trying to process it all," Matthew said. "I felt a little like that when I first saw you. Give her a break."

"I know," I sighed. "It just felt deeper than that. Like our separation hit her the hardest. Like she lost a piece of her with us gone. I can't explain it."

"I'm going today to try again to find her," Matthew vowed.

"I told her that you'd be waiting for her. I hope she understood what I meant."

"I've got to get back." Matthew motioned his head back to his group. "And you don't have much time. Get some training in before you leave. Get the other girls to do it, too." He smiled at me and gave a slight wave to the group of girls beside me. More giggles followed.

"Don't want to keep your new followers waiting," I teased.

The next day, I rushed out of my hangar again. Mom was there, waiting for me at the same spot.

"Lauren, I'm here," Mom called out. She seemed more alert, clearer in a way.

"Mom!" I panted. "You stayed for me."

"I'll be here each day," she assured me. "But before I leave, there's something I need to share with you." She looked around and then lowered her voice. "Some of the women in here—they're pregnant."

I supposed that made sense. Matthew had said there were babies in her hangar. I was happy for Mom. I knew she must enjoy helping take care of them, rocking them to sleep, just like she did with me and Matthew.

"I don't think they were pregnant before the invasion," Mom continued. "It's all highly suspicious. I think the timing of it—it's all off. There are only women in my hangar. And they're having babies."

I wasn't really comprehending what she was telling me. I didn't want to comprehend—it made me sick to my stomach. I rubbed my forehead. "What's happening, Mom?"

"I don't know, Lauren. It's concerning, though," she'd said with a sad look on her face. "These children won't know what life was like for us, outside the hangars. They won't know the love and freedom we knew, the opportunities we had."

I thought about this for a moment. "They aren't going to face the hardships either though, Mom." I responded. "No crime, no wars, no hunger . . . no attacks."

"I'm not sure if the tradeoff is worth it, Lauren. Think about it."

CHAPTER 15

CHOSEN

I couldn't shake what Mom told me about our captivity . . . and that the babies being born would only know life this way.

In this new life, we were closely monitored and controlled, both physically and emotionally. We slept when told to sleep, ate when dragged to our eating station, and learned not to resist, even to the point of our cries being dowsed at their whim. The invisible force moved us beyond our control. The constant presence of the Vellatros reminded us to comply, since they continued to appear and abduct any person who misbehaved. We were powerless to stop it, any of it.

Having the vessel hovering overhead reminded me daily of my—of our—total dependence on them. I only caught glimpses of the white-robed figures moving through the rings in their enormous, ever-present vessel. We'd been given no information about our captors since the Invader's hologram had appeared to us so many months ago, trying to justify our imprisonment and the occupation of our planet.

That was, until the girls' hangar was filled with an unexpected burst of iridescent, multicolored lights. I knew it was them. Worse, I sensed that something was about to change.

We were lifted from our seats in unison, forced to stand and turn toward the pixelation as the image continued to form. Two Invaders emerged out of the image and above our heads, far out of any of our reach. Just as the images came into view, several small objects flew in through the windows. They looked like drones but took the shape of a miniaturized version of their vessel. The drones moved in quickly and darted erratically throughout the hangar, flying so close to our heads that many of the girls had to duck.

While the others watched in awe at the drones, I watched the Invaders. They were in control. When one of them lifted its arm and swirled its long, white hand, the drone slowed and began scanning the crowd with a green laser-like light, as if searching for something. It was then that one flew right toward my table.

Even though we all ducked, it did not leave. It continued hovering overhead and repeatedly shifted gears. It was so close above us that I heard every single ping while it stayed put, as if it had found its target.

I lifted my head up from under my rounded shoulders, still trying to safeguard myself from the drone's blades, to find out which girl it had locked in on.

No one was beside me any longer.

The other girls from my table had taken several steps back, leaving me standing alone inside the circle they formed. They looked at me, seemingly relieved that it was not them in the middle. When I crouched back down and tried to push the drone away, another green light shined, this time scanning my face.

"You are the chosen ones," the drones announced with a deep, electrified voice. "You have been identified and marked. You will now make your way to us."

That was it. No further explanation was given.

The drone hummed overhead.

Click. Click. Click.

With each click, my heart pounded harder. To say I was terrified would have been an understatement.

Thinking I could outsmart it, in a frantic panic I dashed toward the circle of girls, trying to break through, to be one of them—just another one in the crowd. They kept the circle closed tight, not letting me pass. Had Matthew and Mom been here, they would've tried to pull me out of the middle of the circle, to save me. But not these girls. They had gladly moved together, leaving me alone under the drone—a sacrifice offered to save themselves. Maybe I should've tried a little harder to be nice to them.

Before I could get to the other side of the circle, my branded arm rose toward the drone as if it were a magnet, and my feet lifted off the ground.

It had me.

Let someone else be chosen! I screamed silently in my mind, over and over, as I struggled, kicking the air and trying to grab anything or anyone to keep me from being dragged away. I must've looked just like those trying to evade the Vellatros after they had been targeted.

Why me? I'd done nothing wrong, nothing to deserve being carried off, never to be seen again. All those who went before me—*they* did something wrong, not me. I was quiet, just as Mom commanded. I followed their rules. I never caused any problems. I had been through *enough* already. I knew this wasn't right. I was going to fight it with all I had. There had to be some way to get this thing to drop me.

As I ascended toward the ceiling, I kicked and twisted about. But I was already ten feet off the ground, dangling from the drone and looking down on the other girls. I tried to reach up far enough to release its grasp on me, and that's when I noticed that I wasn't alone. From each of the drones, girls were dangling.

Others had been chosen, too.

But why?

We were brought swiftly to the Invaders and dropped, each of us landing onto our own detached platforms, floating lower than the platform on which the Invaders stood. They were, as before, perched high above us. Being so close to them, I tilted my head all the way back to see them and gasped slightly. Another hologram, I noticed. Once again, they hadn't bothered to enter our hangar.

I crawled slowly to the edge of the platform and looked over. I was so high above the floor.

Screams echoed in the hangar. One desperate girl had jumped.

But the girl never reached the hangar floor, stopping midway and suspended in the air. Knowing that it was them in charge, I turned to look at the Invaders instead of the girl. One was manipulating its fingers again. Just as it flicked a hand upward, the girl was flung back up to her platform, her light brown hair flying everywhere.

With another flick of its hand, the roof opened up. A drop of sweat rolled down the side of my cheek as I scanned the sky anticipating that a Vellatros would swoop down to grab me. Instead, I was suctioned straight up at an unimaginable speed. My stomach felt like it had stayed behind in the hangar, and my throat filled with my recent meal.

After that, everything went blank.

◆

My eyelids were so heavy that I could hardly blink to clear the haze from my eyes. But I was alive, which was not what I was expecting. I thought the platform was it for me.

The ground was cold and hard. I rolled onto my side and discovered I wasn't alone.

Across the room lay another girl, motionless, her olive-green uniform as rumpled as mine was. Her light brown hair fanned out next to her. Her back was to me, and she could have been dead for all I knew. My body was still too heavy to get up and find out.

I lay there like a limp rag and let my eyes explore. It was a new room—not part of the hangar. That much was obvious. This room was small and more nondescript than the chaotic, stale, massive-sized hangars. This new room was reminiscent of the materials that made up the vessel: metallic, sterile, colorless.

Still lethargic, I rolled onto my other side to scan the rest of the room, but it truly was almost bare. Nothing was in it but me, the possibly dead girl, and a large floor-to-ceiling window that made up one entire wall, which revealed a view of the beautiful, near-darkened sky. I gazed out the window through my groggy eyes. The sprinkling of clouds looked to be so close that I could touch them.

What are you doing? I scolded myself, upon regaining my lucidity. I had to get up and get my body working again. This was not a time to enjoy the moment.

I made each body part squirm to get feeling back. My fingers flinched . . . my toes wiggled . . . my arms shifted . . . my legs bounced. Upon realizing all my limbs were in working order, I stumbled to my feet—and instantly fell back down with a yelp.

Maybe my body parts weren't working quite so well after all.

The girl moved.

The sound of my yelp must have woken her. She sat up suddenly.

"Where are we?" she asked, glaring at me as if this were somehow my fault.

It was Shaila—and she brought her bad attitude with her.

"I don't know where we are," I responded, "but I don't think we're in the hangar any longer. I woke up here just before you did." I added under my breath, "Wherever here is."

Shaila said nothing, just began taking stock of the room and gazed out the window as I had. She looked like I felt, still trying to regain control of herself and her bodily movements.

"Was that you who tried to jump off the platform?" I asked her.

"I miss my mom and dad and my cat," she blurted out, failing to answer my question. Her voice sounded jittery. "How is all this happening? Why? When will it end? What are they going to do with us?"

I had no answers—only the same questions. "I don't know. I mean, how could I?"

"I just want to know what's going on," she pleaded.

"So do I," I said, trying not to roll my eyes or sound irritated. "Everyone wants to know."

We weren't getting off to the best start—just as we hadn't exactly clicked the first time we met, with Mazie.

"How old are you?" she asked.

"Well, I was fourteen when the Invaders came, but I might be fifteen now. My birthday has probably come and gone for all I know." I certainly *felt* older, especially after everything we'd gone through. Though I wasn't about to share that last part with her.

"Yeah, I think I'm thirteen now, but I don't really know either."

I gave her a friendly smile this time. "It's Shaila, right?"

"You can call me Shai."

"I'm Lauren."

"Yeah, I remember," she replied.

I realized, being the older one out of us, that I needed to take control of our situation. "Well, Shai, I don't see anyone else around, so we'll need to figure this out together." What there was to figure out was still a mystery to me. But when I stood up and offered my hand, she clutched at it, still a bit unsteady from the transport.

Once she settled on her feet, I let go of her hand and walked to the window. The view of the night sky was captivating. I hadn't seen the stars since before the Invaders came. There were so many . . . so clear, so vibrant. There were no city lights to deaden the brilliance of their light.

"Wow," I whispered, breathless by the beauty. The dark sky was endless, interrupted only by the silhouette of a distant tree line and the mountains behind it, with only a scattering of other vessels among the stars.

Then I looked down. Just as I had suspected, the familiar shadowy humps—their shape and size undeniable—were *below* us. That meant only one thing.

I shook my head once, hoping to snap out of the paralysis that came hand in hand when I felt fear. "When you were let outside, did you ever see their vessel in the sky above us?"

Shai gave me a cynical look. "Of course. How could I miss it?"

At least she was observant. Maybe she would end up being useful. "Can you see that?" I pointed to the outline of the hangar.

She walked closer to the window and looked outside. "No."

I took a long, deep breath, trying to calm myself. "I don't think we're on the ground anymore."

CHAPTER 16

REMOVED

Were we in one of the many smaller vessels that occupied our sky? Or were we in *the* vessel—the mothership? I didn't know, but that didn't stop Shai from interrogating me for answers.

"What are you saying, that we're not going back to the hangar?" she demanded, wrapping her arms around herself. "That I'm completely removed from my family now? Is that what you think?"

"You keep asking me all these questions. I don't know where we are exactly, or what we're doing here," I snapped. But I understood how she felt. The thought of being in the vessel was overwhelming.

I reminded myself that Shai was younger than me—about the same age as Matthew. I needed to calm down, to breathe deeply like Mom always told me to do. "Wherever we are, it's above the ground. Look around the room. It's made of the same metal and glass or whatever their spaceships are made of."

I tapped on the window, pointing at the shadowy tree line. The window was cold, so cold.

"See, the skyline indicates we're above the ground," I explained to her. "That's my best guess." It was no guess, though. I was certain about it. I had no way of seeing Matthew and Mom anymore.

My hand slid down the cold window as I slunk to the floor, staring out into the darkness. The coldness was just like the frosty car windows on our family ski trips, which came about when we were closest to the icy mountain air. I stayed there a long time—the only solace I had was that Shai kept quiet.

Until . . . my stomach grumbled.

"I'm so hungry," I mumbled.

"Me too," she squeaked out, falling beside me.

Across the room, a table and chairs appeared suddenly, and a familiar aroma filled the air.

Food.

Were they listening to us somehow?

I was too hungry to be worried about that. I crawled to my feet and rushed to the table, not waiting for Shai to catch up. The same bland, colorless food squares had arrived on plates, essentially out of thin air. Dazed and silent, we ate because it was necessary to stave off hunger—not because it was anything to enjoy. This certainly wasn't the better food Matthew had talked about. The cold, steel-like chairs did nothing to help improve the experience.

As I regained a bit of energy, one of the room's walls caught my eye; it appeared to have rectangular creases, like a hidden door. It occurred to me that there was more to our new living quarters than this one room. I was curious to find out more. Without waiting for Shai to finish eating, I went to investigate.

The door was cracked open slightly, almost baiting me to touch it. Was this a trick, some new type of barrier that would burn my flesh? I had no rock to throw at, like we did with the garden, so I took my chances.

I pushed against the wall and discovered a hallway.

I glanced back at Shai, but she remained at the table, eating small bites in an eerily familiar comatose state. Maybe she was waiting on me . . . waiting to see whether I'd return from my exploration, be burned alive by a barrier, or be carried off by the Vellatros. But no matter what I encountered or whether I'd survive, I was going anyway. At this point, I had nothing much to lose.

I opened the door wide enough to slip through and inched down the hallway, clenching my teeth harder with each step. I saw no sign of a barrier—no unevenness or colorful glare in front of me. Below me, the floor was smooth and cement-like, just like the room I'd left behind. The walls around me were a bleak gray like all the rest.

At the end of the hallway was another wall, with that same faint crease exposing a rectangular outline—another door, perhaps. This was closed, unlike the first one, but had no knob to open it. Knowing that this could very well be protected by the barrier, I held my breath and winced, pressing both hands against the wall.

It popped open.

I released a nervous laugh, realizing I was unharmed. I peered around the door's edge, not ready to fully commit to going through just yet. Behind it was a set of stairs—to where, I had no idea. But I had to go find out. I led with my toes, and just as the top of my shoe extended past the door, a dim light flicked on. I jumped back, hitting the wall behind me, panicking at the thought of what punishment would follow the light.

"Hey," Shai called out from down the hall. "I heard a thud. Are you okay?"

"I'm fine," I called back, straightening up and patting down my pants—it soothed me enough to try again. Just as I'd done down the hallway, I calculated each step I took going up the stairs. Slowly. Touching the stairs with a delicate step, one by one. Although everything looked perfectly normal, I still worried that the next step would be the one to take me out.

I got to the top.

I had survived.

I released another strangled burst of laughter, like I had cheated death.

At the top of the stairs, another soft light turned on, revealing a little white room with two beds, complete with fluffy white bedding. One for each of us. This seemed unnervingly planned.

I inhaled and covered my mouth in surprise. On one of the beds was my backpack. I tore it open and found my tattered old clothes inside. My journal and pens were gone, but at the very bottom was my stuffed kitty—the only thing I had left of home. I held it tight, realizing how long we'd been gone now. I tried to hold back tears.

"Hey, I made it," I called down to Shai, trying to hide the quiver in my voice. "There are some beds up here. One for—"

Before I could finish, Shai was in the room. Her eyes widened at the sight of the beds. "Wow," she whispered, shuffling toward the empty, inviting bed. Her knees buckled just as she reached it, and she fell into the soft, welcoming bedding. With her curled body engulfed in the covers, I heard her faint whimpers from beneath.

I crawled onto my bed and collapsed, sinking into the softness—it was perfectly silky and felt like a cloud. There was nothing like this in the hangars, just hard, cold cots, with the firmest and dirtiest mattresses I'd ever experienced. In the hangars, the shivers never went away during the night with only my layers of dirty, tattered clothes as a blanket to keep me warm.

This bed felt like luxury. I had warmth and comfort—and pillows! I'd only had my rolled-up sweatshirt since leaving home, and that didn't count. The pillow was as inviting and wonderfully soft as the bed.

Closing my eyes and gripping my kitty, I wanted to cry. But I was floating on a pillow cloud, and the tears didn't come.

In the stillness of it all, I realized that Shai and I were still alive, unharmed, and fed. We even had a window from which we could see the dazzling stars. We were significantly upgraded from the all-girl containment. In there, I'd already been separated from my mom and Matthew and survived it. This wasn't any worse than from where I just came, and it could very well be considered *better*. While I was still confused and terrified about *why* we were here, likely in their vessel, I couldn't help but feel . . . comfortable. I was running out of tears anyway.

I fell asleep listening to Shai cry.

For what felt like days, I slept. For the first time in a long while, I even remembered my dreams . . . of home, of the farm I'd once longed for, of sitting on the couch with Thor wrapped in my lap, of laughing with Matthew and Mom, even of walking through the school halls. I almost felt that it was a natural sleep, not one forced by them.

I dreamt I was back at home after the attack on the school bus.

Matthew and I hadn't yet returned to school. He was healing in his way, and I in mine. Once his head was better and my night terrors had eased, Mom said the school wanted us to return.

"They think getting back to your normal activities will be good for both of you," she said. She knew this wasn't the news I wanted to hear. "You're going back to school tomorrow."

Since the attack, I hadn't spoken to or seen any friends, not even Zary. Meanwhile, Matthew had been flooded with get well cards.

Returning to school was worse than I imagined. The other students blamed me, with glances and glares and lots of muttering in the hallways, for the football season ending shortly after Coach Blaizer was fired.

Sitting through classes was unbearable. Only in Mrs. Pickering's science class could I stay focused. The situation was unsustainable. I knew it, the school knew it, and Mom knew it.

Then one day after school, Mom surprised me with a new puppy.

"Oh, he's amazing!" I squealed, kneeling to admire the pup's shiny golden and white fur and floppy ears. He seemed about to wag his tail off. For an instant, my troubles melted away. As usual, Mom knew exactly what I needed.

Playing with Thor and petting his soft ears calmed me before school. I sat through all my classes the next day, thinking things would be okay.

A week later, we were taken.

◆

When I awoke in the strange, sterile new bedroom, Shai was curled up next to me in my bed, still sleeping. Matthew and I had done the same to Mom in the hangars and even back home when we were scared. But Shai wasn't family, and I wasn't her mother. I slipped from the bed, trying not to wake her. I needed some time alone.

Natural light shined up the stairs. Eager to discover the rest of this new living quarters, I started down the stairs, thinking there may be some clue as to why Shai and I were chosen and brought here.

Once I reached the lower level where we'd first arrived, I was awestruck by the bright blue sky and the sea of green just outside the window. It was magical—inspirational. I skipped to the window, surprising myself at how excited I was to see it all. I leaned in with all my weight on the large glass pane that ran from the ceiling to the floor and looked straight down. I was right. In the daylight, I could see we were in the sky—in one of their vessels, many stories above Earth—undeniably removed from all that we had known.

Far below, the hangars were unmistakable—long, massive, elongated cement buildings with tall square doors at the front. I could see the seam where the roof had opened from the top. From high above, the hangars seemed less intimidating. But it would be impossible now to see Matthew and Mom.

Beyond the hangar were the flatlands, where everything had changed for me during captivity. That was when I first got to breathe fresh air, feel the sun's warmth again, and was with Mom and Matthew. From my window, I could even see the garden. Oh, how I wanted to be back in that garden with Mom and Matthew.

I missed them. I missed home. We had been gone for so long now.

I wiped my eyes with the back of my hand and moved to the other side of the window for a different view, unobstructed by the hangar.

For the first time, I saw that the entire panorama—hangars, flatlands, and a band of surrounding land—was surrounded by the translucent and oscillating barrier, brandishing an array of dazzling colors, extending far into the air, similar to the barriers that separated the hangars from one another. What I saw beyond the barrier, though—it was magnificent. It was Earth, unspoiled and flourishing. No national park, no hidden beach, no mountain range could be as radiant as the splendor that existed just beyond our prison walls. Not even the most impressive photographs—in which I recalled each of the smallest of details—captured such beauty.

Our planet was thriving.

The shadow of the trees I'd seen in the night had come to life in the daylight. They were like gentle giants shooting up from the ground, taller and greener than any trees I'd ever seen. The wide-spreading branches of the trees created a picturesque canopy, combining into a thick forest lined by dense bushes just below the sea of branches. Grass plains flowed outward from there, expanding from the edge of the forest. Off in the distance, herds of animals roamed free, uninterrupted, and unafraid of being exposed in the open, which had once been overrun by people.

Strikingly absent was any sign of humans ever existing on Earth. No buildings, no houses, no businesses, no stores, no cars, no streets, no signs—nothing was left. All that remained from our world was locked up in those hangars, and maybe in other places like them around the world. All that we had built as a human race had been eviscerated, as if we were never here. Replaced with a growing Earth and wild animals, unspoiled, preserved, and idyllic, almost as if it should have been this way all along.

Where did it all go?

My mind turned to the bombings we heard from the hangar when we were first captured. None of us knew what had happened then. Our only concern was that we were unharmed and had survived another day. Had the bombings cleared it all away for this regrowth to occur?

Not until I could see from high above had I realized that this vast destruction was kept hidden from us. On the ground, we couldn't see past the bushes and trees that grew just outside our reach, on the other side of the barrier. I never would have imagined that evidence of our past existence was absolutely . . . gone.

I shook my head over and over. None of this made sense. It couldn't be gone. We would need it when we'd be released. Our home had to be there, and Thor would be waiting for us.

We would be released, right? Eventually we would be, I told myself, desperately wanting to hold on to that belief.

But seeing it all from above, my stomach sank, and then I realized I had been clinging to a false reality that we'd be returning home one day. With it all gone, it was clear we would never return home. Thor was gone. Everything was gone. The Invaders had eradicated our way of life.

Stunned by this stark, brutal truth, I slid to my knees. My shaky hands tapped the windows, trying to track the number of days and my mind raced with questions. How many days had passed since we were captured? Could it have been long enough for this much growth to occur? Had we been taken so Earth could flourish? That answer was right in front of me—the Earth was alive, without human interference.

In my mind, I repeated the lecture from the first time an Invader appeared in our hangar, speaking about receiving signals from Earth. What messages had humans been sending into space all that time, about the climate crisis, self-destruction, mass extinction, calls for help? Did Earth's most brilliant minds, as Mom often referred to them, even know what signals they were sending? Had they even thought about what would happen when the signals would be received and exactly *who* or *what* would come to our world? And what had happened to all of them, those who supposedly knew better and were better than the rest of us? Where did they go? I never saw any of them in our containments—the scientists and politicians, the billionaires, and celebrities.

Despite the persecution and destruction of humans, the Earth, itself, was thriving. I couldn't wrap my head around it.

In school, we had always learned how to live greener, how to heal the Earth. That was the whole reason for our field trip to the sustainable farm with Mrs. Pickering. My mind wandered back to the assignment she gave us the night before the field trip.

"Be sure to get your parents to return the permission slip for the sustainable farm trip tomorrow, and for homework tonight, ask them what they did to recycle when they were young." I heard Mrs. Pickering's voice as if I was sitting in her classroom instead of an alien vessel.

The assignment was an open invitation for Mom to start ranting yet again about all the mandatory changes intended to address the climate.

"Oh, no, Lauren. Not this nonsense," Mom complained. "What are they teaching you in school? How is this math or reading? It's just more of their agenda—"

"It's homework, Mom," I stressed. "Please, just answer the questions."

Mom threw up her arms in mock surrender. "Well, I don't remember recycling being as important as it's made out to be today. It was a newer concept. They essentially bribed kids with pennies for cans. Your grandma's car always got sticky bringing our haul to the recycling center, the cans spilled out, and the bags always seemed to break, only to get like a dollar in return. We didn't have recycling automations everywhere, like we do now. Those are the biggest differences I can think of."

"That actually sounds gross."

"As for climate change, I really don't want to get into that, Lauren. Look, as far as I'm concerned, we need to make sure the world we live in is protected and preserved. But we can't go overboard or believe in nonsense."

I grumbled, "Off topic."

"Fine. Rational conservation is what I think we need," she said. "More innovation, less hysteria."

"Like what?"

"The solar panel roof tiles that were nationally implemented by Congress—now *that* was a superb idea. Covering desert lands as solar farms, also cool. Though I didn't care for the mandates that came with them. There's so much more to invent, I think, and I'm not the scientist. I leave that up to those supposed *brilliant* minds." Mom chuckled, seething with sarcasm. "You know, I think they're too reckless and a bit dangerous given the amount of influence they wield," she added.

"You've told me all about it before," I responded with restraint. "More than once actually."

"Why not tell your science class about that time when you were six, crying when I didn't recycle the one can I threw away in the regular trash?" she teased. "Or the time you cried because I ordered calamari. The only way to calm you down was by burying it in the backyard, next to your hamster."

I remembered both moments, of course—every detail.

"Do your own research," Mom had advised at the end of our interview. "Think for yourself. Assess all angles, even from opposing views. Make your own conclusions."

Well, I had concluded that the youth were going to save Earth— that was what we were set out to do. What *I* was preparing to do.

Yet here it was, the new reality, right in front of me. The Invaders had done it, not us—they had saved Earth. Their invasion clearly had profound, positive impacts on the land, the likes of which would never have been achievable by mankind.

But was it worth the price?

As a prisoner, severed from my mom, my brother, and my whole life, I could only answer with a resounding *no*. But gazing upon the beauty and simplicity of the land below, I was no longer sure.

CHAPTER 17

MATTHEW'S INSPIRATION

D ays passed as Shai and I began acclimating to living alone in our quarters, to each other, and to our new surroundings. We'd been given new slip-on shoes and clean uniforms that looked like hospital scrubs, with fitted blue tops and wide pants, soft and stretchy. The olive-green jumpsuits were tossed in the corner, never to be touched again. My clothes and sneakers from home were soiled and torn—no longer wearable due to the lingering, potent smell that I could never wash away in the hangar's sinks. Like everything else, the new uniforms just appeared in our tiny bedroom each day, fresh and waiting for us when we awoke. We thought nothing of it since we'd been given our food and water this same way. Shai and I just stopped questioning any of it. It was our accepted new way.

Our search for any way out was short-lived. We'd already discovered the only doors, neither of which led out. We were trapped, with nothing to do. We spent hours in front of the windows in silence, trying to absorb it all.

Each morning, I was the first to wake, and I often found Shai beside me in my bed even though I'd been alone when I fell asleep. I slunk away early each morning, not waking her. I wanted my alone time, gazing out the windows at the Earth below. Despite my captivity, I relished watching the planet's transformation before my eyes. I hadn't had this expansive view in the hangars—and it was all mine while Shai slept.

I looked out the window toward the grazing herds of animals clearing a path through the grassy plains that were beyond the barrier. The magnificent elk and buffalo that must have been native to this region long ago had returned since we were gone. If I awoke before dawn, sometimes I'd hear animals howl like the coyotes used to do, up in the mountains behind our house. But these howls were deeper and longer . . . wolflike. It was the occasional giraffe herd that stumped me. Knowing that the hangars were near my town, none of it made any sense. I figured that animals traversing long distances across the Earth was now possible without any interference by humans or our infrastructure.

Alone on those mornings, with nothing to do and nowhere to be, my mind was quiet in a way it could never be before captivity. My thoughts had always been about school, friends, homework, my family. Too much to watch, see, and do . . . all the time. There would be a new video to watch or post to follow or gossip or project—it never stopped. All that drama.

But in this new stillness, I found calm. My breathing was collected. My mind was still. The abundance of life evident in nature seemed to reset me. If only I had this alone time and ability to rise above the hurt before the Invaders came, things would have been much easier for me after the attack.

I began meditating in those morning hours—praying even,

just as Mom had always wanted me to do. I hummed that church song Mom loved, remembering especially how she sang it after the Invaders came. It calmed me then, and it calmed me now. It made me feel closer to her, as if she were still with me.

In the hangars, Mom had tried to encourage Matthew and me to be hopeful until we were rescued. As each day passed and our captivity continued, it was hard to believe what Mom tried to teach us—that everything happened for a reason, that it was all part of God's plan. I didn't see it—not under these circumstances. As my stillness grew, my anguish over Mom's words faded, evolving into a quiet faith in what Earth's infinite beauty had to offer . . . a blessed tranquility . . . and then I knew I had to continue to hold on to the belief that we'd be free someday.

After my quiet time in front of the window, I searched the ground below in the hangars, hoping to see Mom and Matthew. I looked for them every day. But the prisoners on the ground below were too far away to identify. Mostly they shuffled along the dirty ground, wandering aimlessly outside the hangar, like creatures caged in a zoo waiting for their next meal. Others just slowly walked around in circles and had seemingly lost their will to live in continued captivity.

If only they knew what was beyond the barrier.

———◆———

"In the hangars, my brother Matthew made me exercise," I said to Shai one morning as we sat in front of the giant window. We were isolated, bored, and in danger of becoming hopeless, like those on the ground. We needed to do something. "I think we should do that in here."

"Matthew is your brother?" Shai's eyes lit up, and she blushed. "I followed him in my first hangar, before I was moved with all the girls."

"We must've been in the same first hangar," I said as I rolled up my sleeve, displaying my brand. "Let me see yours."

She rolled up her sleeve and held it next to mine. They matched.

"My mark didn't match my mom and dad's." She paused and rubbed her shoulder as she let her sleeve fall back down. Hearing her story, I realized how dismayed and just sad Shai was. She'd lost everything, just like me.

"Once I found him, I never missed his exercises, ever," Shai continued, her eyes rounded. She was on the verge of tears. "It really changed things for me. Gave me something to look forward to each day. Matthew's drills made me believe I could be strong—fight back, escape even. He's amazing."

So, Shai has a crush on my little brother.

Even though the Invaders took away everything important to us and held us as prisoners, they couldn't take away our desire for love or purpose. Shai held on to the memories Matthew had given her—and the importance of those memories was something I understood. I decided to be more patient with her, as long as she stopped asking me unanswerable questions and climbing unannounced into my bed.

"When Matthew first started his training, he practiced with me before the group. I remember *all* his routines, every detail. I remember a lot of things, actually—" I stopped. I didn't need to explain to her my grandfather's memory, which had been passed on to me.

"I don't know." Her shoulders slumped forward, and she looked down at the floor. "I don't want to do *anything* right now. What's the point?"

"It's not like we're doing anything else in here," I said, pushing back. I always was frustrated when people wouldn't go along with my ideas.

"I don't have the energy," Shai grumbled.

"I get it," I responded. "When Matthew first started, my mom and I sat out. I didn't want to do any of it. I found a garden, and that's all I wanted to do. But then we tried it, and it made a difference for me, just like you said. We can get back to that."

I jumped to my feet and held out my hand to her.

Her forlorn look gave way to a slight smile. "Okay, I guess." She reluctantly grabbed my hand, and I pulled her to her feet. "Until we get moved again."

She made a good point. We didn't know how long we would be held here, particularly since we had no idea why we were in this effectively solitary confinement. For all we knew, we could be moved the next day.

We started with the easiest of Matthew's exercise routines and pushed ourselves harder each day, committed to making our bodies stronger and keeping our minds active. I always ended up a little more cheerful than when we'd first started.

Shai followed the exercise drills closely each day at first, but after a while she started to fall behind. Instead of trying harder, she would get testy when she couldn't do the same number of sit-ups, push-ups, or squats as I did. Sometimes she would just give up.

"At least we're not doing this in the dirt outside our hangar," I snorted one afternoon as I fell to the floor, trying to catch my breath.

"Not sure this is much better," Shai sneered. "I wouldn't mind being back in that hangar."

I shot her a disappointed glare. Why did she have to be so unenthusiastic? At least I was trying to be better and do *something* in here. This must have been how Matthew felt when I kept avoiding the workouts. He never gave up on me, though, and I was determined to keep pushing Shai to keep up.

"I'll switch things up tomorrow, like Matthew did," I said, sitting up and trying to lighten the mood. "He always seemed to make it fun."

The next day I improvised, doing push-ups against the beds, lifting the chairs as weights, even pushing the table across the room.

If only Matthew could see me now!

Shai tried it and fell. She tried it again and fell.

"Let's just stick to what Matthew did," Shai snapped, and walked away to do her own routine.

I didn't respond. Her frustration was misplaced. It felt like she was trying to compete with me. Did she think that I cared about winning or outdoing her? She could do whatever she wanted. I was not her mother or even her sister. We were barely even friends.

The less I seemed to care about Shai's attempts to create unnecessary rivalry, the more tense and irritable she became. In my quiet time, I moved beyond her negativity and focused on what was important . . . strengthening myself as Matthew had done. I wanted the same for Shai, for her to push herself to become stronger.

"We should start sparring," Shai said one day, scowling, "if you're up to it."

I hesitated. It had been a long time since I'd sparred with anyone during Matthew's exercises. Plus, I wasn't sure about Shai's motivations. Why did she want so badly to fight me?

"Come on," she said again, baiting me.

I laughed, trying to relieve the tension. "Sure, I'll take you."

She lunged at me while I was still laughing, taking ahold of my shoulders, and struggling to throw me to the ground. It didn't take long for me to swipe her leg and pin her to the floor.

Reaching down, I offered to help her up. "Remember, I trained with Matthew one on one. He practiced all his moves on me—knocked me down left and right," I said, hoping to soothe the sting of defeat. "After a while, I kinda kept up with him, and he didn't beat me *every* time."

Shai just swatted my hand away.

I had to give her credit, though. Losing didn't stop her. In the following days, she asked to spar again and again, trying hard to bring me down. She never won, not even once. I wouldn't let her win either. If I did, it would make her weak.

I was tough on Shai, but I was tough on myself, too. My mindset shifted to strength and perseverance, just as Matthew had shown me. We'd already spent too much time doing nothing, just sitting around waiting. That time was over.

As her losses against me grew, Shai started keeping to herself a little bit more, and our meals were eaten mostly in silence. She hadn't crawled into my bed since we'd started sparring—not that I was complaining. But I decided it was time to calm things down. With the sparring, on top of Shai's negative attitude, the tension between us was too high.

"Maybe let's try something different today," I said to her.

"Why? Afraid you'll lose?" she chided.

"Not really. I've beaten you every single—" I paused and took a breath. I avoided responding like her. "I shouldn't have said that. Look, I just want you strong."

"Then let's get started." Once again, she charged before I was ready.

I anticipated her advance and threw her to the ground. Her anger concerned me, but I wasn't going to let her take it out on me.

I walked toward the window, shaking my arms out to ease the

tension. When I looked over my shoulder to see if Shai had settled down yet, her skin was sheer white and her mouth was gaping. She was looking past me, as if I wasn't even in the room.

I turned back to the window.

Floating just outside it, looking in on us, there were two of *them*.

CHAPTER 18

THE APPEARING

My heart nearly stopped. Sheer terror befell my whole body. I did not move or even breathe—I just stared awkwardly at the two Invaders just outside the window. It took everything out of me to remain motionless, thinking that I could avoid detection.

All four of us just stared at one another.

This was no hologram. They were real. They were here.

I had anticipated that if I were to see them close up, I'd see something revolting—alien creatures with slithering tongues and devilish eyes, just like the pictures posted online. But they were nothing like what I had imagined, or anyone had imagined. I struggled with how I felt awed at the magnificence of them.

Just as I had seen during the hologram encounters, the two before me shimmered with a silvery essence along their brilliantly white skin. The seams of those robes were stitched in gold and glistened magnificently in the sun. The previous projection had not exaggerated their size, which dwarfed ours, as if we were little children next to them.

They floated closer to our window, unaided, and removed the hoods of their robes to peer in closer at us. Just as I had previously noticed with their hoods off as they passed through the transport tube, they had pointed ears and long white hair, also with the soft and subtle silvery radiance like their skin. Although nearly identical, there were notable differences between them. One of them moved with a delicacy that indicated to me she was female. Her face had softer characteristics, and her eyes swam with a mix of both sadness and kindness. A few subtle, delicate clear jewels surrounded each eye. The other had bigger, more pronounced facial attributes. His movements were firm and mighty, and he was intimidating.

I was drawn to them . . . unwillingly. Their supernatural presence made them seem . . . pure. Everything about them was peaceful and serene. But their entrapment of our entire species was the exact opposite.

Shai began shifting.

"Don't move—maybe they can't see inside," I whispered through pursed lips.

She threw her hands up in the air. "How can they not see in—we live in a glass bubble. Like lab rats!"

I didn't move, thinking that's what my mom would have directed. I worried for Shai that she showed so much emotion in front of them.

She pointed out the window, directly at them. "And they're staring right at us . . . they see us . . . they definitely see us."

That's when one of them approached, floating right up to our window, tapping it. *Ping. Ping.* I jumped away from the window, afraid that pointy, skeletal finger would stab right through it and touch me. For all I know, it could have. But it just tapped again.

Ping. Ping. With each tap, I caught a closer glimpse of what looked like lightning streaks coursing through what should have been its veins.

Trembling, Shai grabbed my hand. I held hers tightly and whispered through unmoving lips, "Don't let them see you shaking."

Then . . . they vanished.

I dropped Shai's hand and ran to the window, but they were gone. When I looked back, I saw tears on her terrified face—and a wet spot down the inside of her uniform pants. She ran toward our bathroom.

I knocked on the bathroom door. "Hey, are you okay?"

I could hear her shuffling around inside, crying. But she didn't respond.

"I got you some fresh pants if you want." I paused. "I was so scared, too."

She opened the door. "Thanks for the clothes," she muttered. She moved closer and hugged me intensely. She still was shaking.

Despite everything that had happened between us, I hugged her back.

◆

I was hardly surprised to find Shai beside me when I woke. Although this time, I didn't mind as much. Seeing the Invaders so close had terrified me, too. During my quiet time that next morning— praying, meditating, and humming in front of the windows—I cleared my mind, hoping it would help me figure out the previous day's encounter.

Shortly after Shai and I ate, they again returned outside our window.

Thus began a new routine for us to follow. Each visit was just like the first. They floated outside our window, observing us, and eventually tapping at the window. Shai jumped every time, but I tried to anticipate it and remained still. I was convinced they did it just to see how we would react. I felt like a puppy for sale in a store every time they tapped on the glass cage to get my attention, as if considering buying me.

They never stayed long. Afterward, we would get back to our sessions. I worked harder, and so did Shai.

"What if, one day, they decide to come in? We have to be ready," she asserted.

I stopped in the middle of a jumping jack. "What would we even do if they did?" I almost laughed at the thought. "Did you see how big they were? They've got to be like fifteen feet tall."

"We'd fight them!" she shouted, even though I was standing right beside her.

I held my ears and stared at her. I wanted her to know that screaming in my face like that wasn't going to be tolerated. If only I had my headphones to drown her out with music.

"We've been training," she replied in a slightly lowered voice, but still resolute. "We fight back. We escape. We get out of here. *That's* what we do."

My enthusiasm had worn off on her—but now that we'd seen *them* up close, it had worn clean off of me.

Shai's expectations were unrealistic at best. Had she missed the fact that all of humanity had been rounded up and imprisoned? Had she forgotten about the other attempts to escape that were unsuccessful? Or did she miss the early uprisings by some of the captives in the hangars and how they all just disappeared? Did she actually think the two of us could fight back? Had she forgotten about the

Vellatros? Those creatures came unannounced and abducted people right before our eyes, without a chance of pleading or redemption. We were lucky the Vellatros were not the ones outside our windows.

I just shook my head, went back to jumping jacks, and then threw a couple of roundhouse kicks.

"What?" she grumbled when I didn't answer her. "You don't think we can fight them?"

My exercising stopped. "Maybe you haven't been paying attention to what got us to this point, Shai," I said in my firmest voice. "None of our weapons or armies could fight them. They abduct people on their whim. People have disappeared instantly, and we have no idea what happened to them. But yeah, the two of us are going to fight them and win. Keep dreaming." I turned away from her, refusing to engage in her delusions any longer. I went to look at the stars outside our window, wondering where my world had gone . . . and when I would wake up from the nightmare.

Despite our argument, I found Shai next to me when I woke the next morning. It seemed she was more afraid of the Invaders outside our window than she was upset with me yelling at her. I snuck out as I always did, eager to get to the window to find new animals roaming the ground below.

Before I took another step down the stairs, I gasped. "Whoa!" An unfamiliar squeak from me followed.

It was them. I was so engrossed with the idea of my morning alone that I almost ran into them.

The two Invaders were *inside*—right in front of me.

I never expected it.

The surprise knocked me backward, and I stumbled, scrambling up the first few stairs on all fours. But when the larger Invader lifted his hand and flicked a long, spiny finger, I involuntarily rose to my feet, forced to stand upright. Some invisible pressure was at my back, like two massive hands preventing my escape. The pressure grew stronger, inching me down the staircase step by step, closer and closer . . . to *them*.

My jaw clenched as I fought the strange force with everything I had, grunting and backpedaling to avoid moving forward. My sweaty hands slid down the walls of the stairwell, seeking a grip, but my efforts were useless. The pressure behind me was too powerful for me to overcome. With a mere flick of its finger, it had control over me, just like everything else we had faced in captivity.

Even my voice failed me. When I tried screaming out to Shai, I couldn't. Only another weird squeak escaped my mouth.

I was on my own.

My feet slipped and my stomach twisted as I was pulled down the last step within inches of *them*. I held myself against the wall, flattening my body, trying to stay away from them as much as possible.

I couldn't move, breathe, or even think . . . I wanted to stay frozen against the wall, but my entire body trembled. I shook uncontrollably. The terror of them being inside took hold of me.

Suddenly, they just disappeared. Maybe they weren't ready to be close to me, just as I didn't want to be close to them.

I collapsed to the floor. Heaving and crying.

I screamed out, "*Shai!*"

She came running down the stairs and knelt beside me. "What happened? What's wrong? Did you fall?"

For once, I couldn't be the strong one. I reached out for her and held her tight, shaking. "They were in here," I said, my voice cracking.

"What? I don't understand," Shai questioned, her voice panicked. She knew this was unlike me. I never leaned on her for anything before.

"They were here. Standing right in front of me. Inside!"

"Did they . . . hurt you?" Shai asked.

"No, but what happens next time?" My voice deepened. "We aren't safe in here, Shai. They breached the window. Came inside—"

Shai released me. "We've been preparing for this, Lauren. Did you use any of the moves we've been working on?"

I shook my head. "What? No, I froze," I responded defensively. I sat up, clearing my nose and eyes with my sleeve. I held up my hand to see it still shaking. "I never thought they'd come in here."

"We need to train harder for when they come back," Shai grumbled.

"You're not getting it, Shai." My fear was gone, replaced with my annoyance with her insistence that I could've done something to stop them. "It'll be useless. I was powerless against them. They controlled me . . . completely and with a mere finger flick. Just like they've done from day one."

Shai gave me a disgusted look.

"They're going to do to us whatever they want, and we can't stop it," I insisted. "I don't know how to explain this any clearer to you. They were at the bottom of the stairs, forcing me toward them. I couldn't fight it. I couldn't even see it, couldn't grab at it. It was an invisible, powerful force, and I was at its mercy."

Shai just stood up and walked away. She worked harder on the drills that day than I'd ever seen her do before, while I could do nothing. My body felt like it had been hit by a car.

The rest of the day, I just sat in front of the window, rocking and grasping my stuffed kitty—the only thing I had to remind me of home. I just wanted to be back home. But my memories were all I had left of it.

CHAPTER 19

FORCED TRAINING

The next morning, I didn't go downstairs on my own. I poked at Shai to wake her up. She slowly stirred, even tried to go back to sleep.

"Hey, we have to see if they're downstairs," I whispered. Before I could finish uttering the words that they could be inside, Shai jumped out of bed as if ready to fight them. She finally remembered what happened yesterday.

We crept downstairs, hands clasped together. With each slow and decisive step we took, I gave her hand a squeeze. Just as we took that last step, we found . . . nothing. They weren't there. I could finally breathe, releasing Shai's hand and running mine down my pants for a familiar comfort.

But then I saw them.

I bumped Shai to see.

Floating above the floor in their shining white robes, the two Invaders were waiting and staring. I reached back for Shai's hand. My heart was pounding.

They glided across the room toward us, appearing serene.

As I went to step back to get away from them, my back met that invisible pressure, holding me in place. Watching Shai twisting and turning to pull away, I knew she felt it, too. She dropped my hand in her quest to fight against what neither of us could even see.

Before we knew it, we were pushed forward, meeting *them* in the middle of the room. They towered over us, their iridescent robes swaying along with them. Despite my fear, I wanted to reach out to touch those stunning, shimmering robes.

But my arms were frozen in place beside my body. My body was frozen, too. At this point, I was unsure if this was something they ordained or if I was paralyzed by my fear. Standing before them, the larger, male Invader lifted its spiny, elongated finger toward my direction. Not knowing what it was going to do to me, my stomach clenched so hard I released a faint whimper. I wanted to yell out, but I felt verbally detained.

Its nail slowly poked at my shoulder, at my brand. Though it was as sharp as a needle, it didn't penetrate my uniform nor my skin. The Invader quickly retracted its finger.

Then it poked Shai's shoulder in the same way. It quickly retracted again.

Maybe they were testing us to see how we would respond.

I realized it was my turn once again when the Invader's finger approached my direction. This time it touched my face and then caressed my hair, gently wrapping a strand around its finger. Despite its tenderness, I was about to vomit.

It retracted its finger. I could finally breathe.

"What the heck!" Shai blurted out, and she swatted its hand away from her belly. "Leave us alone. We aren't pets!" The Invaders quickly withdrew their hands, hiding them within their sleeves.

My eyes widened in alarm. I couldn't believe she just did that. I was afraid of the repercussions that would come from her defiance. I kept watch for a Vellatros to appear to take us away.

None arrived.

Instead, the two Invaders just looked startled.

My fear turned to confusion. How could *they* be startled by *us*? It was as if they were unaware of their total dominance over us. Their movements and intrigue about us made me think that they were as unsure about us as we were of them.

The larger Invader's hand reappeared from his robe, releasing each of his five spiny, long, porcelain white fingers one by one until his palm was flat. He lifted his flat palm upward, exposing more of his thin, skeletal arm. My eyes followed his hand, and I moved nothing else. From the corner of my eye, I saw Shai glaring directly at him in defiance.

He repeated the movement, lifting his flattened palm.

We just stared.

His forehead wrinkled, and his thin lips tightened. If I were looking at a person with the same expression, I would assume frustration. But I didn't know what had prompted that reaction. We were just standing before them, staring.

With a flick of his finger, I felt a sharp lash against my right leg.

Shai and I fell to the floor, each grasping at our legs. Nothing had struck us, but the pain was real. My leg was throbbing. I pulled up my pant leg to see and try to rub the pain away. Reddened slash marks appeared across my calf, as if I'd been whipped. Shai hastily rolled up hers, revealing a matching mark. Shai looked up at me, tears filling her eyes. I slowly shook my head no, just as my mom had done when we were branded. *We can't show any emotion*, I thought, wishing she could hear me.

As soon as we got to our feet, the Invader's hand rose again.

We just stood there. I still didn't know what he wanted.

Again came the sharp pain, this time across my other calf, bringing me to the floor. Shai fell, too. The tears now streamed down Shai's face, and her bottom lip quivered. He lifted his finger, forcing us both to our feet again.

We were supposed to be following his command, but what was it?

Suddenly, I understood.

When he flattened his palm again, I sat down immediately, pulling Shai with me. We thumped to the ground, and no lashings were delivered. We were safe—this time.

We followed the same process several more times. Shai caught on and sat on her own. Then they left.

"How did you know to sit?" Shai asked me, still rubbing at her injured leg. "You saved us."

"I—I guess I just . . ." I stammered under the difficulty of explaining what happened. "My mind just kind of understood it. The command was just there, embedded in my thoughts. So I followed."

Shai had closed her eyes, looking defeated.

"Did you hear it?" I asked her.

"No. All I could think about was the brutal pain in my legs," Shai responded as she rolled up her leg pants to see her swollen skin. "Were we invisibly lashed by them? What's going on?"

"I don't know, Shai. I just don't know."

He was training us to sit, just like a dog. It was humiliating and defeating.

Shai had insisted that we weren't pets, but to *them*, that's exactly what we were.

After that, not a day went by without the two Invaders appearing inside our living pod, each time with a new command.

They came to train us.

It was always the male Invader who commanded us, and if we failed to follow along, he seemed to take pleasure in watching us writhe in pain. The other Invader—the more delicate one—just watched from the side. I felt that maybe she wasn't entirely in favor of his brutal ways.

The male Invader was tricky, too, sometimes adding new commands we had not learned before and then punishing us for not knowing them. I wasn't always given a mental clue, and the punishment for not knowing was severe and rapidly doled out, just like the slashes from the first day of our training. But the visible damage didn't remain long—only the pain.

The one thing I gained from these penalties and the prolonged captivity was a hardened heart.

With each session came a new hand signal to obey. A hand went up, it was to sit. When it was brought down, it was to stand. My memory served me well: I moved toward the Invader when he signaled, spoke when prompted, and sat when commanded. But Shai forgot them, even the easy ones, which made me wonder if she was doing so intentionally . . . as if to defy them.

"I'm afraid of what comes next if we can't figure this out," I confessed to Shai after training one day, as I dragged my damaged leg across the room to reach her.

"What is there to figure out? We can't read alien sign language," Shai said, struggling to sit up. "And they don't speak English."

"I just didn't know what he wanted today. I'm sorry."

"Lauren, this isn't your fault. You've been great, better than me at this." Shai grabbed my arm. "Today was unbearable. I feel like my tailbone is smashed into tiny pieces." She lay down beside me with a hand behind her back.

"I hope they don't come back tomorrow," I moaned.

We never made it to our beds that night, and we didn't even move to eat the bland food that likely appeared in our eating area. The pain was too much.

I was not sure how much longer I could go on with the struggle, the burden, and the pain. What if they just ended up killing us? Was this some wicked game to them? Was this just a slow, tortuous path to our ultimate demise?

If we wanted to survive, I had to learn to communicate with them, no matter how hard it was. As I told Shai, their commands were sort of in my thoughts already. To understand them, I just had to clear away the other thoughts swirling in my mind. Instead of blocking the aliens out, I had to be open and receptive to them—no matter how harsh and painful the punishment was. I knew how to calm my mind like this. I had been doing it all those mornings alone at the window. All that quiet time had taught me how to have the silent mind I needed to survive. Or so I hoped.

The next morning, before the Invader could flick his wicked finger at us, I closed my eyes and released a long, loud breath. Shai elbowed me, but I ignored her. I thought about sitting alone in front of the window and letting go of any anxiety that rose up within me. I sought to clear away any mental obstructions that would interfere with understanding the Invader's signals. I relinquished control, freedom, and individuality, opening my mind to *them*—because if I didn't, Shai and I would not survive.

When I opened my eyes, the female Invader had moved closer to us, and the male Invader had stepped to the side. I waited for her signal.

No commands were given.

No lashings were handed out.

Instead, as she raised her hand, Shai and I lifted off the ground and floated toward the window. I felt no need to struggle. I felt no pain. It was delicate, not punishing. We were placed carefully into a sitting position, exactly where I used to sit during my quiet time. Her placement of us was as if she had peered into my mind and seen the very picture I just imagined. Could the female Invader have understood my thoughts?

The Invaders kept us there for what seemed like hours, in silence. Then I heard a quiet word, directly in my mind.

Calm.

Another word followed, gentle and whispering.

Still.

Over and over, simple, encouraging, peaceful messages emerged in my mind.

Quiet.

Open.

Oneness.

As I reached complete calmness and the clearest mind I had ever known, I heard a new word in my mind.

Stand.

I stood.

Sit.

I sat.

I didn't just understand or intuit these messages—I *heard* them.

The Invaders had transmitted messages that I could understand and obey. And in seeing my thoughts, they had discovered what I, or rather we, needed for this to work.

It was exhilarating yet terrifying. I had connected with *them*.

CHAPTER 20

BROKEN

While I listened and followed, Shai struggled. She was unable to connect with them as I did. She stood only after seeing me stand. As I lowered to the ground, I pointed down for her to follow. She huffed and begrudgingly sat after I already had made my way down on the floor. She was delayed, and it was noticeable. Her resistance to listening to them and following their commands were noticeable as well. And not just to me.

They, too, caught on, then adjusted accordingly. The male Invader's training tactics dramatically changed. He positioned his body only toward my direction, not to both of us. He gave me the upward signal. I sat. But when Shai followed, he flicked his hand, raising her swiftly to her feet. I stood; she got pulled down.

We were now on differing paths in training, and Shai was on her own.

As I complied and listened to his messages, he flung her around more and more forcefully to ensure she obeyed. Hearing Shai's moans, just after he slammed her to the ground for failing to sit, was gut-wrenching. I couldn't stomach watching her arm get contorted in such an unnatural way, forcing her to rise. He seemed to know just how far to bend it before it snapped. He finished her off with a deep slash across her leg. Shai looked at me through swollen eyes and seething pain.

I was left untouched.

That was the hardest part of her punishment. It was hers, and hers alone. Dutifully complying with the messages, I no longer received the lashings. Training disparity broadened between us, and once it did, it also became an emotional punishment for Shai.

It worsened once they began to reward me for my willful compliance. Little by little, simple comforts and remnants of my old life returned to the living quarters. I found my journal and pens on my bed, while music played in our pod that only I could hear. The rewards confirmed for me that we were under endless surveillance, and not just by watching. The only way they could know what to reward me with was by piercing my thoughts even beyond our training sessions.

Even so, the rewards were constant reminders that Shai was second-best to me. I sensed her ever-growing resentment, and I was not surprised when she stayed in her own bed most nights.

After one particularly hard day of training, I found Shai lying in front of the windows. Unmoving . . . emotionless. Just blankly staring out. Broken.

I sat beside her. "Hey," I said softly, handing her the cookie I earned. "I don't know if this is even allowed, but I think you need this more than me."

She rolled away. "Why are you getting so close with them?" she hissed. "Why do you obey their every command?"

"Whoa, where is this coming from?" I stood up with my cookie in hand. After all, I could have gotten in serious trouble sharing it with her. "What else am I supposed to be doing? We're captives here. I have no other choice."

She sat up, glaring at me. "We need to be plotting our escape, not rolling on our backs for a belly rub and a treat."

"I do what I have to do to survive, Shai. I don't ask for rewards, but I'm not going to turn them down either." Frustrated, I swallowed my cookie whole right in front of her.

"I don't have that!" she shouted, pointing at my stuffed cheeks. "All I get are more lashings."

I understood that her anger was coming from her pain and the inequity of our treatment. But having an attitude like hers was not going to make things better for either of us. If the roles were reversed, I would be just as angry and hurt as she was. She tried just as hard as me, but she couldn't connect with them as I could.

Wanting to help, I turned back to her, quickly swallowing what was left of the cookie. I grasped her hands, just as Mom would do for me when I couldn't breathe.

"Maybe I can help you hear the messages," I said. "It's just more of the same from them, their mind manipulation. They've done it to all of us from the start. Making us sleep, pacifying us to prevent us from trying to escape. We all fell into their routine, complying with our tingling brands. They're teaching us what they want from us. Let me help you learn it."

"I don't want to." Shai yelled through her tears. "I want to go home!" I knew she was afraid and angry, and that stopped her from being receptive to the Invaders' commands. Getting past that defiance somehow was the only way forward.

"Look, at my school, they gave us time each day to relax and clear our minds," I continued. "We could close our eyes and sleep. We could read. We could pray. We could just breathe and relax. It was up to us. But the idea was to have dedicated time each day to be calm and relaxed. Can we try it together?"

"Why would I do that?" Shai asked angrily. "I want to fight, not relax."

"I'm just trying to help." I responded softly, to subdue her anger.

"I don't want them in my headspace."

"When we used to sit here and stare out this window, didn't you marvel at all the changes? Take in all the beauty? Watch the animals down below?" I asked her. To me, it was all so amazing that I allowed my feelings to clear, gaze out the window, and just sort of be in the moment.

"How can I appreciate any of this? Look at the price we've all paid." She threw her hands up in exasperation. "We need to be devising our escape, not enjoying ourselves up here, Lauren."

"I get it. I feel that way, too," I said truthfully. Earth's beauty sometimes felt like torment after I had lost my freedom—and Mom and Matthew. "There's no way to justify what they did to us."

I paused to breathe and look out the window, still mesmerized by the beauty below us—its magnificent transformation was nothing I could ever have imagined.

"But what do we do, Shai?" I asked. "How do you suppose we escape if that's even an option? Or instead, do we try to make the best of this awful situation until it changes?"

"I don't know, but we have to try something. Try to escape, try to help our families."

"I *am* trying something," I insisted. "I'm complying to survive. I'm trying to coexist with these Invaders in the circumstances handed to me. I'm hoping one day I get to see Matthew and my mom again.

None of it is easy. But I can help you try to learn their ways, if you'll let me. Besides that, I cannot help." I wanted to make it clear to her that I would not be escaping with her. I believed any attempt to do so would be futile.

"I guess I could try," Shai muttered, much to my surprise. "But I just don't understand any of this."

Shai's training began.

"First, your defiance to them or being disgusted by them must go," I explained. Shai's face lightly spasmed.

I continued, "You can hear their messages, but you have to allow them into your mind."

"Why would you do *that*?" she huffed. "That's all we have left of ourselves. The only thing we still own and control is our mind."

"Do we, though?" I replied.

Shai stormed off. I heard her down the hall say, "*Unbelievable.*"

"If you want my help, you can't judge me," I yelled back at her. I had already placed enough guilt and torment upon myself for obeying—I did not need her to pile more on. I already feared for myself that I was becoming too compliant and vulnerable to the Invaders.

The next day, the Invaders came back to train.

With the female Invader leading us through common commands we both easily knew, the training went smoothly, even for Shai. Maybe she had gotten past yesterday's reluctance and decided to use some of my advice.

Then the male Invader stepped up. As the female Invader moved behind him, she momentarily grasped the male Invader's arm, but he rebuffed her reach. I had never seen them touch before, and it raised an inner alarm for me—as if the female Invader was trying to prevent something from happening. The intensity in the room was far beyond the familiar.

Shai must have noticed it, too, because I saw her hand began to quiver. I reached out to reassure her, but my hand was forced back painfully, slamming to my side—the first discipline I had received in some time. I heard a warning in my mind.

Do not move it again.

He began. It was a new command, and one we had never seen before. He swirled his arm up and around toward the ceiling. It looked like he was commanding us to spin around in a circle, but I heard something entirely different.

Bow on the floor.

It was abject compliance he was looking for. I fell to my knees and let my forehead touch the floor. I could not see what happened next, but I heard it.

Shai was slammed to the floor. I heard her moan.

Then another slam down.

She screamed in pain. "Stop!"

With a third slam, I heard nothing.

Silence.

They left.

I rushed over to her, finding her unconscious, but intermittently twitching. I lifted her head on my lap and brushed aside her hair, with my trembling hands. As I did, a pain ran through me remembering that I had done the exact same for Matthew after the attack.

She moaned. She was alive.

She slept for several days, waking only when I tried to help her eat. She was on the edge of death, and there was no emergency room I could rush her to for help. I worried about whether she would ever recover. I vacillated between my fear of losing the only person I had left and seething with anger that they had done this to her. How could they do this? I realized that there was no way I could comply with their commands anymore. I wasn't going to listen to or follow them. Never again. They would have to hurt me, too. I could not turn my back on this torture against Shai. My defiance was not tested, though. The only solace I had came from the Invaders staying away.

Shai stirred. She finally was awake.

"Shai, you were out for days." I sniffled. "I thought you were going to die this time."

"I know. It scared me, too," Shai answered as she sat up slowly. "A picture flashed in my mind of you crying over me trying to move me. I wasn't alive. I don't know if that really happened."

"I don't think you died, Shai," I responded. "You were really hurt, but you were still breathing."

"Then it's what I feared. They must've implanted that vision in my mind, almost like it was a message to me to understand the severity of my noncompliance. Lauren, I have no other choice. I need you to teach me."

"Are you sure you're up for this?" I asked her.

"My body hurts all over, but I don't know when he's coming back."

"You can't connect with them when you're trying to fight them," I warned. "Clear your thoughts of anger and resentment. When they're here with us, you can't be thinking about home or escaping. All has to be set aside so you have a blank mind for them to enter."

Shai nodded. "Yes, I understand that now. I'm ready to learn their commands. If I don't, I'm afraid I won't live through another training session."

She was finally ready to give in to their mind control. They had broken her, just like they had broken me. It was exactly what they wanted.

CHAPTER 21

A TURNING POINT

I helped Shai down the stairs and placed her at my favorite spot in front of the window.

"I sit here and try to forget where I am, forget trying to change my circumstances, forget about how bad it is on the ground for my mom and Matthew," I began. "I've learned to accept things here, as hard as it is. I gaze silently down at the Earth and take in all of its changes, the vibrant colors and the tremendous overgrowth of the forest. Or I'll watch an unknown animal in the grasslands and marvel at its delicateness through the grass. I put aside all my fears and worries. You can do this, too."

I glanced at Shai. Was she listening? Was she understanding?

She nodded. There was no pushback from her. She did not judge me this time. She just listened and seemed to want to learn.

"I do the same when *they* arrive," I went on. "Rather than be apprehensive about what they'll do to us, my mind goes to this place and replays what I see out this window. I repeat in my mind:

Quiet . . . still . . . calm. In that state, I'm more receptive to their implanted messages."

I was careful not to push Shai to adopt exactly what I did. This would have to become a matter of self-exploration for her. She had to discover for herself how to receive their messages. But I needed her to follow through with something, for the sake of her life.

I continued, "What helps me the most is—"

I paused, not knowing Shai's beliefs. I did not want to offend her in any way.

"What?" she pressed.

"Well, my mom brought us to church, and she encouraged us to lean on God. You need to find yours or what works for you. As captives, we do what we must do to survive. While I let them into my mind to hear my messages, I'm still free in my thoughts and feelings afterward. My soul is intact. My core remains. In the silence and stillness, I still feel it. Now it's your turn—try to connect to it."

For weeks, we were not visited by them, and we sat in the silence together. What was once my alone time in the mornings before their abusive training began, Shai joined me, and we began our day together in my favorite place in front of the windows. She no longer questioned my process. Her body healed, and she seemed calmer— there was no more talk of escaping. She no longer judged me for letting *them* into my mind. I felt that the progress she made during this time would help to avoid the punishments and possibly even death the next time the Invaders visited our pod.

Then they reappeared. The time had come for Shai to be tested.

I grabbed Shai's hand and whispered, "I believe in you."

Shai's legs shook, and she slowly buckled toward the floor. Her fear overpowered her. That last beating almost took her life. Nothing that I taught her could control her involuntary bodily reaction. All she had worked on was marred just by their appearance alone.

I reached under her arm and lifted her up before the male Invader could react. I whispered, "Remember what I taught you. Your fear will keep you from hearing them. I'm here with you."

Then they began.

I released a sigh of relief once I noticed that the male Invader floated back. The female Invader led us through training exercises—delicate in her commands, soft in her requests—while the male simply looked on. There was no punishment, no lashings, and the female Invader even showed Shai a bit of grace for her efforts to learn and hear.

Instead of seeking connection, Shai adopted an attitude of mechanical compliance. She seemed to have lost her way—she was a shell of her former self.

"You're doing well," I said to Shai gently after the training ended and we were alone again. "You didn't get hurt."

"Yeah, I guess," she muttered.

For weeks Shai complied, while the female Invader led our training exercises. I was proud of her for changing and allowing them into her mind to save herself from harm. Without having to worry about Shai any longer, I focused on my own advancement and connection with them.

With the female Invader, I was able to learn additional commands. Her cues were seamless and clear—no longer one-word demands exploding in my head, but a deeper, encompassing feeling, an expansion of my senses. As I willingly granted her more control over my mind, she was able to sway me mentally and emotionally through her transmitted messages. I felt a sense of calm from head to toe as she sent the messages to me, almost as if in a trancelike state. It evolved to where both her thoughts and mine intermingled.

"They're downstairs," I announced one morning, just as we were waking up. Without even seeing them, I knew they had arrived. I felt an immediate connection with them. And that spark came to me each time they entered. "I sense them."

"Lauren, that's unnatural," Shai sneered.

After Shai's angered response, I knew I had to keep from her how vast my connection with them had grown. If I had explained to her the nearly seamless compliance I had achieved, she would have been very worried, even troubled over it.

I doubted she would ever give up control to the extent that I had. *She just needs time*, I told myself. Eventually she'll get there, I believed.

One morning, Shai missed our quiet time in front of the windows, obviously forgetting my instructions that this was a necessary precursor to the training with the Invaders. She was particularly on edge, which I found odd given that she'd been spared for weeks from any punishments, while the female Invader showed her much patience.

Soon after the Invaders appeared, and as we had been trained to do, we rose and stood across the room from them awaiting their commands. Just before I closed my eyes to clear my mind, Shai darted across the room, lunging and wildly swinging at the Invaders. A shiny object slipped from her hand and lines of blood spilled through her fingers with each swing. A shard of glass from our mirror. She targeted her attack at the male Invader. She was after him.

I released a strangled yell as she continued her enraged swinging.

When none of her swipes made contact, she leapt on him, plunging the shard into his torso until a trickle of gleaming, silver fluid oozed through the robe. Although this was retribution for all the harm he inflicted on her, I knew it would end only one way—and I was not ready for Shai's death. She was all I had left.

Just as quickly as the Invader flung her to the floor with a twirl of his finger, the silver stain disappeared from his robe. Apparently, they had the ability to self-heal.

"No!" Shai growled, lunging at him again, screaming and scratching at the air. But this time she couldn't reach him. His finger had risen again, and she became suspended in the air.

The broken pieces of the mirror from her hand fell to the ground. He snapped his fingers.

I had never heard a snap from them before, and I was petrified of what that meant for Shai.

While still suspended in the air, she rose quickly to the ceiling and was slammed to the ground. She wailed, kicking and screaming, unable to rise or move, restricted in place on the ground. Her body slowly thinned, like she was being flattened from something above—an invisible crushing of her body.

I heard a terrible popping noise. She went limp and quiet.

With a rise of the Invader's hand, Shai was lifted by her branded arm from the ground—her broken body suspended in the air. She was held there just above where the two of us would sit in front of the window, her legs and arms dangling down. Blood dripped from her nose onto the blanket that I had placed in my favorite viewing spot shortly after we arrived here.

"You're killing her!" I screamed after seeing her blood.

I charged, knowing that I was powerless against them. I didn't care what they would do to me. No longer could I watch their cruelty against Shai in silence. I couldn't allow the horror of their torture continue to paralyze me from helping. I had to do something, anything to make them stop no matter what the consequences would be.

The female Invader raised her arm and flung it to the side, and my body followed. I hit the wall and slithered to the ground, unable to move and hardly able to breathe. All I could do was cry.

CHAPTER 22

ALONE

Shai was gone.

How had this happened? I thought Shai had changed. I thought she *wanted* to survive. I never considered that she might plot to kill the Invaders. She had not shared her plan with me. She no longer trusted me, or maybe she worried that I could not keep them from learning about her plans through my thoughts. I had gotten too close to them, and she knew it. She knew it before I did.

I was alone.

I didn't get out of bed. I didn't want to move.

I stayed there in the darkness, stunned and numb, drowning in all the losses I had endured. All the suffering had finally hit me. I could not suppress it any longer, no matter how much Mom wanted me to. My will to survive had carried me this far—but now it had been sucked out of me.

I had no desire to look out onto the Earth or to relive my favorite memories from before captivity. There would be no deep breathing and calming exercises. I did none of it. I would never be receptive to them again.

After Shai disappeared, they stayed away, and I did not leave my dark, cold room. I only slipped downstairs for a fleeting moment to satisfy my hunger pains but would hurry back up to hide under the bed covers. This went on for days.

Until I felt them—despite my attempts to fight it. They had arrived downstairs. I knew they were there. I could feel their presence, but I refused to move from my bed.

They would not leave, repeatedly sending me mental messages to come to them. I wrapped my pillow over my head to block them out. When I failed to comply and stand at attention before them as they expected, the invisible force came, pulling me with my branded arm and thrashing me down each and every stair. My body tumbled and thumped all the way down. I didn't care; I wasn't complying in any way. I *hated* them for what they did to Shai—for what they did to all of us. I sensed that they were equally affronted at me—but their reasoning made no sense. I had nothing to do with her attack.

After receiving what they wanted, I refused to comply. I had never before ignored them this way, even refusing to get to my feet no matter how many messages they tried to embed in my mind. What was the point of complying? I likely would be killed eventually anyway. And what they had done to Shai was unforgivable. I *was not* going to comply ever again.

When the male Invader raised his skeletal, silver-hued arm, forcing me to stand, I went limp and flopped to the ground. A hint of red permeated his otherwise sparkling white skin just as he pointed his finger at me. A burning sensation burst from the brand on my arm, traveling down to the tips of my fingers. My arm pulsated in pain, feeling as if it was on fire. Not only was the brand a painful visible reminder of my endless captivity, but now it was singed and swollen from the physical abuse I endured at the hands of my captors. I closed my eyes and let the tears stream down my cheeks, but still I was *not* standing.

He pulled my branded arm up above my head and lifted me off the ground, as if to demand my compliance. My distress did not matter to him. My legs wobbled below me, remaining limp as he tried to place me on the ground to stand. The only response he got from me was the occasional body spasm with each of his lashings.

I fell back to the ground and rolled myself into a tightly rounded ball, waiting for more invisible lashings.

But the strikes never came.

After a long pause, I peered out of my ball. Why was I being spared when Shai had been murdered for her defiance?

I heard soft noises and whispering words, although nothing that I could recognize. The Invaders were communicating with each other, and I could hear it all even if I couldn't understand it. I sensed that his anger with me was growing, while she became more and more worried for me.

When the male Invader noticed me watching them, he raised his finger to the ceiling, readying to strike me. I noticed again that his porcelain face turned a reddish hue. The female Invader grabbed his arm, pulling it forcefully down.

I heard a message in my mind: *Safe.* I suddenly realized that it was *she* who had sent me the messages all along. She was the one guiding me, helping me follow his commands, showing me the quiet grace that could surmount his destruction. She had made sure that each lashing was followed with the transmission of a calm feeling to my mind, seeking to temper my fear of him.

Just before they disappeared from the pod, an unseen ball of warmth surrounded me with tranquility. Once again, I felt she was trying to defuse his abuse. I wasn't certain if the male Invader was even aware of what she was doing.

The next day, she arrived . . . *alone*.

My shoulders sank in relief, though I wasn't entirely convinced that I was safe with her. After all, she was the one who had slammed me against the wall just before Shai was taken.

She extended her fingers from the cuffs of her glistening robe, curling them in my direction, motioning me to join her at my favorite spot in front of the window. I heard her in my mind: *Come.*

I convinced myself that maybe I should go to avoid punishment, if all she wanted from me was to be by my window.

In response, I heard a single, whispered word in my mind: *Yes.*

The female Invader and I had conversed *in my mind*.

I heard her again: *Come. Here.*

She stood by the window, and I moved toward her, one slow step after the other, in disbelief. I felt her staring at me, but I didn't want to look up at her. I stood beside her, my arms tightly folded. I cast my eyes downward and found the bloodstain left over from Shai. A single tear rolled down my cheek, and I thought, *I shouldn't be here. I shouldn't be next to this thing that took away my last friend in the world.*

Her presence was demanding. Looking up at her was unavoidable.

Next to her, I was like a little child. I raised my head to meet her gaze. She slowly blinked her large, rounded eyes—not pitch-black as I had thought, but swirled with a hint of silver. The jewels aside her eyes sparkled exquisitely. I blinked back at her as we watched each other for a moment.

Her hood was off and folded down along her back, halfway

covering her white hair, which shone brightly from the light of the sun gleaming in through the nearby window. Strands of silver ran through it. Her skin and features appeared even more delicate than before.

She broke her gaze and turned to stare out the window. I followed her lead. We stood side-by-side looking out the window. No messages were sent. No commands were issued. I feared no lashings from her. We just stood and stared.

My arms fell to my side. My shoulders rolled back and down. My forehead relaxed. In this moment, I could breathe again. I could look out the window and take in the beauty of the Earth below. I almost got lost in it, forgetting briefly that *she* was beside me.

She spoke no verbal words. But I could *hear* her speak to me.

I am Ula. The other is Jun. I know you are Lauren.

I jumped, staggering backward a step or two, shrinking away from her in surprise. How did she know my name? I thought of Shai and how she would have been so spooked to hear this Invader in her mind, giving us their names.

The friend, Shaila, has not been harmed. She has been returned to the others.

"Not harmed?" I blurted out loud, keeping my distance. "I thought she died! She was limp. You dragged her body out."

Ula softly responded, *It was not real.*

She had to be kidding. "But I saw it. And I felt pain," I insisted. "He struck us. It was torture. He *killed her!*"

Put aside what you saw. It was not real, Ula repeated in the same soft voice. *Only an illusion in this place, for that moment.*

Her messages were soft and precise—no more words or details were provided other than that which was necessary. I was left stunned and unsatisfied with her explanation. If she was not going to tell me where Shai was, I decided to disengage from her, refuse to communicate.

But she would not let me. She was in my mind, whether or not I wanted her to be.

The truth is revealed to all of us in natural creation, Ula continued. *When you look out this window, what you experience through Earth's transformation is natural revelation—a natural revitalization. We have charted a new course for Earth. The atonement has occurred, and now the enlightenment will happen for all. I feel that you feel it. You have learned it and become part of it.*

I just blinked at her, bewildered. I had no idea what she was talking about.

Come near me to receive a gift, she said gently, *as you have been most loyal and most willing to embrace our message.*

Ula closed her eyes and drew her spiny hands together in front of her. A faint golden glow radiated from within her cupped hands, forming a tiny whirlwind of light. I gazed at that heavenly light, unable to look away. The longer I looked in, the more different I felt—less anxious, more calm. Within me, an intense undercurrent of rage was replaced with a feeling of peace and of simply existing in the light. The animus I felt toward Ula slipped away.

My chest expanded, and I inhaled deeply, pulling the whirlwind of light into my mouth, swallowing it down. It warmed me, flowing into my chest and down into my stomach—a tender warmth that spread throughout my body. My arms floated up as if they were weightless, and a golden hue infused my skin. Tranquility penetrated my bones. It was unlike anything I had ever experienced.

Then Ula left the pod, leaving me with this heavy, mysterious interaction to reflect on alone. For the rest of that day and evening,

I just existed, without all the trauma and guilt I had accumulated. It all just . . . dissipated.

I did not want.

I did not miss.

I did not worry.

I just *was*.

I was a light-filled being, observing the natural revelation outside the windows of my living quarters in an alien spaceship. It was absolutely wild.

My sleep that night was deep and long.

When I woke the next morning, the golden light running through my skin was gone, and my normal state of mind had returned: worried about Mom and Matthew, anguished over Shai, missing home and my puppy, and trapped in a room with no exit. The gift from Ula—that brief time of knowing equanimity—had been truly remarkable. But my mom, my brother, and so many other humans were caged up like wild animals. How could I feel so wonderful amid all the suffering endured by everyone else?

Plus, I missed them . . . all of them, even the ones I didn't know. I missed just having people around. I was alone . . . all the time.

When Ula appeared by my side at the window, I clutched my stuffed kitty and curled up in a ball on the floor, hoping she wouldn't make me train. But Jun—as she called him—was not with her, and even more interesting, she brought an unusual object. It was very large and taller than me, though Ula suspended it in both hands in front of her effortlessly. It was rounded and looked to be of a crystalized, nearly clear material. I only got a peak of it. Ula waved her hands over it, and the clear transport ball disappeared. She beckoned me to come near, but I didn't want to get any closer. The idea of any physical contact with her frightened me. As far as I was concerned, I was close enough to her.

I shook my head. *No.*

She lifted one spiny finger as a warning, waving it slowly back and forth, and then pointed to the spot next to her. Before I could refuse again, I was filled with a sense of assurance: *All will be okay. Trust.*

Whatever it was, it persuaded me to obey, and I walked to her side.

Without further instruction, she waved her hand over my head. The glass ball reappeared, surrounding my body and enclosing me in it. She lifted the ball in her hands, with me trapped inside of it. My mind went blank, and the room faded to black.

When I awakened, the glass ball around me had vanished, leaving me on a cold, cement floor.

I returned to the hangar.

Maybe they were done with me.

CHAPTER 23

AN UNEXPECTED TRIP

W hy had I been returned? Would I be a prisoner again, with all the others? Strangely, the thought excited me. How could I *want* to be back and held as a captive?

Before, I dreaded waking up each day in the cramped, cold, bleak hangars. And now I had been living in luxurious quarters in their vessel with my own space, amazing views, and a comfortable bed with pillows and plenty of soft blankets. The answer, of course, was obvious: I wanted to be with Matthew and Mom again.

Thank you, I whispered to Ula, while she was perched high above, near the ceiling of the hangar, looking down. *For releasing me.*

I stood alone in the middle of the hangar. I figured all the girls had been cleared out for their outside time.

Through the massive doorway, Matthew appeared, his branded arm leading the way.

He saw me and looked just as confused as I felt.

I heard Ula, *Go see him. There is no barrier.*

I ran toward him. My little brother. My heart ached, just as my tears swelled in my eyes. There was no holding them back. "Matthew." I never thought I'd utter his name with such relief, such overwhelming joy.

Matthew stopped short and waved his arms before him, as if to warn me against getting too close. He obviously was worried about a barrier.

"There's no barrier." I waved my arms in the space between us. "They told me it's not here."

Ignoring the puzzled look on his face, I jumped into his arms and gave him the tightest hug I could, never wanting to let go. How long had we been separated?

He squeezed me back, and then grabbed my shoulders, stepping back as if to confirm it was truly me. He seemed even more stunned than I was. "Lauren, how are you here? You haven't been at the barrier in . . . well, months. I thought you were taken by the Vellatros." He pulled me back to him with bulky arms and squeezed even tighter, sniffling. "I thought I'd never see you again. What happened to you?"

"What happened to *you*?" I wriggled from his sturdy grasp, which actually started to hurt. He was more a man than the little boy I remembered. His arms were noticeably bulkier, much stronger than before, and he even towered over me. "You're all grown up. And so strong!"

"We've all grown stronger," he replied. "After you went missing, I began training harder and pushing the others more and more. There are more of us now. We've organized. I keep my men ready and strong for that day to come."

"Oh, wow," I responded. I hit his chest to test how strong he'd gotten, but he swiped my hand away after my fourth hit.

"They consider me a leader now. I tried to fight off one of the Vellatros."

"You did *what*?"

"It was trying to abduct one of my guys. I jumped up and grabbed the boy's ankle and threw the thing off. It was slithering around on the ground. . . . They're not as big as they look from below. I stood on its tattered robe while it struggled beneath my foot until it flew away, squealing. It didn't come back for him . . . or me."

"Geez, Matthew, you could've been taken away," I responded.

He shrugged. "The boy just made a mistake. He should have been given a second chance. I was angry. Plus, I thought *they* took you. I hadn't seen you for so long."

"You saved him, just like you saved me that day on the school bus." I hugged him again, not knowing if I'd ever get the chance again. "Matthew, I need to know. Have you seen Mom?"

He nodded. "I still visit her at the barrier. Not seeing you, not knowing where you've been—or if you were even alive—has been *really* hard on her."

I imagined the grief my mother must have been going through.

"Lauren, she's different—detached, sometimes even unresponsive. Like a part of her was lost when you went missing. What happened to you?" he asked again. "Where have you been all this time?"

"They've been holding me in one of their vessels." I pointed up. As I uttered those words and upon realizing how long I had been removed from him and my mom, my eyes swelled. I continued, telling him everything all at once. "I have my own living quarters with a great, big window. From up above, I can see the hangars and people and the garden. I look for you and Mom every day from above. I'm just too high up to really tell who I'm looking at. There was another girl up there with me, but she disappeared. She tried to fight them. They took her away after that. Now I'm all alone in there. There are two of them that visit me in my living quarters. But they take care of me. I have a soft bed, and they feed me—even cookies sometimes, chocolate ones. You know how I love chocolate." I paused, not knowing if I was even making any sense to him. "I really wish you were there with me."

Matthew just looked at me and listened intently.

"I've even seen beyond the hangars. There's a vast forest in the distance, Matthew, and grasslands just beyond the barrier. The bushes block your view on the ground, but it's all out there, and I can see it. There's nothing left of what humans built. It's gone. All of it." I lowered my voice and leaned in closer, whispering. "They've been training me. I—I really don't know what for, but I feel like . . . an experiment."

"An experiment?" he snarled. "What do you mean? Are they hurting you, Lauren?"

"Not recently." I couldn't lie and tell him no because they *had* hurt me . . . and Shai. "Not since I figured out how to communicate with them and follow their commands."

"What do you mean? You can . . . talk to them?" Matthew probed, his voice rising. Repulsion dripped from his questions.

I gestured for Matthew to see her, perched at the ceiling of the hangar, in the same spot the holograms had been before.

"Is she real or a hologram?" Matthew asked, narrowing his eyes.

"This one is real. She's my designated Invader." I had no other way of explaining Ula's role with me. "She is nice to me; she sometimes protects me." I had to convince him that Ula was not his enemy.

"But she *hurt* you," Matthew growled, his fists clenched. He grew noticeably angrier while he continued to stare at Ula.

I thought about my training with her and suddenly saw myself at my window, surrounded by the golden light. All other thoughts cleared from my mind, exactly as I performed the training with Ula. Calm overtook me, and I thought of the nothingness she had made known to me. My palms tingled as the light spread through my mind, transmitting tranquility to my brother.

Don't be angry. I'm okay.

Matthew shuddered, jiggling his head as if trying to shake something off.

I was stunned. Was this really happening? Had I learned how to receive and remit Ula's messages? I tried again.

Be calm.

"Whoa." He exhaled. "Did—did you do that? Is that the experiment? Is that what they're training you to do?" Apparently, he caught on much quicker than I had.

I shrugged. "Until now, I didn't even know I could. I just did what they do to me."

Matthew seemed unsure how he felt about it, but when he spoke again, his voice was calmer. "That's what they've been doing to us all along, Lauren. They force us to sleep, to calm down, to keep us complacent and compliant as they shuffle us around. It's mind manipulation. And you're doing that same thing to me now."

"I don't know, Matthew. Sometimes it helps. It calms me. You've been training in your own way down here, building your army with your followers. I'm all alone up there. I'm not sure why they trust me with it, but I don't have much of a choice."

Matthew mumbled to himself, "If we could use it somehow . . ."

"Matthew!" He was no longer paying attention to me.

"Are you in their main ship?" he asked, seemingly fixated on plotting to use my skill for his purposes.

"I'm not really sure. I'm kept in my own quarters. I—"

He grabbed my shoulders again. "How long are you staying here? Will we see each other again?"

"I don't know. They didn't even tell me I'd be coming." I gestured again to Ula. "She somehow knew how lonely and upset I've been. I think that's why I'm here." Hearing myself explain this to my brother, I realized how absurd and defeated I sounded.

"Look, I don't know what's going on up there. But you need to remember where you come from and who you can trust—who your *real* family is. Don't let yourself be controlled by them." Matthew looked deep into my eyes. "Get them out of your headspace, Lauren. We're going to need you. Stay strong. Protect your mind."

"I will, I will." His grip was tight, and I tapped his hand to release it. "I got it, okay?" I reached out to reassure him, but his arm began tugging, and we both knew what that meant. In just a moment we would be separated again.

I held onto Matthew as long as I could. As he was pulled away, Ula appeared beside me with the glass ball that quickly formed around me. Matthew gasped as it enclosed me.

"I'll stay strong, Matthew!" I splayed my hands against the translucent side of the ball. "For you and Mom!"

Everything went black.

◆

Just as the crystal transport ball opened around me, I watched it dissolve into Ula's hand above my head. I was not back in my living quarters. Once more I was sitting on the cold, hard ground of a hangar. Matthew was no longer around.

Three older ladies were looking down at me, whispering among themselves: "Who is she? What is she doing here?" One poked at my leg, as if I wasn't real. Maybe they reacted that way since I arrived with an Invader. I found her, Ula, resting high above, near the ceiling . . . watching. I assumed that meant I was not staying here either.

Behind the women, a familiar figure sat on a rocking chair with a bundle of blankets in her arms. Her faint humming reached my ears. It was the song my mother hummed to me whenever I needed comforting—the same song I hummed to myself in my living quarters whenever I missed her most.

Missing her was so overwhelming.

I sprinted toward her, and cried out, "Mom!"

My mother rose from the rocker and stumbled, nearly dropping the bundle. An older lady steadied her and reached for a baby from my mom's arms, depositing it in a nearby crib.

Quietly, Mom stretched out a shaky hand, grabbing and pulling me in. I placed my head on her shoulder, just as I had always done. In the safety of her arms, I forgot everything else. Her hug swept me away from the hangars and everything that had happened since that purple dome had appeared so long ago. I never wanted to let go.

"Mom," I whimpered. She lifted a finger to her mouth.

"Shush," she whispered, pointing at the cribs all around us, leading me away.

"Not seeing you for so long, Lauren, I was afraid . . . I thought the worst." She grasped both my hands into hers and held my gaze with her eyes. "My baby is here. I want to see your beautiful eyes. I've *missed* you so much." She pulled her hands up, still grasping mine, to wipe the tears from her eyes with the back of her hand. "I still remember when I rocked you to sleep . . . my precious baby girl . . ."

"Mom, I missed you so much. I couldn't—"

"I've gone back to the barrier every day, still writing you messages.

I never stopped looking, and hoping. . . . But so many days passed, and then weeks . . . I thought you were gone forever." She looked despondent, childlike—lost, just like Matthew said.

"Mom, I'm here," I said gently. "I'm here."

"But where have you been, Lauren? I haven't seen you in the hangar with the other girls."

I explained about being chosen and held in their vessel. "I don't know why it was me. But none of that matters. I don't want to be separated from you anymore. I want the three of us together, even if that means we're still held captive here. I just want to come back."

Mom's eyes were sad. "It's always better when I have my babies with me." Her head dropped into her hands, and she sobbed uncontrollably. Matthew was right, being separated from us was worse for her than for us.

"Mom, I don't know how long I have here with you."

Her sobs turned to light sniffles until she finally stopped crying altogether. She composed herself upon realizing we had limited time.

"I just came from seeing Matthew. He seems . . . intense. He says he's the leader of his group," I added, probing whether Mom knew anything about it.

She did. "He's strong and determined. He seems to like the role of being in charge and what they call him, MatX. Though still so young for such a responsibility, I see no harm in it if it helps him during captivity. I get to tend to the babies, and he gets his warriors." She wrapped her arms around me again.

I squeezed her back, enjoying the time with her before we were pulled apart, just as Matthew and I had been. When the transport ball came for me, before everything went black, I took comfort in knowing that they were still alive.

When the crystal transport ball dissolved around me and things grew light again, I was no longer in a hangar. I was in my quarters on the vessel, but the view through my huge window was very different. Instead of the sky or the Earth below, I saw another window. It opened onto a gigantic vessel, and my pod was floating directly toward it.

I was on a collision course with the mothership.

CHAPTER 24

NEW BEGINNINGS, AGAIN

J ust as my pod was hurling toward impact with the main vessel, I became transfixed upon what I saw through the other window. It was a room, just as sterile and cold-looking as mine—made up mostly of glass paneling, steel, and white accents. Except everything was considerably larger.

Only inches away from the other, my pod didn't slow. I braced myself against the wall furthest away from the window, expecting shattering upon impact. But there was no shattering, no window blowout. My pod didn't even shake. Just as they collided, the two windows liquefied, melding together as my pod inserted itself into the larger vessel, becoming a single unit. My sole window now looked into the massive room. Any previous uncertainty I had about whether I was in the main vessel was now gone.

The massive room—on the other side of where my window once was—opened to marble-like floors that glistened and contained minimal furnishings: an oversized seating structure, and a rectangular white credenza, with a wall of monitors. I had more comforts in my tiny pod than what they had in this gigantic room. Strikingly absent was anything resembling a door.

Looking into this room without any separation from it, I realized that just as I could see out, anyone in that expansive room would be able to see in. My living space was open and exposed, leaving me even more vulnerable to *them*. I no longer had any privacy at all. I'd be fully enveloped by their world, connected to them at all times.

I wanted nothing to do with it.

I turned to head for my tiny bedroom, where I could hide in the dark under my covers. Before I took a single step, I felt Ula's presence and heard her in my mind.

Lauren, come.

Aside from the trembling in my legs that arose after I scanned the connected rooms, I refused to move. I felt a wave of calmness settling over my fear, and I knew it came from her. My heart pounded as my true distress struggled against her calming transmissions. She must have sensed my tension and the deep, underlying confusion I had while I tried to fight against her emotional manipulation. I no longer found her efforts comforting. I had Matthew's warnings to me to keep her out of my head to thank for that.

But her power was overwhelming, and the calmness strengthened during our unseen and otherwise undetected power struggle. She easily quelled the fleeting attempt I made to override her forced emotion.

I let out a deep sigh. It was beyond my control. I relaxed, just as she ordained.

When I turned back, Ula was there at the edge of these two worlds—my little pod on one side, and their massive room on the other—looking in. With my pod attached higher up from their floor, my tiny face was now aligned with her much larger one. I blinked, peering into her eyes as she gazed back at me. She slowly unfurled her porcelain-white fingers, exposing a piece of chocolate set in the middle of her hand.

I knew she was tempting me with this delicacy. I didn't care. The reward—my first since Shai had been taken—was too tempting.

I snatched the chocolate piece and lost myself in its delights, savoring the smooth, rich flavor. Suddenly I realized I was leaning against her finger, unintentionally touching her. All this time, the only contact with them had been from afar, just the unseen force dragging us around and the invisible lashings. This time, I felt her skin—cold, thin, and supple. It moved easily with my touch, over the hardness of the bones just beneath.

I gagged, triggered by the unbearable physical contact, and dropped the remaining bit of the chocolate. I fled up the stairs as fast as I possibly could, diving under my covers.

She was gone. I no longer felt her in the living quarters. She left me in my panic, without calming me, even though my panic and disgust hadn't subsided. I wondered if she'd been startled too, or if I had hurt her feelings.

Cocooned in the blanket, the calm came to me on its own. With my clear mind, I realized that Ula didn't want to hurt me. She gave me a treat, after all. Unlike Jun, she'd been kind and gentle, for the most part. Why shouldn't I trust her?

With her gone, I tiptoed down the stairs to find that last bit of chocolate exactly where I left it. Still a bit wary, I sat between the two rooms with my legs hanging over the edge of my pod and stared into the other, larger room, enjoying the final bite.

Ula returned. I tensed up, unsure whether to run again or stay in hopes of another treat.

Stay calm, I thought. *Don't run.*

Ula's unexpected response followed: *Good. Calm.* She held out another piece of chocolate. I must have been a good girl.

Behind Ula, a small creature appeared.

I gulped.

I was less than half the size of Ula, and this creature was half *my* size. It was chunky and covered from head to toe with white fur streaked with several faint black stripes. I once saw a white tiger at the zoo, and this could have been its cub, walking on two legs, except for the humanlike face, which was bronzed and heavily wrinkled. A tattered brown cloth necklace was loosely wrapped around its neck, with several strands of beads hanging down its chest. With deep-set brown eyes and a hunched back, this creature had a consuming depth and sadness to it, like a wise old shaman. It spoke aloud with Ula, in a language of clicking sounds that was unfamiliar to me. Ula must have been communicating in the creature's native language, just as she was able to do with me.

It was shy and submissive, obeying her every command. It succumbed to Ula entirely under her enslaving power. I had to wonder if this, too, was my fate. Did either of us have any other choice?

"This is my doulesthe," Ula said with a lisp, as her slivery tongue slightly protruded past her thin lips. The odd sight of her tongue interrupted my obsessive watching of the creature perform its tasks around the room.

Stunned, I turned away from the enchanting little creature to Ula. She had spoken these words *aloud*. I stiffened, but the sense of calm came over me quickly this time. *She did it to me again.* I was starting to find it violating.

"We will proceed with our training in here," Ula explained, pointing to stairs that were forming just below me, leading from my pod to the floor of the larger room. She wanted me to leave my safe little world and join their alien territory.

I stepped back, shaking my head fiercely. I wasn't ready to breach that divide.

"Lauren, come," she called out. "Here is your space to take beside me."

I took another step backward, trying to get as deep into my own pod and as far away from her as I could.

Her bony, porcelain-white hand moved toward the ceiling as she commanded, "Follow me."

Effortlessly, my body followed her hand, my feet lifted off the ground, and I drifted along the floor. Before anxiously reacting to the fact that she was *floating* me, calmness ran through me. Not only did she control my body movements, but she manipulated my mind, too. I should have remembered that disobeying her was pointless.

She kept me floating, suspended in the air, while I moved to *their* side of the living quarters. Any separation between us was entirely gone. I had breached their space.

Still floating, she transferred me across the room, stopping at the main vessel's enormously tall windows, which were exquisitely outlined with a thick golden frame. In front of the windows facing outward were oversized furnishings, with one smaller seat, just my size, right beside it. Plush blankets sprawled around the ground. Ula had replicated what I had created for myself in front of my window in the pod. Prompting Ula to release me, I squirmed to get loose and back to the ground.

Just as my toes touched, I dashed to the windows to take in the utterly breathtaking new view of the Earth below. From this vantage point the forest was closer, with a clearer view of the little animals darting in and out of the rim. I now could see the intricate details of the overgrowth, the density, and the tree's rich thickness. I sat above the brilliant green canopy and gazed upon the different tree species growing strong and deep together, all without any threat of destruction by humans.

"It's beautiful, yes?" Ula asked.

I simply nodded, still uncomfortable with having a verbal conversation with her.

"Come, sit with me," she directed. I knew I had no choice. "For our training."

I fell into the velvety, thick blankets beside the chairs. As I lay there running my fingers over its softness, a golden light formed above my head and continued to grow between us. The light fully surrounded her. Just as it made its way to my skin, I panicked and jumped away. Before I could explain myself, the light disappeared, and I stood alone in my pod. In an instant, there was no longer a view out the windows, no plush blankets beside me, and no cloud-like, soft chair to sit in.

I sensed her disappointment in my reluctance to trust her. But what did she really expect of me? After all, I had just arrived in their living area, my only friend since being taken from the hangars nearly had been beaten to death, and everything changed again. Her expectations were unrealistic.

Your people are unenlightened. This message rang throughout my pod, but she was nowhere to be found. *We train to change this within you. You cannot resist it.*

Despite everything they had put me through, a part of me wanted another chance to prove myself to her. I also wanted to know what she meant as enlightenment. As I turned to return to her, I was stopped. The familiar multicolored, oscillating, translucent barrier formed between our two spaces, preventing me from leaving my pod.

Beyond the barrier, I watched as she floated across the room, leaving our new training area and over to what I initially thought was a solid wall. But with a wave of her hand, a circular energy source appeared, through which she walked and then was gone. The passageway closed before the doulesthe could join her. Each time I thought of the doulesthe's name, Ula's lisp was heard, and glimpses of her wretched tongue came to mind. The creature quickly retreated elsewhere beyond my view.

But more importantly, was that a secret, hidden portal in their quarters?

CHAPTER 25

MEMORIES

Ula began another day of training in front of the windows.

"Open up to the indwelling presence of the calm, the intensity. You must learn to live entirely within its realm. In the realm of the power," she instructed, while trying to invade my mind. All I could think about were warnings from Matthew and Shai's refusal to obey them. I stiffened in opposition . . . and in fear of what this all meant. The golden light continued extending toward my direction until it fully engulfed me.

I allowed it. I gave into it. I felt relaxed and unburdened. I soaked in the warmth of the golden light.

The transference from her ended, and the golden light faded back into her.

She returned me to my living quarters, drowsy and intoxicated. Despite my hazy state, I noticed the doulesthe walk by, staring in, almost as if it was checking on me. I giggled at its unbearable cuteness and waved. It walked away, seemingly unamused. My trancelike state faded as Ula's spell wore off.

Not long after, Ula returned. "You experienced the transcendence of the light. For a permanent implanting of this gift, you must overcome your unrest."

My eyes grew heavy, and I fell into another daze. My memories overtook my thoughts.

I was back home. I remembered that day vividly. A memory of a month before we were taken, just after the new school year had started. Matthew was in sixth grade, and I just started high school. We were getting ready for school while Mom was getting ready for work.

My memory jumped ahead to Mrs. Pickering's class. I could hear her as if I were sitting in her classroom.

"Coach Blazier is waiting on the bus," Mrs. Pickering called as we shuffled out of the classroom. "Let's get going."

I tried to fight it. I didn't want to get on that school bus. Not again.

Do not fight. The voice was Ula's.

Entranced, I gave in to the golden glow and became part of the memory.

Zary boarded the bus ahead of me. "I'll get us a seat," she mentioned as she breezed past Coach Blaizer in the driver's seat. She turned back at me, squeezing her nose, laughing. She leapt past him. I was next in line.

Beneath the overwhelming stench of cologne came a powerful smell of booze, oozing from Coach Blaizer's pores. "There's my favorite girl," Coach Blaizer slurred as I approached him. He wasn't normally this cheerful. His typical greeting to me during P.E. class was his whistle in my face, as he shouted, "Run! Faster!"

"No running for you today, young lady. Not that you need it. You're just too cute!"

A chill ran down my arms, and I laughed nervously, walking past him as fast as I could.

"That was kinda awful," I said, pushing to the back of the bus and plopping down next to Zary.

"Ugh!" she agreed. "He flirts with all the pretty girls, you know."

"I guess I made the list." Pretending to gag, I shoved my backpack under the seat. "Should we be worried? About him driving?"

"Why? Does being a creep impair his driving?" Zary joked. It took me a second to realize that unlike me, Zary wouldn't recognize it. I could never forget that smell. I gripped that armrest all the way to the sustainable farm while Coach Blaizer somehow managed to get us there without crashing.

Time skipped. We were watching the farm-raised chickens enjoying the sun and being outside.

"Forget what Pickering says about the chicks at the farm, boys. You have some fine ones of your own right there." Coach shoved Bodie with his shoulder and pointed in Zary's and my direction. The other boys laughed, and one whistled.

"*Never* let me marry someone like that," Zary said under her breath.

I snorted, grabbing my mouth to hold it back.

The boys grew silent, and their expressions turned dark. They were not accustomed to being laughed at. They were the champion football team, after all.

"I just hope we make it home alive," I said loudly, hoping Mrs. Pickering would hear.

Coach Blaizer's nostrils flared as he lifted his chin, staring right at me . . . and only me. I turned quickly away. No other adult had ever looked at me like that before.

I held on to Zary tight for the rest of the farm trip, not letting go until we were in our seat on the bus for the ride home.

"I told Mrs. Pickering what he said to me," I explained. "I also kinda raised how badly he smelled."

"Is that why they were arguing before we got on the bus?" Zary asked.

"Most likely. She better not have told him I said anything."

I was back at the school parking lot, relieved to have arrived safely. We returned from the field trip later than expected since Mrs. Pickering drove us back. I knew Mom and Matthew would be looking for me. Hurrying past Coach Blaizer in the front passenger seat, I practically jumped down the steps before he could say anything else creepy to me.

Zary caught up to me. "Sucks for you, you have P.E. with him tomorrow," she chided.

"I know!"

"Hey, where's your backpack?" Zary asked.

"What?" My backpack. In my rush, I had left it under my seat. "Crap! I gotta go back. I'll call you later. I'll let you know if Coach Blaizer is a weirdo when I grab it."

The bus door was ajar.

When I stepped back on the bus, Coach was the only one left. He rose unsteadily from the driver's seat, blocking the aisle.

My body tensed, and my stomach clenched. "Um, Coach Blaizer, I left my backpack."

"Well, go get it," he snapped. By his response, I just knew that Mrs. Pickering mentioned me when they were fighting in front of the bus. "I win championships. I don't clean up after you kids."

I made my way down the aisle, touching each seat as I passed.

My backpack was on the ground, pushed under the seat where I left it. My stomach dropped realizing this was not going to be easy for me to grab it and go.

Let me wake up, I called out faintly. My muffled call for help echoed in the vessel's large room my body was in, while my mind was elsewhere—in the past, to the memories I tried so hard to repress. The daze would not lift, no matter how hard I tried to shake it off.

You must go through this to get past it, Ula explained from inside the memory. She refused to release me from this trancelike state.

I reached down to grab my bag.

A bottle dropped.

The sound of shattered pieces dropping to the ground broke the silence of the bus.

Before I could look up to see, my neck whipped back by the force, pushed down from behind.

I struggled to get up, but he pinned me down.

It was Bodie. The quarterback.

His mouth hovered over my ear. "You girls think you're so much better than everyone else. Kissing the teacher's ass in class, trying to make me look bad. Laughing at Coach. Telling on him."

Where *was* Coach?

"Coach could lose his job because of you, and you're gonna pay," he hissed. The alcohol on his breath was unmistakable. He smelled even worse than Coach did.

I thrashed and kicked, trying to escape his grip, but he pinned me down harder. When I cried out, he covered my mouth. "Hold still. You're going nowhere." Bodie grabbed my arm tighter.

I tried to scratch at the hand that clinched my wrist. He was just too strong, and it was all happening too fast.

"Get off her!"

Someone was here. It was not Coach's voice.

Bodie looked up, while his grip loosened. I fell still. It all stopped in an instant.

"What're you going to do about it, little man?" Bodie sneered, and turned back to me, his breath in my face.

"I told you . . . get off her!"

It was *Matthew*.

Bodie flew off me with an unexpected force.

A loud *thud* followed. Bodie groaned.

Did Matthew do that? Was he strong enough to do that?

Matthew reached down, pulling me up through the seats. "He's down. Let's go."

We rushed toward the front of the bus, Matthew pulling on me to hurry. Before we reached the steps, Bodie grabbed my hair and threw me aside. He zeroed in on Matthew.

I struggled to get up as Matthew turned and lunged toward Bodie, seemingly empowered by his early victory. Bodie backslapped him with such a force that Matthew flew back, hitting his head on the metal pole.

Stunned, I watched as Matthew rose to his knees, blood streaming down his face and rage in his eyes. Thrusting up from the bus floor, he punched the star quarterback right in the gut with a swing so powerful that Bodie wrenched over, crying out in pain.

Matthew collapsed.

Hurriedly, I lifted Matthew's arm over my shoulders and dragged him off the bus. My heart hurt with every moan he made as he slid down each step and onto the ground.

We were late for pickup. Mom was just beyond the bus, looking for us.

She called out, "*Lauren!*"

I stopped. Dropped Matthew. Then, I vomited.

Finally, I folded over and fell to the ground.

I woke with my head on Mom. I felt her shaking uncontrollably.

"You're awake!" Mom grabbed me. I flinched and pulled back from her. My body was still tense. I feared Bodie was going to rush us from the bus, or that Coach was somewhere in the distance to come back for revenge.

"You're safe, honey." Mom assured, pulling me closer to her. "I'm here. The police are here." Mom scared me in those times when she knew exactly what to say to me, without me even saying a word to her.

The EMT interjected, "We've got to get your son to the hospital, ma'am. He's still bleeding." Mom nodded in agreement. An emergency vehicle had arrived, and a medic was wiping the blood from Matthew's face while two others lifted him onto a gurney.

Beside the ambulance were blue flashing lights. Police cars were parked next to the bus, with Coach Blaizer locked in the back seat of one. Several officers started to assist the principal with a growing crowd. He was trying to hold everyone back, with students and parents craning their necks to see what was happening.

Zary's worried face appeared among the others. She reticently waved in my direction from behind the principal's arms.

My heart sank. The whole school knew what had happened.

I rolled my head into my mom's arm, trembling, wanting never to let go.

———————◆———————

Still a bit fuzzy, I awoke back in the vessel. Ula was no longer beside me, but I sensed her presence somewhere within the living quarters while the doulesthe kept watch over me. Instead of returning to my pod, I kept my head on the pillows and wrapped myself in a blanket in front of their window, hoping to lose myself in the comfort and forget the memories forced on me by Ula.

But I could not shake how my idealistic belief about my life had burst that day after the farm. Mom quit her job to take care of us, and we struggled financially, waiting on a settlement from school over the incident. My dad sued them without delay. Matthew was still recovering; his head remained bandaged. Mom said none of it was my fault, but it was hard for me to feel any other way.

"I just want you to be better." I remembered those words uttered by my mom one night after rushing into my room during one of my night terrors. "I just want you to be back to your old self, be my little girl again."

Matthew was healing, and his hair bristled through the shaved area on his head. But I was struggling, and Mom knew it. She worried about us all the time.

"I'm trying, Mom. I really am. I don't *want* to feel this way," I explained, not believing she would ever understand the way I was struggling. Caressing my head, she didn't respond, just quietly hummed her favorite song. She was the only one able to help me through—with her song, by her tenderness.

Being held in the vessel, with the doulesthe watching over me as I lay before the window, I realized that Mom's perfect, contrived life was no more after that, with my constant worrying that none of us were truly safe. I realized that we all just pretended we were safe to get through our daily tasks, but it was only a matter of time before something bad could happen to any of us at any time. My intuition on this point was remarkably accurate. Something had been triggered in me out of that experience that made me see life as it truly was, as opposed to the false sense of normality.

"You are correct," Ula said aloud. She had appeared beside me, from behind the surging wall. "With your heightened understanding and intricate memory, you were *chosen*. Chosen for this training, for this very purpose. You have no choice. You must receive what we offer." Her glow arrived and intensified around me.

With that I was lifted from my seat, although I could see that my physical body remained firmly planted in the blankets.

I did not fear.

I did not react.

I was overwhelmed with a sense of acceptance and calm. I was just *in the moment*.

What happened to Shai felt like a lifetime ago. The torment of being separated from Mom and Matthew faded. The fear that arose in me again and again, ever since that day on the school bus, subsided. Captivity became a nonissue. I was calm and felt only peace. I understood that as long as I remained at ease and silent, my training with Ula would progress.

"Do not worry," Ula intoned. "My covenant is to protect you. With the transference from me to you, this power will indwell in you permanently. May you experience the perfect unity."

I let out a giant sigh of relief. I had survived another change.

CHAPTER 26

THE OTHERS

My adjustment to the Invaders' living quarters was surprisingly seamless and even disturbingly enjoyable at times. The training with Ula was amiable. Although my solitude otherwise was unspoiled, I felt Ula's presence often, more than when she was in view. While Jun had been uninvolved in my recent training, I sensed him in the living quarters without seeing him.

Ula took what had been Shai's place next to me at the window. Ula and I sat together often, silently observing the magnificence of the Earth's transformation. My view from the vessel's window looked out toward the rocky peaks of the nearby mountains, and it reminded me constantly of my family's rush to reach the boulders and avoid capture. I longed to see Mom and Matthew again.

When Ula appeared with her crystal transport ball one morning, she must have sensed my loneliness, as she took me to visit the hangars again. This time, she placed the ball on the ground, held up two fingers, and swirled them in a circular motion.

"You may walk in," Ula explained, holding out her hand for me.

As I stepped closer, the glass ballooned large enough to close around me, locking me in. All around me was seamless glass, offering no way out. I panicked, looking around for any slight opening.

"Have you learned nothing from our time together? Do not be afraid," Ula scolded.

I ceded to her and knew what she wanted from me. I turned my focus to calming my panic, while I rested my hands against the side of the ball to feel the consistent smoothness. Understanding the experience instead of fearing it.

With my palms flattened on the glass, a tiny surge of energy zapped me, running through and up my arms. I released my hands trying to shake it off.

"Take in the energy," Ula urged. No matter her suggestion, I didn't put my hands back on the glass.

The transport ball lifted from the ground with me inside and floated to Ula's side as she began to move toward a solid wall in our living quarters. Just as I began to worry, a circular door instantly appeared before us and slid open.

"You will stay alert as we travel," Ula explained, while behind us, the portal rejoined the wall, seamless and secure again.

It was dark on the other side. Buzzing electrical sounds surrounded us and faded lights flickered in the distance. I felt weightless for a moment, and then came a sinking feeling. My stomach dropped, just as we plunged downward through complete darkness, until a blinding light appeared just below my feet.

As the light softened and my eyes adjusted, a multicolored floor moved furiously below us. While Ula remained suspended above and I still was held in the ball, we moved. I was certain that we were gliding through one of the hollow rings surrounding the vessel—the same ones I discovered when the hangar roof was opened that one early morning when I was the only one awake. That morning seemed so long ago.

With this unfettered view from the vessel's rings, I ran from side to side, looking all around and viewing the living Earth, now more majestic, pristine, and blooming than ever before. All my prior views had been limited by the window before which I sat—first in my pod, then in the alien's living quarters. But being so high and in the ring, I could see all four hangars below us, along with the vast dirt space between and even the faint outlines of the pixelated barriers separating them. As we passed over that space, the air in the transport ball changed; it became stagnant, with a hint of decay.

We continued on through the corridor, passing over the bushes surrounding the pixelated barrier and coming to the rim of the forest. The panoramic view from the ring displayed the vibrant green of tremendous growth, the blue skies dashed with cotton-ball clouds. For the first time, I was close enough to the dense, rich canopy of the trees to notice the mist rising from the forest floor. My transport ball cooled, and the air became refreshingly crisp, with a hint of wild jasmine and pine—a stark contrast to the air that the people living in the hangars were breathing. The air that Mom and Matthew had been breathing.

With a wave of her hand, an opening in the transport appeared, allowing Ula to step out of the corridor and onto a small square stage surrounded by empty space hundreds of feet off the ground. Like an open elevator, the stage took us up through darkness, lit only by faded, flashing lights as before. Reaching a circular portal like the one Ula had created earlier, we entered another area of the main vessel—a room that looked much like her quarters, with bright white floors, glistening walls, and an enormous, windowed wall.

From this window, a large, grassy platform extended far out of the vessel and into the open air. The long platform was bordered with bushes, lined with beautiful flowerbeds and scattered trees, which was uncannily reminiscent of my playground from elementary school. Ula led us to the window, which liquified and then melded together behind us, sealing shut.

We were on the platform. Outside. She was hovering above the grass, and I was still in the transport ball. My eye was drawn to one of the trees that lined the platform park, where a sparkling white bird rested in the branches, its feathers contrasted with the green of the park surrounding it. How was it possible for this small bird to find its way to this alien park—a park suspended high up in the sky, surrounded only by sky and clouds, hundreds of feet above the Earth's ground below? The bird's delicate cooing reminded me of the first bird I saw on the other side of the hangar barrier the first time we were let outside. This was the same bird, I convinced myself, sent to me by a guardian angel to watch over me.

Ula placed my transport ball on the grass, and it disappeared from around me.

I hadn't been outdoors since before I was plucked as a chosen one from the hangar. As a soft breeze tousled my hair, I pulled my head back, closed my eyes and took in a long, deep breath of the living air. My sigh of relief was louder than expected. In all the time I'd been held captive in the vessel—what felt like months and months—I breathed only stagnant, manufactured air.

Just like the fake air, the ground I lived on in the vessel was hard and cold. But on this platform and below my feet was clean, vibrant green grass, and all I wanted to do was feel that grass between my toes. I kicked off my slip-on loafers and felt the soft blades against my skin. Sweet memories of hunting for four-leaf clovers with Matthew as kids came back to me.

Without a care of what was around me, I sank down on that grass and closed my eyes, running my fingers over each blade and listening to the cooing of my guardian angel bird. I took in another long, deep breath of the fresh air. Opening my eyes, I stared up at the clouds as the sun warmed my cheeks, feeling grateful. It was all simply perfect.

"Lauren," Ula called softly, prodding my side with her long, pointy finger.

I sat up and saw several other Invaders coming through the window as we had. These new Invaders resembled one another, with only slight distinctions among them. Ula's contrast to them was evident; she had a unique gleam. Missing from the others was Ula's golden stitching that ran along the seams of her shiny white robe and the silver interwoven in her longer white hair, both of which glistened in the sun. The others were covered with noticeably duller white robes; some were even graying.

The other Invaders were holding similar transport balls containing other humans. They were released, just as I had been, with the balls set on the ground and the glass disappearing from around them.

Stunned, I just stared blankly at the other kids as they scattered into the park.

Ula poked at me again with her sharp fingernail. Wondering what I was supposed to do, I got to my feet while Ula retreated to join the other Invaders. I had become so used to being forcibly pulled about by my branded arm that I seemed to have lost the ability to make my own decisions.

I watched Ula for further instruction as she settled beside two of the only other unique Invaders of the group. These two had darkened, silvery robes, with matching dark streaks through their white hair—much like the shining silver that ran through Ula's hair. Sitting beside these Invaders were two younger girls locked hand in hand, each with a bracelet attached to her wrist. They were skinny and wore clothes that were tattered and soiled instead of a uniform like mine, and they flinched every time their Invaders moved. Bald patches were scattered throughout their brown hair, which was knotted up throughout. They seemed unapproachable and not willing to engage with any other human. They occasionally picked at the grass with their free hand as their only source of entertainment and in a somewhat hypnotic state. I had to turn away for fear of breaking down in tears. I suddenly understood that things could be much worse for me. Ula had truly been taking care of me.

Across the platform, another girl about my age sat under some jacaranda trees, alone and as far away from the Invaders as she could be. I knew these violet-blooming trees from home; the city streets were lined with them. My dad used to point them out to me and Matthew each year as they bloomed and dropped their gorgeous purple petals on the ground. The trees on the platform were in full bloom, sprinkling their flowers on the vivid green grass below.

I was eager to go meet her—to talk to another person. But I hesitated, thinking about Shai. Did I really want to make another friend, only for her to be taken away from me?

I stared so long at the tree that the girl underneath it noticed me at last. When she waved, I raised my hand timidly, and overcoming my shyness, started over to join her.

"Hi," I said, taking a seat next to her on the grass. "I'm Lauren."

She responded with hope in her eyes. "I am Rose."

CHAPTER 27

ROSE

Rose had creamy brown skin, long, curly brown hair, and a piercing hazel eye. Her other eye was covered by her long, thick hair. Her beauty was striking.

Dangling from her neck was a golden cross.

"Where are you from?" I asked. "Or were from, I guess."

"Rio de Janeiro," she replied, pulling at her bangs to cover over her face. "I was on the beach with my friends and then taken away. Now I'm on this *shiiip*. I have to get to *mi mama*." Her accent was strong, but we understood each other.

I felt her pain and her longing for her mother, but my curiosity about our current situation was stronger. "Have you been here at this park before?"

"Um, no," she replied. "First time here. You know why?"

I shook my head and shrugged. "No idea."

She squinted and turned up the side of her mouth, as if straining to devise a plan. "Is open," she said, standing up and pointing around the outer rim of the platform. I noticed that she was taller than me. "Maybe we can be . . . free?"

I scooted away from her to put distance between us. She seemed to misunderstand the nature of the platform park. Didn't she realize that we were high above the ground? That there were no doors, so without the transport ball somehow pushing us through the windowpane, we couldn't even get back into the vessel? If Rose had been through what I had been through thus far during this captivity, I wondered how she could even have such a thought. I seriously doubted that we would just be set free. Ula certainly would have shared this important detail, if it were true.

"It is very long time that I am outside of ship. What if this our only chance?" she urged. "We should take advantage."

"Not much of a chance," I replied. I had a bad feeling about where she was going with this. I moved further away from her, worried about what Ula may have thought about my interacting with Rose and her thoughts about escaping. "We're so high above the—"

"We run back inside," she whispered nervously, taking a couple steps over to get to me. "We hide, take tunnel in ship. Find exit."

I lowered my voice and asked, "Have you tried this before?"

Her bangs stayed in place as she shook her head slightly. "No, not here. At home, yes. I was taken by the C.V.—"

"The what?" I interrupted.

"A gang. They took me, just like these . . . creatures." Rose explained. "I was almost gone from my family by them forever, but I took a chance to escape. Another girl was with me. She did not run, did not come back. I have prayed for this same chance." She grabbed at her necklace and held it in her hand.

I was starting to wish I had not joined Rose under the tree. She seemed to be cut from the same cloth as Shai—they both wanted to escape. Not me; I just wanted to survive and see my family in the hangars again. Surely, she could see that escape was impossible. There was no way out. If Ula thought this interaction with other humans would be a positive experience for me, she was mistaken.

"Well," I scoffed. "Another girl was held in the same room with me. She tried to fight back, and they took her. She's gone, maybe even *dead*."

"Our chance is now. Here," Rose quietly voiced, undeterred. "Let us try. Let us go. Is better than to stay. When the door opens, we run out." She cast a nervous look over her shoulder.

I glanced at Ula and saw her ears extend slightly, like she was listening. Her keen surveillance was unnerving. I sensed that Rose's nervous movements raised Ula's suspicions.

I stood up to walk away, wanting no part of Rose's plan.

Just as I gave Ula a reassuring look, I was yanked backward and pulled along with Rose, who had started to run toward the window. I tried to shake her off, but she was bigger and unexpectedly strong, dragging me along. I stumbled over my own feet, trying to pull her back.

The lashings were swift and harsh. We both immediately fell to the ground, grabbing our whipped legs.

It had been a long time since I experienced such harsh consequences, and the punishment was even more agonizing coming from Ula instead of Jun. Didn't Ula realize this was all Rose's doing, not mine? I thought she knew me and knew I wouldn't try to escape. I had tried to *stop* Rose, only to be used as an example to the other kids on the platform. As with the Vellatros' abductions, the message was clear: *Do not try to escape.*

I tearfully looked at Ula, trying to make her understand that it was all Rose, not me. She ignored me. Then I noticed him.

Another kid had just walked away from the group of Invaders. I hadn't seen him with them earlier. I would've noticed him if he had been, particularly with his nervous scratching. He caught me staring and looked away.

I turned back to Rose and glared. I was fuming.

Rose's voice was flat. "To me, this happens many times. Every day they hurt me." No wonder she was obsessed with escaping.

Like Shai, she wanted to flee because they hurt her. Rose had seen an opportunity to flee and tried to take it—while trying to help me, too, I supposed. My anger subsided, replaced by grave concern. If Rose kept trying to escape, one day she could meet the same fate as Shai.

I was struck by a devastating reality. I had chosen an Invader's forgiveness over this human girl. How could I do this? Matthew had warned me.

"Are you okay?" I murmured. "Maybe I can help."

I told Rose that once I learned to obey the Invaders' commands, the beatings had stopped. Maybe things could get better for her, too.

"I understand them now. I know what they want, and I do it, Rose. To *survive*."

Rose looked confused. "What commands? How do you talk with them? How do you know what they want?" Just like Shai, apparently she could not connect with them. That explained the daily beatings she told me about.

I turned to Rose. "Let me show you some things to help you communicate."

Positioning her to look out beyond the platform and to focus upon the Earth's beauty, I began teaching her techniques to calm herself through breathing. She had trouble settling, though, and repeatedly reached for her bangs, patting them over her eye.

"Rose, I feel hesitation from you, like you want to relax but something prevents you from doing so."

"I do not know," she responded, looking down. Then she dropped her head into her hands and sobbed.

After a moment, I placed my hand on her back and tried to transmit calm energy and healing as I had done with Matthew. When her head lifted again, she pushed her bangs aside, displaying her hidden eye. Only half an eyebrow remained, interrupted by a large, gash, as if someone had tried to cut her eye from her skull. She was permanently disfigured.

"Oh, Rose," I whispered, taking her hand and folding it in mine.

Rose started to explain. "I was taken by the gang with my best friend when we walk home from school. I try to escape before they sell us, and they gave me this . . . this scar . . . not from the aliens." She pointed to her brow. "But I still not give up. I got away."

I closed my eyes to transmit more of me to her: more healing, more grace, more love. Everything I had, I sent to her. After a few moments she released a long breath and her shoulders relaxed, and her bangs fell away from her face.

"I don't know what you do, Miss Lauren," she said as a smile came to her face, "but I am not so sad anymore. Thank you." Both eyes widened as she looked past me.

Two boys on the platform were looking our way. They witnessed the whole event, Rose's failed escape and our punishment.

I was so embarrassed.

One was tall and exceptionally good-looking. Wisps of curly black hair hung in front of his soulful, dark brown eyes, which seemed to hide a deep well of pain behind them. He had an athletic build, with broad shoulders, and a strong face with a well-defined forehead and a chiseled jaw. With all this and the outlandish blue outfit he wore, he could have been a model. That is, if it weren't for the strange habit of scratching his neck and arms again and again. I recognized him. He was the one leaving the side of the Invaders when Rose and I were punished.

The other boy had a strong upper torso and equally strik-ing physical traits, from his bright white skin to his penetrating, crystal-blue eyes. With weak, thin legs, however, this boy seemed fragile—unlike all the strong, healthy boys who remained in the hangars with Matthew. Was it possible that some of the Invaders had chosen their "pets" for their unique beauty?

I did not mean to stare, but I hadn't seen anyone disabled in a long time. He was in a wheelchair—one unlike any I had seen before. The chair was sleek and slender, conforming around his body, almost as if it were connected to and an extension of him. The graphite-looking wheels spun in the middle when the boy moved, while the outside of the wheel stayed still. With each move of his arm outward, the chair moved along with him—without his need to even touch it. The metal of the chair mirrored that of the materials of the vessel. Had this been created by them for the boy? And how had this boy survived this long since the invasion? I had so many questions to ask him, and strangely, I felt like I knew him from somewhere.

"We saw what happened," said the tall boy with the bright blue suit, while both boys approached us. "Are y'all okay?" His Southern drawl was unmistakable.

I opened my mouth to respond, but the boy in the wheelchair beat me to it. "I would suggest not trying to escape again," he announced. "An energy barrier surrounds this platform—and the entire vessel, actually. It prevents us from ever getting out."

I was both intrigued and baffled. How had he come by this

knowledge? Could he possibly answer my other questions about captivity and the Invaders themselves? He seemed so smart and the only one that knew what was happening around us.

Then it clicked.

But it couldn't be. In a wheelchair? Plus, he was so skinny. His intelligence and piercing blue eyes were instantly recognizable.

"Milo?" I whispered.

CHAPTER 28

MILO AND BENNETT

t was Milo from my science class.

"Hello, Lauren. Yes, it's me." Milo responded, smiling. "You look older. I didn't recognize you at first."

I could not believe I was seeing someone from home. I wanted to hug him.

But before I could, Milo reached out his hand to shake mine. "It is nice to see you again," he said, oddly formal. "As I was saying, even if you did make it off this platform, you would be burned alive by the barrier. I would have thought any human here would have realized this by now."

"That attempt to escape was *not* my doing," I corrected.

And I would have thought that ever since Mrs. Pickering's science class, Milo and I were closer than a simple handshake. After all, we were the only two ever to answer questions in that class, which I thought gave us an unspoken understanding about each other's superior intelligence over all the others. But now I was glad about holding back my hug. I didn't need anyone talking down to me.

Who was he to give us a lecture? But then it dawned on me that kids at school must have thought the same about me, with my similar judgmental tone. Was I also that unsufferable?

"Hola. I am Rose," she offered. I anticipated her to take the blame for the failed escape attempt, but she said nothing else. Not even an apology to me.

I huffed.

"I have not seen either of you on the platform before," Milo precisely observed. "I'm guessing this is your first visit outside since being selected and brought to their vessel?"

I nodded. "Yes, this is my first time to the platform," I replied, matching Milo's formality.

"Well, y'all have some learnin' to do," the handsome boy chimed in. "Milo and I have been comin' here for a bit now. Y'all need to *relax* and enjoy what we have. Stop fightin' it."

I could have listened to that thick Southern accent forever, but my attraction to him disappeared when the unusual scratching began again—not just his neck and arms this time, but down to his legs. He caught me watching and quickly dropped his hands to his sides.

"That's Bennett," Milo said dryly after Bennett had skipped right over his own introduction. "You can count on Bennett if you ever need to be persuaded not to escape."

"That's right," nodded Bennett, grinning. "My place is up here, and I'm not leavin'. They feed me, give me gifts, and I've got a warm, comfy bed—not the dirt I used to sleep on. Now, don't you two go and muck it up." Bennett scratched under his arm ever so slightly.

"All they do is beat me," Rose replied. "It's awful. I cannot relax. Being dead is better."

Bennett chuckled. "Sweetheart, you keep up with them lashin', you're fixin' to be traded out."

I reached out in front of Bennett to get him to stop.

"Rose, the beatings were bad in the beginning, but once I learned their commands, it got a lot better. It's possible, it can get better for you, too," I shared. While I certainly did not enjoy captivity like Bennett, I learned to survive and even found myself content in those rare moments.

"What does that mean, commands?" Bennett asked.

"It's hard to explain, really," I said slowly. "I . . . connect with her. We become bound in a sort of golden light that extends from her. It balances and calms me."

Milo let out a long, low whistle. "Fascinating."

"You'll be able to hear them soon, Rose," I assured her. "And then things will be easier for you." It also occurred to me that if I could help Rose communicate with her Invader, maybe Ula would trust me again.

"I'll help you learn to charm 'em," Bennett added, with a wink and a great big smile.

"And I will help you learn their protocols," said Milo.

That got my attention. "What do you mean, 'their protocols'?"

"Well, for one, they have a hierarchical system of societal classes, from the supreme rulers down to the workers. And as you have seemed to have learned, Lauren, they have certain demands around assimilation and obedience—regarding not only their orders, but also their method of communication."

It all sounded familiar based on my experience. "There's a furry little creature where I live. Is it a worker?" I asked. "She calls it doulesthe."

"Oh, yes. *Doulesthe* is their word for 'lowest of servants.' You must be paired with very important Invaders, quite possibly at the very top," Milo explained. "There is a doulesthe that dwells among me in my living quarters, and I know my Invaders are very important within their mission here."

"How do you know all of this?"

"They've given me limited access to their technology, the likes of which I have never seen or experienced before, and it is all accessible through my chair." Milo pressed his fingers in the air, as if he knew where secret, invisible buttons existed. Unfolding before him were three luminous screens and flashing lights that covered his entire upper body.

I walked to his side to peer in, finding the screens displayed no words—only symbols.

"This is all unreadable," I complained, and frowned.

"While it is indecipherable to most humans, I read and think in code. But still, I can only understand a fraction of what this is all about."

"I'm not surprised, Milo. You always were the smartest one in our class."

He scoffed. "The Invaders are amazed that I'm able to understand any of it. I surmised that it entertains them as I struggle through it. Either that or they are studying me. Perhaps a bit of both. I believe that my ability to think in code is why I ended up here as opposed to being left to die in the hangars like the others like me. Or worse, removed by those terrifying shadow-beings."

As he spoke, I felt an overwhelming feeling of genuine wonder emanating from the Invaders across the park, near Ula. I sensed that they marveled at his intelligence and capabilities, which contradicted their original belief that his disability prevented such gifts.

I gasped under my breath. It was astonishing to be able to perceive the thoughts and feelings about Milo from the other Invaders, not just from Ula.

"Y'all make it so complicated aroun' here. Just don't piss 'em off," Bennett interjected. "I learned that a long time ago to avoid the beatings back home. Just figure out what makes 'em happy. Dance if you need to or wear silly clothes. Even let 'em brush your hair if that's what they want." He flashed his blue jacket.

"Don't you have a uniform like the rest of us?" I snapped.

"Not me." Bennett itched his head. "I get new clothes all the time from them aliens. Heck, I put on a damn fashion show for 'em sometimes. I'm not too proud to strut my stuff. I'm serious about the hair brushin'—it feels good. My Invader takes good care of me."

"It's true," Milo agreed. "The Invader dotes on him. Bennett is like a surrogate baby."

Bennett stood up tall, patted down his bright blue jacket and grinned from ear to ear, almost as if it was one of his biggest accomplishments in his life to date. And then he itched.

I turned to Milo, ignoring whatever Bennett was doing to get everyone's attention. "Milo, what happened to you?" I asked, delicately. "How did you end up in that chair?"

"My paralysis happened during the transport, after my family and I were captured," he explained. "No pain, no obvious injury. I just arrived and couldn't stand up. I have yet to figure it out."

"And those shadow things? They did not take you?" Rose asked, her eyes wide.

"You were saved from the Vellatros," I insisted. "We all know what they did to the others they saw struggling on the ground, and I didn't see anyone in wheelchairs in the hangars."

"Veela-tross?" Rose asked.

"The shadow creatures. That's the name the Invaders called them during the first appearance," I explained.

"You are right, Lauren, I heard that name, too." Milo finally responded. "And I was fortunate. My dad picked me right up, and my family took turns keeping me on my feet. All my family landed next to me, but not my sister Luci. I never saw her again."

I reached out and touched Milo on the hand. "I haven't seen my dad since the invasion. I know how hard it is."

"I feel much better now. But I'm not entirely sure I know why." Milo glanced down at my hand and then looked at me strangely before pulling his hand away. My touch had calmed him. It had worked on Matthew and Rose. It had worked on him, too, without me even trying to help him.

"It's curious that you were still chosen by the Invaders to be up here," I said.

Milo shrugged. "I don't know why. Though what I have come to learn is that the Invaders seem to know everything that happens in those hangars. Somehow, they knew that I was capable of understanding, at least to some extent, their technology. I believe that is the only reason why I'm here with them."

"I know why *I* was selected," Bennett chimed in.

"Why is that?" I asked, a bit irritated.

"I'm irresistible." Bennett chuckled and pranced around dancing. I remembered those moves; it was the last dance trending before we were taken.

"Lauren," Milo interrupted Bennett's exhibition, "why do you think you were chosen?"

"I don't really understand it," I responded slowly. "But it may have something to do with my memory capability and . . . a past traumatic event. At least, that's how she explained it." I looked over my shoulder at Ula.

"You mean after the field trip to the farm?" Milo asked quietly.

My shoulders dropped. I hoped he would not have brought that up—the lowest point in my life before being abducted by aliens. I wanted to forget that day. Even worse, Milo brought it up in front of Rose and Bennett, two people who didn't need to know anything about my past.

"So you were there," I muttered to Milo, still wishing I could avoid the topic.

"Yes," Milo replied. "I walked up just as your dad was threatening the principal with a lawsuit."

I wanted to avoid everything about that memory, but the details came rushing back.

As the EMTs loaded Matthew in, Dad ran through the crowd and held up his hand, stopping them from finishing until he gave his approval. Dad had no problem interfering with Matthew's care to make himself look important. Without hesitation, he turned to Mom.

"The court holds you responsible for their safety," Dad said through tightened lips. He always threatened court with my mom when he wanted to be particularly cruel. With her two kids lying injured, Mom looked away, avoiding what would otherwise be an inappropriately timed, intense exchange. This was the first time I had ever seen her back away from him.

Then he started in on me. "How did you get your brother into this mess? Why weren't you more careful?"

Mom hugged me so tight it felt like she was shielding me from his verbal arrows. I didn't respond to him.

Dad stormed off toward the principal, shouting the same sort of accusations. "How could you let this happen? The school's going to pay for this!" All my friends were there, and worse, the entire school heard him.

He stormed back to me and finally asked, "Are you okay, at least?"

Still nuzzled into Mom, I muffled, "I'll be okay."

"Lauren?" Milo pulled me out of the memory.

"Maybe that's why I was chosen," I said to Milo. "What the attack on the school bus taught me, and how I've been trying to calm myself ever since. I think that's why I can hear *them* in my mind during their training."

Milo nodded. "Possibly a change in the white matter of your brain," he mentioned, which I didn't understand. "But I want to revisit this training, Lauren. I surmise it is something truly special. We should explore it together. I'll investigate what I can through my access into their encoding, and let you know what I find."

"That really would be incredible, Milo. Thank you. I want to know all that I can about what they're doing to me." I responded with a sigh, grateful he changed the subject.

Across the park, the Invaders rose at the same time and placed the transport balls on the ground, summoning each of us to enter. One by one we were taken by our respective Invaders after we entered through the passageway.

Alone that evening in my pod, I thought about the three of them—Rose, Milo, and Bennett. All three were interesting and unique in their own way. What was it about all of us that caused the Invaders to select us? Why were we chosen to live among them instead of in the hangars like the others?

Milo made sense; he was undeniably brilliant. Rose was strikingly gorgeous, and she had the most caring nature about her. Bennett was both beautiful and entertaining. Had he not been such an ass, I would have completely crushed on him, which would be incredibly awkward in captivity. Plus, I didn't understand why he scratched all the time.

Yet I had none of these traits to make me special. I had my trauma and an exceptional memory, according to Ula. I'm not sure that made me very special to have been chosen.

CHAPTER 29

A PERFECT GIFT

After Rose's escape attempt, Jun returned. His discipline was as severe and relentless as ever. If I did not sit down fast enough, he slashed my legs. If I did not jump up to my feet right away, he raised me from the floor and slammed me to the ground. Despite my compliance with his commands, Jun continued to punish me. But none of it was justified. I was *obeying*.

His harsh penalties were unnecessary, and his violations of my mind through his mental commands left me nauseous. After all, they spoke aloud and in *English*. Even worse, Ula never intervened to protect me. Through this, I better understood the fury that rose up in Shai against him. Had he continued beating me, I have no doubt that the same intense anger likely would have taken hold of me. After these beatings, though, a slow, burning ire began to form in the pit of my stomach.

It took several days for me to heal after his multiday punishment had finally come to an end and he left. Although, at times, I could still feel his presence in the living quarters. Not until I fully recovered did Ula come to see me. I sensed she knew my anger toward Jun and my embitterment toward her.

"Lauren, come join me," Ula said upon her arrival, as she stood by the enormous window in the living quarters. I still was hesitant to interact with her after Jun's beatings. But I was drawn to the metallic object she held, with it floating and spinning just above her outstretched hand. This was smaller than the glass ball she normally arrived with when it was time to transport me somewhere.

Next to Ula was a steel frame, with four metal supports extending outward like spider's legs forming a circular stand with an opening at its center. When she skillfully set the metallic ball in the center of the stand, it stopped spinning and hovered above the steel frame, suspended in the air. The ball's metallic covering disappeared, revealing a radiating see-through outer rim that enclosed a cloudy projection.

As I got closer to the frame, I noticed on each of the legs meticulous sculptures, brightly lit and colorful. One of the legs mirrored the symbol that had been branded into the flesh of my shoulder. Instead of flesh color, the leg markings were in blue, carved into two half-circular lines that faced each other but never connected. Within the two blue lines was a bright ball of light that sparkled.

The other three legs also were intricately carved. One had displayed several illuminated rings in various colors, attaching and overlapping to form a star in the middle. Another carved leg had a single-pointed crown with a blue ball of light sparkling in the middle of it. The last carved leg was a lone circle formed by illuminated dots, each of which emitted a mist of color. I marveled at the mystical and illuminating elements over each of the carvings.

The sphere hovered in its place above the metal frame, which reached just below my chin, allowing me to stand over and peer down into it. While it was small in Ula's hand, it was large to me and covered most of my body.

With a flick of Ula's fingers, the ball swirled slowly, the cloudy projection cleared, and inside grew a clear image. Ula's robe fluttered, and a light breeze ran through the strands of my hair, as if both had been touched by wind. Until that moment, the Invaders' living quarters had always been sterile, artificial, and stagnant.

"This orb elucidates the ground below," Ula explained, pointing out the window and then back to the strange device.

Whoa!

I looked deeper into the orb to figure out what Ula meant. The image within was identical to my world below. I suddenly felt that I was standing on the Earth and connected to what I once knew: my home on the ground.

Another breeze grazed my cheeks. It came from the orb. I detected the bold smell of grass, with a hint of sweet wildflowers. It was just as I'd imagined it would smell when looking out my window to the forest. I closed my eyes and breathed deep and long, delighting in the aroma emitting from the orb.

When I opened my eyes, an image of an animal appeared inside the orb. Surprised, I looked up at Ula.

"Look to the ground," Ula directed.

I ran to the window. Far below, the same animal was walking through the tall grass, apparently in range of the orb. This was a live transmission.

Within the orb's projection, I watched as an entire deer family with small, fluffy rumps trod carefully from the forest into the grasslands for an afternoon snack. Their flimsy-looking legs parted the grass, and their noses wiggled as they chewed. Big ears thrust upward every so often, startled and on alert for predators. On display were all the intricate details of the deer that I had missed seeing, being so high above the ground in the vessel.

"Press." Ula pointed to a tiny button that blended into the stand's designs, just between the metallic ring and one of the carved legs.

After I pressed it, the orb spoke in a robotic voice. "The animals within the sphere are a family of mule deer, found in California's open grasslands and mountain ranges. They feed on grasses and grasslike plants. They can be identified by their large, mule-like ears and the distinctive white patch on the back of the animal. Their predators are humans, cougars, coyotes, wolves, and other meat-eating animals in the similar region. They were vulnerable to the previously existing human infrastructure, including highways, vehicles, and fencing, which caused death and prevented natural migration for this species. Despite being subject to sport hunting by humans, the species was not subject to extinction."

"If you wish, the orb will answer your questions about the projection inside," Ula explained, placing her finger on the side of it. As it moved under her touch, different views of the ground below appeared within the orb.

I looked up to Ula with a small smile and gratitude in my heart. She reached down to my face and wiped away a tear with her long pointy white finger.

I was awe-stricken by the fact that my alien captor had gifted me this magical glowing ball. I hadn't believed it was ever possible for her to comprehend my feelings or the importance of what a gift such as this meant to me. But, in that moment, I realized that Ula completely and undeniably understood. Nonetheless, her touch was unsettling, and I hoped that she would never do it again. Maybe sensing my discomfort, she quickly turned and disappeared beyond the forbidden wall, where I couldn't follow—leaving the orb with me.

Nothing from my reality seemed real, even though it was possible that I had lived this way for years by now. Dates and time no longer mattered, and I gave up tracking it all long ago. Maybe Milo knew how long it had been. Did it really matter anymore? I stopped myself from the consuming thoughts about the unanswerable time of our captivity.

The dazzling, enticement of the orb called me back to it. I remained entranced by it for hours that day. I wanted nothing else, only to watch everything happening on the ground, with the many animals slowly crossing into and out of the orb's range. With excitement in my step, I ran back and forth from the window to confirm that the orb's view was accurate.

Ula had shown me how the orb moved along with her touch. If I could see the ground and the orb frame moved, just maybe I could see Matthew and Mom. I placed both hands on the frame and gently gave it a push. It floated over. I pushed it delicately across the floor to the very corner of the window where the end of one of the hangars could be within range. Unexpectedly, the hangar did not appear within the orb's imaging. I moved it even closer to the corner, considering that the hangar may have been out of the orb's range. Still nothing showed.

The hangar seemed to be entirely untraceable . . . untraceable to the one thing that allowed me to see details on the ground, to see Mom and Matthew. Heartbroken, I didn't understand it, but I knew I had to get the orb back to where Ula first placed it to avoid detection of my attempt to find people on the ground.

As I was pushing the orb back, an odd-looking horse or maybe a zebra-type animal captured my attention. I moved the orb around, trying to get the animal back into the orb's range. There it was, in plain view. I pressed my face against the orb and waited for all the creature's features to become clear.

It was cindered-colored, with an equine head and zebra stripes encircling its body. Was this some sort of glitch in the orb? No, there it was far below the window. I could see faintly this striped, weird-looking animal—like some crossbreeding program gone wrong.

"Orb, tell me about this animal," I commanded.

The orb responded in its sophisticated, mechanical tone: "The animal is a quagga. It once roamed the lands of South Africa. Growing to eight or nine feet, it foraged in the same grasslands as the cattle and horses that were domesticated by humans. It was slow and helpless, however, and became a food source for humans, until becoming extinct in the late nineteenth century as measured by the humans. Despite breeding efforts to save the species, the last remaining quagga died in human captivity."

I watched the herd of quagga for as long as they remained in view, pushing the frame around to keep them in sight while they grazed. Amazing that an extinct animal from a different continent could be roaming the grasslands below this vessel. How could that be, and could other extinct animals be roaming the Earth under the vessel, too?

CHAPTER 30

CONTROL

Ula arrived with the transport ball to return to the platform. Rose, Milo, and Bennett were already there, talking together under the shade of the jacaranda trees. Seeing humans interact in a normal way was refreshing, breathtaking even. In any other circumstance, it would have been a perfect place for a picnic, where friends could laugh and enjoy the day.

But that was not our reality. All one needed to do to understand the depraved circumstances under which we were held was to look at the two fear-ridden, skinny girls in tattered clothes who never interacted with the other kids. Having endured Jun's cruel punishments, I just wanted to help those poor, petrified girls. But whether they were paralyzed by the bracelets they wore or by their own traumatic experiences, they never left the side of their Invaders, and there seemed to be no way to reach them.

Milo waved me over, but Bennett—as before, and probably always—was the first to speak. "There's the escapee. . . . Glad you're still with us, darlin'." He gave his leg a big, long scratch.

I frowned. Bennett's Southern charm already faded on me, but I did see a smile sneak onto Rose's face.

"Ignore him," Milo interjected. "Though I have to admit we were all a bit worried when you didn't return after your first visit here. We were uncertain about the forgiving—excuse me, *unforgiving*—nature of your Invaders."

I shook my head. "It's not her, but the other one. Jun. He's cruel. It wasn't good. It took me a few days to recover." I wiped my hands down my pants, remembering the beatings. "Ula—the one who brought me here—isn't so bad."

"And yet she beat you, too," Milo interjected.

He was right.

It was disturbing. Although Ula's treatment of me vastly contrasted to Jun's, and she seemed to understand what I needed and when I needed it, she was still willing to hurt me. And even though she no longer communicated with me directly in my mind, I felt certain that she continued to intrude into my thoughts and feelings. How else would she know exactly when I needed to see the others or my family? I needed to learn to prevent her mental intrusions somehow.

"How do you have names for them?" Rose asked, interrupting my plan to block Ula from my mind.

"She told me."

Rose pushed her bangs behind both ears. "I use your . . . techniques," she said. "To hear them in mind. To understand what they ask of me."

"And are you feeling any better these days?" I asked, taking her hand in mine, hoping to transmit calm. "Are things getting any easier?"

"*Si* . . . yes," Rose responded. "I thank you. You help me to understand. I do not like it, but . . . no beatings."

"Good," I whispered, patting her hand. "And don't try to escape anymore. It will only cause you pain. And we may not see you here again."

"We were concerned that we wouldn't see you again," Milo murmured.

"And give up our play dates?" I joked, trying to lighten the mood.

Milo chuckled. "Like pets being taken out for a walk. If I didn't enjoy it so much, I would be a bit offended by the whole thing. But it is my only human interaction, so I always look forward to it. Though I wish it occurred more frequently."

"I do, too," I agreed. "We both know why they're limited."

"Lauren, you *do* realize they have an ulterior motive for our meetups?"

I shrugged. "They don't want us to go mental in captivity."

"Well, no. Actually, when we are here, each of us shares our knowledge and discusses what we've learned from the Invaders or otherwise what we know," Milo explained. "The Invaders share whatever we have taught them with the other Invaders. This includes our interactions, differences between us, feelings of joy from dancing or fear of reprisal, and our thoughts."

I knew we were being watched and listened to, and this confirmed it for me. Milo knew it, too.

"However, they don't want us to become a threat either. That is the main reason why our meetings are limited," he continued. "They don't want us sharing too much information amongst ourselves."

"I think I understand what you mean. But I'm not sure what Ula could learn from me to share with any other Invader." We decided to keep our conversations vague and incomplete to interfere with them tracking us. I sat down on the grass next to his chair. "Have you learned anything new lately?" Milo seemed to be the only one that could access the Invaders' secrets, and I wanted to know about all of them.

"Well, I broke through some of their encryption and discovered that the Invaders know how to heal our bodies."

I gave him a weary smile. "Not too surprising, Milo. I mean, they can make us feel a whole lot of pain without leaving any visible damage. Plus, I saw the male Invader heal himself."

Milo's half-grin was sad. "Yes, and basically it means I could be walking right now—if they wanted to help me. Instead, I remain a disabled captive, fumbling around their systems, trying to break through it all."

"Do you remember researching that science project at school, about geneticists trying to bring back extinct animals?" I asked him.

He nodded. "But they were never successful."

"What if I told you I saw an extinct animal roaming the Earth?"

I told him about the orb, that it had informed me about everything I saw below the vessel, and how I had seen the quagga with my own eyes.

"Incredible," Milo responded, with widened eyes. I was baffled that I knew something that Milo had not yet discovered through their code.

"But that's not all the orb can do," I confided. "Milo, I'm pretty sure that I touched a fox on the ground through the orb."

"What do you mean? That makes no sense."

I explained to him that, while interacting with the orb earlier that day, a little brownish-red fox had come bouncing into view, prancing through the tall grass while swirling its big, bushy tail. Its theatrics humored me, and I wanted an even closer look. My instinct was to zoom in as I used to do on my phone's screen. Just as I touched the orb to zoom in over the fox's image, the animal jumped, startled.

"No other animals were around, at least not within the orb's view. Nothing that could have startled it," I explained. "So I touched the orb again, poking the fox's image." I paused and looked over my shoulder at Ula to ensure she was not listening.

"And," Milo prodded.

I turned back to him. "The fox hopped off the ground, exactly at the same time I touched it. Then it ran into the forest."

"That could all just be a coincidence," Milo said dismissively. "You cannot legitimately deduce a cause-and-effect relationship the way you are explaining it."

"I get it, Milo. I thought the same." I had to remind him who he was talking to. After all, we had competed for the top grade in science class. "But I tested it again when some deer wandered into view. As I touched the buck's image on the orb, his head popped up from grazing and one of his back legs kicked out to shake something off. I tested it again and pushed the buck's antlers. He reared his head and stood straight up on his hind legs, as if being challenged. Every time I tried it, the animal reacted. And every time there was *nothing* around to make the reaction—only me, far above, with the orb."

Milo did not respond right away. He just sat, squinting his eyes, as if trying to compute it all.

"Well, what you are explaining is much like how the Invaders pushed and pulled us against our will, all controlled invisibly and instantaneously. I previously thought that it was done through their telekinesis power, having the ability to influence our bodies without physical interaction," Milo responded.

"Jun throws me about with just a flick of his finger, so they definitely have that." I added. "Ula mentally manipulates me, too."

"Based on what little I know about telekinesis, it is often limited in scale. I never could have imagined it was possible to be used to move hordes of people all about collectively. Maybe it had nothing to do with this power at all, but through this advanced alien technology that was gifted to you by your Invader. It is quite possible that that orb is a miniaturized version of it. If that were true, interrupting the technology could possibly break their hold over us."

"Why would Ula share such a secret with me?"

CHAPTER 31

MOTIVES

Milo had promised to look into the orb's technology and try to figure out how it might lead to deciphering the Invaders' control over us all. I desperately wanted to get back to the platform and find out what he had learned. But as Milo had pointed out, I had no control over when that would be. I could hardly complain, though, because not long after our last meeting at the park, Ula sent me to see Matthew and Mom again.

When the transport ball disappeared, leaving me standing in the hangar, I barely recognized Matthew. Shocking would be an understatement about what he morphed into. Everything about him—his arms and legs, torso, even his neck and face—was thick and strong. He rivaled the fittest bodybuilders. He certainly was bigger and taller than any thirteen- or fourteen-year-old I'd ever seen.

I held him tightly, and he squeezed back but not for very long. He was serious and determined, more so than before.

"I've forged a small, elite group of us here in the men's

containment," Matthew began explaining, not wasting a moment. Over his shoulder, I noticed several men going through practiced maneuvers—lining up, grunting out orders, marching, wrestling with each other. "We created a council, formally electing me as their leader. We're getting stronger every day. We're making plans to—"

I held my hand up to stop him, concerned that Ula may overhear Matthew's plans. I bumped my head up for him to notice her at her usual perch, hovering high above us at the top of the hangar. She became distracted by an altercation with the other inmates. They were trying to reach Matthew.

"Don't worry about that. We planned for it, to distract your captor. Lauren, I need you to focus on me." Matthew grabbed my hands. "We need to talk, now, about the plans and how we'll use you from within. We're going to overtake them, free us all."

"Okay, Matthew . . . okay. I really hope you can. You're the only person I know who can do it." I let go of him and ran my hands through my hair, nervous about how long Ula could remain distracted. "But you can't tell me your plans. It's too dangerous."

"What are you talking about?"

"I tried to explain to you before about the connection between Ula and me, and how we communicate without speaking. It terrifies me. I can't stop it, even if I wanted to. She'll learn about your plans just from me knowing it. You just can't tell me."

"Lauren, you can't get close to them," Matthew pleaded. "They've infiltrated your mind. You need to fight it. Think about what they've done to all of us. They took you away from Mom and me. And what about those who've gone missing? Those who've been hurt right in front of us? Something's gotta happen—and soon."

He knew that reminding me of us being separated would get my attention.

"I know, I know. I'll figure it out, how to block them from my mind. I just haven't yet. If I don't comply, the male beats me . . . for days sometimes." I held up both hands to stop him from reacting the way I knew he would after that disclosure. "Don't freak out. She's nice to me. She teaches me, and I think she trusts me. She brings me to visit with other kids held in the vessel. Remember Milo from school? He's up there. Things have changed so much since the last time I saw you."

"But *they* haven't changed, Lauren," he responded, raising his voice and staring into my eyes. "You're a prisoner. You have no freedom. You were stolen from us. All of us were stolen from our homes."

He squeezed my shoulders with surprising intensity. I had only seen him this angry once before: on the school bus, when he attacked my attacker. After that day, I had worried for a long time about Matthew's tenderness disappearing. It was part of what made him so different from anyone else, so special. And now it seemed to be all but gone.

"There's something you need to know, Lauren." He lowered his voice again and released his grip. "We've watched as the older boys are . . . taken. They seem to age out, or something. They reach this pinnacle—remarkable strength, phenomenal speed, indescribable agility—and then they're just gone."

"Gone where?"

Matthew shrugged. "We have no idea where they go or what they've done to them. We're at their mercy, Lauren. I'm begging you, do *not* get close to them."

I sensed that time was running out, so I hugged him again and held on tightly. What else could I do?

"Remember your home, your true family," he repeated. "Don't give in anymore. And don't lose hope! We will prevail."

He had gained this inexplicable confidence, this self-assurance that I still didn't have, even with all my mindfulness techniques. I was disappointed in myself, in the situation—and worse, that I couldn't be there for my little brother.

I didn't want to let him go. I wanted to bring him back to the vessel . . . to keep me safe . . . to remind me what I needed to do. Instead, I was leaving him behind, grabbed by Ula and ushered out. My brother was left standing alone, looking up as I was forced out of his reach . . . again.

◆

"Mom!" I called out, just as the glass receded from the transport ball.

"Lauren! My baby!" she called back, holding out her arms to embrace me as I ran to her. I buried my head into her shoulder, sobbing.

"It's been so long," I whimpered.

"Too long." Mom stroked my hair. "Do you know why they've kept you away?"

I pulled away and cleared the tears from my face. "One of them keeps me away from you as punishment. But the other sends me here as a reward, I think. Others have tried to attack them or escape, but—"

"You've met other humans?" She reached out to smooth my hair. Looking into her sunken eyes, I saw that, like Matthew, she had changed. Her beautiful long blond hair had turned mostly gray, her wrinkles had deepened, and she had noticeably less energy than before. She could no longer hide how hard life was on her, how captivity was taking its toll.

"Yes, several others, boys and girls. It's crazy, one is from my science class. He was the smart one, Milo. We meet sometimes on a platform in the sky that looks just like a park from home."

Mom smiled sadly. "You have friends. I hope they help you through. Get close to them. They're all you have up there."

With Mom, our survival was always dependent on keeping to ourselves, just the three of us. Her suggestion to get close to others was a noticeable shift in her. I surmised that this change was prompted upon her realizing that this captivity was not ending, and that comfort and companionship was more important than isolated survival. She finally succumbed to the realization that our family would never be together again.

"I just saw Matthew," I said, trying to smile and shift the conversation topic. "He's even bigger and stronger now."

Mom stiffened. "I'm not sure what they're feeding those young men, but they've all grown well beyond their years—taller and stronger."

I chuckled.

"No, Lauren, it's serious." Mom leaned in closer. "I see him changing by the day. I watch how he trains the other young men. Even from a distance, I can see that he's come up with some highly sophisticated moves. Why does he think he's been allowed to train so hard for so long? Does he think that the Invaders don't keep watch over his group—that they don't know?"

I worried about the same thing. "I think they know *everything* about us."

She nodded. "I've warned Matthew, but he disagrees. He believes he's untouchable. And he is so intense . . . I caution him about steroids—maybe they put it in his food."

"What does he say about that?"

"He just laughs. He doesn't care. Believes he poses a threat to the Invaders. But you know what I believe?" Mom whispered ominously. "I think they're letting him train because they intend to use him to their own advantage, before he ever gets a chance to free any of us."

The idea that the Invaders were letting Matthew build an army of warriors for their own purposes had never once occurred to me.

But Mom had more to share. "Remember the pregnancies I mentioned before?" Her pace quickened, worried that I would be taken away soon. "Some of the younger women here are *still* having babies."

How could that be? We had been in captivity for so long and separated strictly by gender. In such conditions, natural conception was not even possible.

"And it seems to happen overnight," Mom continued. "The pregnancy symptoms arrive suddenly and progress quickly. I don't know how they're getting these girls pregnant, and, frankly, I'm afraid to find out." She paused and looked over her shoulder. "And most of the babies are boys. Very healthy, strong boys. Lauren, I'm so worried . . ."

What did this mean? When the Invaders first came, they said it was to save Earth from humans. But what Mom was telling me did not fit with that message. How did creating strong human boys and men have anything to do that?

"We've been misled, lied to. We've been locked up for so long . . . and there's no relief, no help. No one is coming to our rescue. This can't be how it all ends, Lauren. Can it?"

Mom had always been the calming figure in my life, the one with all the answers, always leaning on her faith. But now she was looking to me.

Seeing Mom on the edge of losing hope would have triggered a troubled reaction from me in the past. But now I realized that I had to look within and somehow remain calm, get past my lost feelings. I reached for her hand and gently squeezed, looking directly into her eyes. The frown lines on her forehead relaxed. The sadness in her eyes softened. Her shoulders dropped as she released a sigh.

"Did you do that?" she asked, her eyes searching mine. "You made me feel better somehow, didn't you?"

"Yes, Mom. I can—"

Before I could finish, the crystal transport ball began to form around me once more. I reached out to my mom, but it had fully enclosed me already. I pressed my hands against the glass and mouthed *I love you*. Mom slowly waved goodbye with one hand and wiped tears away with the other.

———◆———

Seeing Mom and Matthew again had been unsettling. I could no longer avoid the truth about our circumstances. I became too comfortable with life on the vessel: my training, visiting the platform, observing the animals through my orb. I forgot all too easily what was happening down below.

Ula had let me believe that the Invaders were helping our planet, regrowing its resources and repopulating its wild animals, and that any consequences to us, the humans, were incidental and necessary. She explained that the universe was a vast system where the planets reigned supreme, not the individual inhabitants—that the Invaders were doing only the good deed their conscience required by restoring the Earth's ecosystem to undo centuries of humans' destruction. And I had believed her.

But there was all the human suffering. Weren't we part of Earth, too? We were torn away from our families, our homes, and our planet, separated from all we knew and loved. They converted us into alien playthings, and now it seemed they were procreating us and even turning some into ruthless warriors.

I understood why Shai had been disgusted with me. She saw the Invaders for what they were and what they were doing and refused to comply, while I accepted and even encouraged it. I remained blind—and justified my blindness with excuses that I was powerless and just trying to survive.

Shai had seen through it all before me. My mom and brother knew it, too.

CHAPTER 32

COMFORT

Since returning from the hangars, I knew Ula could sense my distress from that visit. There was much I wanted to ask her—about our captivity, about the Invaders' intentions. Yet I resisted, partly out of fear but also because I wanted to keep her out of my mind. I kept hearing Matthew's pleas:

Do not get close to them, Lauren.

Don't lose hope.

We're going to need you on the inside.

I held on to those words day after day, but there seemed to be no opportunity for change. Now something *had* changed.

"Lauren." It was Ula, her voice unusually melodious. In contrast to her usual serene and calm demeanor, Ula sounded excited—gleeful, even. "Come join me."

Curious, I hurried downstairs from my bedroom. She held the transport ball in her elongated white hand, which meant we were going somewhere.

The ball closed around me, and we passed through the wall and into the dim corridor. But instead of the dreadful drop that meant we were heading to the platform, we moved forward along a dimly lit interior corridor leading toward steel doors reminiscent of an elevator. With a wave of Ula's hand, the doors parted.

On the other side was an energy field of sorts, a collection of blue light that flowed upward. She walked into the light with my clear transport ball following. We were swept up, moving rapidly through the light. Suspended in the ball, my body experienced none of the nausea or tension it usually did with the sudden drop—just a serene timelessness as the light sped past my eyes.

When we stopped, Ula stepped out of the blue energy transport and stood before a shiny white door that glistened like so much of the Invaders' clothing and possessions. With another wave of her hand the door opened, and we entered an enormous, circular room. My guess was that we were inside the wide, steel-and-glass tower that rose from the center of the vessel.

My eyes grew wide, and my jaw dropped open. The room was filled with animals—baby animals.

It was a nursery.

I let out a nervous giggle before covering my mouth with my hands. All around me were incubating eggs, infant mammals suckling on artificial bottles, and animal toddlers wrestling with one another, all in cubes separated by glass walls with breathing holes. It was like a pristine zoo or the cleanest farm you could imagine— a dream come true for me, and everything I'd wanted before we were captured.

Ula nodded ever so slightly, acknowledging my excitement, and placed the transport ball on the floor, releasing me. Unsure of how much I'd be permitted to explore, I stepped slowly toward a wall of incubators that extended impossibly high. Before me was an uncountable number of eggs. Each seemed to be assigned an optical code, appearing below it in blue light. Was this the coded language that Milo had been able to decipher? I certainly couldn't read it.

Ula glided toward me. With the swipe of her finger, the coded writing flashed to English. The display under the egg before me read:

ANIMAL: TASMANIAN EMU

INCUBATION TIME REMAINING: 100:01

The Invaders do have some sense of time. But I had no idea what a Tasmanian emu was. I moved on.

Beyond the egg section were tubes of various sizes, filled with undeveloped creatures suspended in a gelatin-like substance. The purpose was clear to anyone as interested in animals as I was, that these were artificial uteruses, holding fetuses in an artificial amniotic sac. The umbilical cord leading from the creature to the top of the tube was a dead giveaway. It transferred whiteish fluids, with just a hint of silver, into each growing baby. Artificial milk, I surmised. But what was the sliver tint?

"Here we have collected the requisite matter once held by human scientists," Ula explained. "You would understand it to be DNA, bones, teeth, fur, and the like. These fossil specimens have been used by us where your people failed."

I understood. While we were unable to genetically engineer the revival of extinct animals, the Invaders had succeeded. My mind had trouble comprehending, but I wanted to know all about it nonetheless. This exceeded anything humans had done on Earth, and I was a witness to it. Had any other human seen this?

"No," answered Ula. "No human is permitted in here, except for you. As the overseer of this program, I am authorized to bring you. You will be instrumental to our development of the animals."

She violated my mind again. I thought I was stronger than that, especially after Matthew's warnings. While I was intrigued and delighted that I had a role to play in all of this, I was terribly distraught that I couldn't keep her out of my thoughts.

Ula had twisted the situation entirely. I moved away from her to think about what sort of work I would be allowed to do, without her unilaterally answering me.

I peered into one of the larger glass cubes at a baby animal with brown furry patches scattered across its rough, rugged skin—like a rhinoceros but with buffalo fur. Most fascinating of all was the long horn on its forehead, almost like a unicorn's. But this creature wasn't horse-like and certainly didn't have the legendary beauty of a unicorn. Instead, it looked a bit monstrous, nothing like I'd seen in any zoo or exhibit. Instead of re-creating historical animals, could they be creating new hybrids?

A fuzzy brown eyelid opened unexpectedly, and I jumped back with my heart pounding. Just as startled, the creature kicked out its legs, mirroring my panic. It soon calmed and looked directly into my eyes.

"This animal was just born," Ula announced, "and will need your assistance."

◆

Outside of its cube, the newborn animal stood as tall as my thighs. When it expanded its large nostrils toward me, I looked at Ula. She bowed her head in affirmation. "Your kind called it a Siberian rhinoceros," she said, attaching a harness to the four-legged creature. "It has been revived from extinction."

I reached out gingerly, allowing the animal to smell my hand as I would for a dog or a horse. Ula watched, seeming a little puzzled about what I'd done. The baby Siberian rhino inhaled and then released a ribbon of wet mess into my hand.

"Yuck!" I exclaimed, wiping my hand against my uniform pants.

The animal stomped on its wobbly legs, unsettled by my smell. Ula placed her hand on its forehead, and a tiny flash of golden light sparked from her fingers. The animal calmed.

"Prepare the feeding mechanism for this baby," Ula called out.

Another Invader appeared with one of the largest baby bottles I'd ever seen, containing some sort of milky substance with a silvery tint reminiscent of Ula's skin.

"Hand the bottle to the human girl," Ula instructed the Invader. When I stepped forward and reached out, my body was violently lifted from the floor and flung against the nearby wall.

I hit the hard surface with a thud and slunk to the ground, groaning and holding my side, utterly confused. Why would Ula punish me so harshly and so suddenly? Then I sensed the displeasure coming not from her, but from the other Invader. I thought I needed to prepare for another attack, but I was in too much pain to stand back up.

"It is because of them that these animals no longer exist!" the other Invader roared.

I clutched my chest to hide my pounding heart. Never had I heard another Invader speak out loud in a language I could understand—not even Jun.

Ula didn't stand by and watch me get hurt, as she had when Jun punished me. With a red glow swelling around her like an aura, she faced the other Invader. I knew instinctively what it meant.

Ula was angry.

I knew they were communicating angrily with one another—about me. Clearly, the other Invader didn't want me involved with the animals, the program, or anything in that room. When the other finally left us, I stood up and waited for whatever punishment might come.

"I alone have authority and responsibility over the revival program," Ula said at last. "My rank is supreme. The other is below me in status." She was speaking about the hierarchical system Milo had told me about. Even so, I was surprised and a bit touched by her devotion to me. She'd refused to allow another Invader to threaten or hurt me.

Ula pointed to the bottle for me to resume our efforts. As I raised it for the feeding, the furry rhino's nostrils flared and retracted, jerking its head toward the food. With every bump of its head, its long, thick horn nearly speared me, forcing me to maneuver the feeding just right. I angled the bottle off to the side and then shoved the artificial nipple into the baby creature's mouth. The beast slobbered as it sucked down every last bit. Ula watched on with curiosity. With every interaction I had with the animal, she seemed to be learning from me.

Spitting the empty bottle from its mouth, the animal plopped down by my feet and grunted before rolling from side to side with his stumpy legs flinging in the air. "I'm going to name you Elmer," I said, scratching the brittle fur on his thick, fuzzy neck to get him to stop rolling.

Ula handed me the leash connected to the harness. "Lead him to walk," she ordered.

Although still a bit bruised from hammering against the wall, I grabbed the leash and tugged gently. But Elmer stayed put and even

gave a slight snort of derision. I tugged some more until he begrudgingly pushed up on his stumpy front legs and heaved his back legs
up. I tugged again, giggling, and he sauntered behind me. After a
few steps, he got the hang of it and broke into a loping trot. When
I stumbled and fell to the floor, he dragged me along for a couple of
feet, seeming to think it was a game.

Ula watched it all patiently, and I sensed an unexpected soften-
ing, almost a fondness. Her feelings toward me mirrored what I felt
toward Elmer. I couldn't help but think about Shai and why Ula had
not shown the same patience and kindness to her. I forced myself
to remember Matthew's warning: *Do not get close to them.* Thinking
about any of this in Ula's presence was dangerous.

"May I help take care of Elmer?" I asked, holding my breath as
I awaited the answer.

"You may assist until the animal is sustainable," Ula declared.

I didn't understand. "Sustainable?"

"Our intention is to repopulate the Earth with species like this
one that have been eradicated from Earth by your people. When the
animals are ready, they will be released. The revival program operates
under my oversight. And in this, I include you."

This was an extraordinary opportunity—one I could only experience while being held captive by the Invaders. But then it struck me,
this baby beast would someday be released, free to roam the beautiful Earth, while I would remain a prisoner on this vessel. I blinked,
caught between a range of emotions, swaying from my excitement
about Elmer and the other creatures to disbelief and then to complete disappointment.

"You plan to release these animals, but not us humans? Not
me?" I whined. I was so overcome with anger and confusion that I
didn't think before I spoke. I never posed a hard question to Ula in

this way. Instead, I complied with all her commands, demands, and training. There was so much I wanted to ask her about our captivity and their intentions, but I never did—mostly out of fear of what would happen to me if I did.

"That is beyond my control." Her tone was resounding and unwavering. All the kindness seemed to drain from her, and I knew that was the end of the discussion—and that I might have just narrowly avoided another beating.

◆

"This animal is ready to return," Ula declared unexpectedly. "And it will soon be released."

Under my care, Elmer had grown fast to three times his size at birth. I returned again and again to the nursery, under Ula's protection, to care for him. When I did, I stayed out of the way of the other Invader assigned to nursery duty. The Invader often glared in my direction but quickly turned away when Ula was near.

Elmer was hesitant to enter the pen where the other young Siberian rhinos jostled and stomped and snorted. He didn't want to leave my side, despite the fact that all the other animals looked just like him. I maneuvered around his hazardous horn and gave him a big squeeze, scratched the rough fur of his neck, and quickly slid back through the gate. My heart ached almost as dreadfully as when I had to leave Thor behind, but I was happy to think of Elmer running free. Still, leaving Elmer was yet another loss to me . . . out of a long list of losses.

I placed my chin on the pen and pet Elmer's head while he stayed right by the door that I just closed on him. A couple of my tears dropped on his fur, but he likely never felt them on his thick, rough skin. I knew it was time for him to go with his own kind, and I was just delaying it.

My shoulders slumped as I reached into the pen to pet Elmer one last time.

I ambled through the nursery, not wanting to disturb the animals but mostly to avoid any interaction with the other Invader, particularly since doing so brought the risk of being slammed against the wall.

"You may choose another to care for," Ula directed, speaking firmly and louder than normal. The message wasn't just for me to hear, but also for the other Invader—an instruction not to interfere.

I wanted another baby. That I knew for certain.

High-pitched squeaking from the baby pens caught me ear. Puppies? I followed the sound and found a small litter of sandy-brown newborn pups, scurrying and wrestling in their glass cube, chomping on one another. Watching them play, I noticed their remarkable markings—tigerlike stripes along their back—and unusually long tails. Their foxlike faces didn't match their smaller, pointy ears. And once I saw the pouch on their stomach, I realized that these weren't puppies. In fact, I had no idea what this animal was.

The display outside the animals' enclosure read:

TASMANIAN TIGER

I was looking at another extinct breed.

A familiar yapping came from nearby. I moved on to the next enclosure and found them—the puppies. Just what I was looking for. Although I could have chosen an exotic, previously extinct animal, what I really wanted was one of them—something I could cuddle and love. When the puppies noticed me, they scampered against the glass and climbed atop one another like a puppy ladder, straining and sliding in their vain efforts to get to me. The smell of puppy breath escaping through the cubes' holes took me back to the day Mom surprised me with Thor.

I had to have one.

I stepped closer to the glass and was struck by invisible pressure preventing me from approaching the enclosure. Over my shoulder, I saw the other Invader's hand in the air. With a flick of its wrist, I was pushed backward. The other Invader didn't want me to disturb these animals.

Ula had the supreme rank and authority over this program, but she was across the room and seemed utterly unconcerned with me. I took a chance and disregarded the other Invader's force, pushing against it with all my strength.

I was shoved back again, even harder this time. The other Invader didn't appreciate my defiance. I lost my footing and fell to the floor, but I refused to be overpowered. Surely, the Invader wouldn't dare challenge Ula a third time. Getting quickly to my feet, I dusted off my uniform and stood tall.

When I stepped forward again, the force was gone. I seemingly won.

I stretched my hands against the glass and watched the puppies play—one of the littlest ones in particular, with a thick coat made up of a mixture of white, brown, and gray fur. Any concern about the other Invader faded, replaced by my gigantic smile.

I read the display:

DIRE WOLF

I pointed to the pup I wanted. His name would be Darwyn.

CHAPTER 33

THE SHARED SECRET

I got to bring him home. Wherever I went, Darwyn was by my side. As I fed him his bottle, he whimpered while my heart skipped. He even had a spot next to me in my bed. From the start, I loved him with everything I had.

Darwyn was a wild wolf, not domesticated as Thor had been. He was confused and a bit uncomfortable with all my smothering. But I did it anyway, and he eventually grew to enjoy my constant petting, hugs, and kisses. I spent hours brushing his thick, majestic coat—so soft, unlike Elmer's. Just as I'd done with Thor, petting his long ears calmed me, and he particularly liked it when I scratched behind them. Although bottle-feeding had tempered his innate aggression, he still nipped at my heels and leapt at me, testing his dominance. He was my baby, and I became his mother.

One day as I came downstairs with Darwyn in tow, I sensed something was different in the Invaders' largely barren quarters. And there it was, jutting out from the gigantic window: a small platform similar to the one where I met Milo and the others. It was my own private platform, which opened with a swipe of Ula's hand and under her supervision.

Darwyn and I spent most of our time together on the outdoor platform. He craved the outdoors, soaking up the smells and fresh air and far-off animal sounds he could access only outside of the vessel, and he whimpered if kept indoors for too long. We played and napped out on the platform, and I fed him his raw meat there.

Ula initially watched our interactions from inside, but she eventually joined us on the platform. As Darwyn chased me around, Ula would flick her fingers, lifting me up in the air, with Darwyn jumping as high as he could to reach me. Darwyn released a broken, slightly clumsy growl at me while I was up in the air and out of his reach.

One afternoon after his feeding and our playtime, I sat down with Darwyn to take in the cool breeze and feel the warm sun on my skin, while he lifted his majestic head into the air. Ula came beside me and lowered herself next to us. It was so calming and serene that I fell asleep beside her, with Darwyn sleeping beside me. That platform changed things for the three of us, so much so that Ula lifted the restrictions and opened the passageway for Darwyn and me to get to the platform without her. There was no reason not to; I had no plans to test the oscillating, multicolored barrier that surrounded it. I knew what happened when people tried. There was no escape, it surrounded everything—to keep us safe, to keep us in.

After that, Darwyn and I spent more time on the platform than inside.

Each night, after Ula disappeared into the Invaders' secret room, Darwyn and I would sneak out to the platform. No doubt Ula could have stopped us if she wanted to—she knew just about everything that was going on. But she never did, so I presumed that meant I was allowed.

The evening was Darwyn's favorite time to visit, particularly since that was where he practiced his muffled, squeaky howls, although there were no other wolves to be calling. From my constant pampering, his coat had grown full, soft and thick. He was a royal and would have been king over the wolf pack if he were in the wild.

One night, he sat tall and peered into the darkness as if ready to pounce. I knew his instinct was to protect me, though nothing could reach us that high up on the platform.

"It's okay, buddy." I patted a space beside me. "Here, lie down."

He turned his growling muzzle to look at me and then back out into the darkness.

"What's out there, buddy?" I murmured. Of course, he couldn't answer me, but I had no one else to ask. If Matthew were here, he would call me out for talking to the animal. I draped my arm over him and looked out in the same direction, hoping to understand whatever he was so focused on.

A faint light flashed.

That can't be, I thought.

It flashed again.

"Darwyn, did you see that?" I whispered. How could there be a flashing light on the ground? All human-made things were gone, wiped out by the Invaders at the very beginning of the invasion. I remember the bombs distinctly, every single blast. Only animals were down there now. And animals do not flash lights in the night.

The light blinked again and again, like a signal.

I jumped to my feet. It was unmistakable.

Darwyn whimpered. He was sensitive to my movements and feelings.

"It's okay, boy," I said, patting his head and stroking his neck, which calmed me, clearing my mind to think. That light was nowhere near the hangars—the only place where humans remained on the ground. They were all contained inside.

"Where could a light be coming from?" I mumbled under my breath. Was it at all possible that there were some that had managed to avoid capture when the Invaders first came? After all the time that had passed, I would have thought it impossible.

Throughout the evening, the light flashed intermittently. With each flash, I watched and wondered . . . until sleep took over.

At dawn, when my eyes blinked open, Ula was standing over me. "Lauren, go inside," she scowled. "We will have training today."

I did not move, too afraid about the training to which she was referring given that I was found sleeping on the platform.

"The servant will take Darwyn," she instructed. I held him tight as the doulesthe came to leash him. With a flick of her wrist, she distanced me from my wolf.

Each time the servant got close, Darwyn held down his front paws in front while his hind legs stood ready to go. He scampered away each time. Darwyn was much too smart to comply.

"Lauren, help the servant control this animal," Ula demanded.

"He is playing," I explained. "He's still young. He won't leave my side."

"Then lead him to the training area."

Having Darwyn with me provided a necessary distraction for my mind. I could not let Ula sense my excitement about the strange blinking light I had seen. I had not yet perfected a way to keep her out of my mind.

To my relief, Ula brought back the golden light training instead of a beating. Through the glow, calmness emanated from Ula—and began to emanate from me. The light from me extended to and enveloped Darwyn. While the light swirled around him, he slept deeply. Not even his typical whimpers were heard.

"You are doing well with this one," Ula commented, following the training. Darwyn woke with a long, exaggerated stretch. "You must avoid any close attachment. It will return to its kind." My heart sank.

Although I knew his release was part of her program and that was what was best for Darwyn, I just wanted to keep him with me forever. I felt protected by him and . . . loved. He was my best friend.

Ula sensed my distress. "He can stay with you for now," she clarified. Her kindness always confused me. The Invaders had, after all, been so brutal to the humans. I wanted to trust her and confide in her about the light. But I could not risk it.

"May I bring Darwyn to show the others? They may enjoy him as much as I do."

Although I had been busy with the new wolf pup to visit the larger platform, I was eager to talk with Milo about the flashing light I had seen in the night. Once again, I thought if anyone might know more about what it could mean, it was Milo.

I was delighted when Ula nodded her agreement.

Upon our arrival on the platform, Ula released Darwyn and me from inside the transport ball. Rose, Milo, and Bennett were already there and rushed over to see.

"Filhote? But how?" Rose asked, kneeling to get a closer look. Her bangs had grown, and her hair was pulled back, exposing her scar without shame.

"He's a wolf, Rose." I explained that Ula had taken me into the omnipresent steel-glass tower that rose straight up toward the sky, high above all our heads. "This is Darwyn. He's from their animal revival program."

"Extinction reversal? So it's real." Milo let out an exasperated sigh. "I found nothing within their code that reveals anything about this."

"It's real," I confirmed. "They're bringing back extinct animals. I had to stop coming here for a while because I was raising a Siberian rhinoceros."

"A what?" Rose asked.

"A Siberian rhinoceros," I repeated. "Milo, you might remember I did most of my projects about animals. I thought I was somewhat of an animal expert even, but I'd never heard about many of the animals in the vessel's nursery."

"It has walls and walls of eggs, fetuses, babies," I continued. "It's really crazy. Ula oversees the program, so I get to spend a lot of time there. But another Invader is part of the program and does not like humans *at all*. It blames us for the animals' extinction."

"That other Invader is speaking truth," Milo responded.

I glared at him, surprised that he would side with the Invaders.

"We weren't exactly kind to the animals, after all," he continued. "Many species became extinct because of us."

Milo was right. Humans were awful to animals. But I never imagined he would defend the invasion of Earth and the mistreatment of humans.

"If they're bringin' back extinct animals, why do you have a wolf pup?" Bennett asked. "They ain't extinct. I heard them beasts howlin' when we went bear huntin' in the deep woods near my house. Frightnin' creatures." He scratched at Darwyn's neck and then his own. "But this one is stinkin' cute."

I patted Darwyn's head to get him to stop trying to nip Bennett each time he went in for a pet.

"This is no ordinary wolf pup," Milo explained. His voice held a warning. "This is a dire wolf."

I nodded. "That's right. How did you know?"

Milo ignored my question. "You don't know what a dire wolf is, do you?"

"No, not particularly. I just figured it was a wolf pup, like a gray wolf," I responded.

"Did you ever notice how big he is for such a young one? He's already almost a full wolf's size, but he's still young. He still acts like a puppy," Milo pointed out as Darwyn pranced around, nipping at Bennett again.

"Yeah, he's big, but he's a male, and they always are large in animals. Plus, I take good care of him, and he eats constantly. And you know how time kind of gets away from us here—"

"Your wolf is going to be enormous, Lauren. Well over two hundred pounds and very tall, maybe up to your shoulders. Dire wolves have been extinct for a long time. They are from the same era as the saber-toothed tiger. You are in over your head with that one."

"You don't know that." I knelt down and hugged Darwyn's neck. "Darwyn is receptive to me. He even sleeps with me at night, just like my puppy at home. Don't you, buddy?"

"'Buddy'?" Milo shook his head, smirking. "Dire wolves aren't very friendly by nature. They would rather eat you than be your friend."

Darwyn flipped his head back and nuzzled me with his nose. "See, he kisses me," I insisted. "He's not going to eat his mama."

After all, Milo didn't know *everything*—and with the things he had just been saying, I refrained from mentioning the flashing light.

◆

That evening, after Ula retreated beyond the wall to the forbidden area, I slipped outside with Darwyn to our private platform. We waited, both of us staring off into the distance with a light breeze blowing against our upturned faces.

There was no light.

I grew impatient and paced around the platform, with Darwyn pacing beside me. Every now and then he would raise his nose in the air to take in the smells, and each time that prompted me to closely examine the darkness for any indication of the light. Still nothing.

Darwyn finally settled on the platform floor, just as I was almost ready to give up. But then a light flickered, faint and quick, from the ground. My heart jumped. Given how badly I wanted to see it, I had thought that I invented it.

Another flash appeared. This time, it was brighter and lasted a little longer. I didn't make it up in my mind, after all. The light was *really* there.

I jumped up and ran to the platform's edge for a closer look, stopping just before I reached the barrier. Although it was faintly visible at night, I knew it was there. Barriers were around . . . always, to prevent any escape attempts.

Without me by his side, Darwyn startled awake, bounding toward me with his oversized paws, and I feared he wouldn't stop in time. Uncertain that Darwyn knew the consequences if he got close to the edge, I jumped on his thick, scruffy neck, hardly capable of pulling him to the ground. With no odor of singed fur, I sighed in relief.

How much *had* he grown?

The light faded into the darkness.

I ruffled Darwyn's thick coat. "It'll be back," I whispered.

CHAPTER 34

TORMENT

I tried to stay awake with Darwyn on the platform, continuing to stare out in the black void of the night and watch the shadow of the trees lightly sway back and forth. I felt a slight gust of wind each time the birds flew by. I suspected, given their unusually large size, that they had been released from Ula's revival program.

The next morning, though, I found myself back in my bed with Darwyn snoring beside me. Ula must have found us asleep on the platform and transferred us to my bed.

After we made our way downstairs, Ula was there and waiting.

"You may bring the animal with you," Ula directed. That meant we were going somewhere.

Back on the platform, Milo remained unconvinced that I was able to domesticate Darwyn, and I noticed he was not as receptive to the others as he was with me.

"Ouch!" Rose yelled after trying to pet him. "He bit my toe! Bad *cachorro*!"

Darwyn flashed his large fangs and growled. He was not accustomed to being yelled at.

I pulled on his leash and rubbed his neck to settle him down. "That's just what puppies do when teething," I explained, trying to defend Darwyn. "He's never growled at a person before."

His teeth had broken through her shoe, ripping open the skin on her toe. "It won't stop bleeding," Rose exclaimed, fighting back tears.

I didn't expect Darwyn's nip to cause that much damage. His bite must have been much deeper and more forceful than a normal puppy's. Milo was uncharacteristically silent considering that my dire wolf had precisely proved his point. I realized that he may be right—this was no ordinary canine.

The bite didn't deter Bennett, though. Underneath his blasé character, he was tough. I learned about how much he had endured on the ground before captivity, and Milo explained to me the origins of Bennett's itch. Bennett had grown up in a cramped apartment filled with trash, beer cans, and dirty diapers. No one cleaned. Bugs swarmed the walls, in the cracks of the walls, and in the one bathroom—shared by five of them. When he slept, bugs crawled all around him. When he woke, he found them every morning all over him.

Milo explained, "That's why he scratches. He still feels them, crawling all over him, all the time. He said it was so bad in school, kids made fun of him and called him Lil' Itchy." Bennett had confided in Milo, sharing the worst of it with him.

I felt guilty for being annoyed by Bennett all this time and his ostentatious personality. I should have tried harder to understand him. I realized I would need to help him.

When Bennett grabbed Darwyn's leash from my hand and announced, "I'm takin' him for a run," I didn't stop him. I needed Milo alone to tell him about the light from the ground. I did not want to risk the others knowing about it—not yet anyway.

I remained suspicious of Bennett, especially after seeing him so close to the Invaders when Rose tried to escape. Bennett's motivations may have been to curry favor with the Invaders, and I knew Rose could not endure any repercussions from keeping the secret of the light. Although, after my training, Rose was getting over her timidness with the Invaders and communicated with them more easily. I just would not be the one to trigger for Rose the same fate as Shai. I would need to keep this secret between Milo and me.

Rose was still between Milo and me, holding her foot as the blood pooled around it.

"Rose, you should ask the Invaders to help you." I cast a quick glance at Milo, prompting him that I needed to talk to him alone.

"They can fix?" Rose asked, sniffling.

"Yes, they can," Milo affirmed, his eyes narrowing. "They don't always do it. Just look at me, still in this chair. But maybe they'll help you."

"Go to mine, Rose, and ask out loud," I said, pointing to Ula. I waved slightly for Ula to notice Rose hobbling over. I hoped Ula understood that I was asking her for help.

Once Rose was out of earshot, Milo spoke up. "You just gave me a strange stare. What is on your mind?" I paused, uncertain about his reaction if I told him about the light, and I had to be calculating with my words so as not to trigger the Invaders to listen to our conversation.

Milo interrupted the silence. "I would be careful about trying to domesticate that dangerous pup." He gave me a serious, knowing look. "I suppose they will release this animal once it can survive on its own. That would be the obvious reason for their de-extinction program. They did explain their coming here was because of human destruction of the Earth, which includes the animals, of course. It was not to let humans keep them as pets."

Milo had heard that message, too, back when we were still in the containments. "But we didn't need their help," I insisted. "People were doing just fine here on Earth, on our own. We were working on doing better."

"Were we?" Milo shot back. His cheeks reddened. "Depleting our Earth's resources . . . animals becoming extinct on a daily basis . . . the endless wars . . . the centuries of pollution, which, mind you, could have even reached to outer space, for all we know. Who else were we willing to pollute with our nonsense, our greed, our lust for the bigger cars, bigger buildings, bigger companies, bigger intentions for the neighboring planets? Is it any wonder they are here? All I can think of is, why didn't they come sooner?"

I slid my hands under my legs to hide them from Milo, my anger about him defending, again, the invasion.

Milo looked over his shoulder at the Invaders. One seemed to be helping Rose while the others continued to interact as if they were on a social outing with their pets. He turned back to me and lowered his voice. "I find myself questioning if they *really* are *here* to help us, Lauren. It sure doesn't seem that way, does it?"

I was stunned for only the briefest moment. I understood now: His bold statements were just for show. I shook my head, relieved to know that we shared the same struggle. "So I'm not the only one driving myself mad," I whispered. "Do they really think what they're doing is what's best for our planet?"

"It's not!" Milo snapped, far too loudly. "We were sovereign beings on a sovereign planet. They should have stayed away."

I gasped slightly and froze, concerned that the Invaders had heard him. I tried to calm myself. Were they looking over at us? Had their ears perked up? I did not want their attention directed at us. Declaring our belief in and longing for freedom did not go unpunished around here.

Milo looked away, and we sat in silence for some time. I picked at the grass and kept an eye on Darwyn and the Invaders, hoping that Rose and Bennett were distracting enough that the Invaders weren't listening to our conversation. But what was the best way to tell him about the flashing light?

"Milo," I said finally, almost whispering, "I saw something the past two nights. I wonder if it was just my mind playing tricks on me."

Milo's eyes tightened, and his mouth pursed, as if telling me I should shut up. I was a bit annoyed by his overt judgment of me, albeit a silent one, especially after his unusually loud outburst just a moment ago.

I tried to pretend to be interested in the far side of the platform. There was nothing to look at there—but it didn't matter, as long as the aliens lost interest in us.

At last, I heard Milo mumble, "I've seen it, too."

I whipped about to face him. He held a finger to his lips.

After Milo's confirmation, I knew that what I saw—the flickering light from the ground—*was* real.

Now I just had to figure out what it was.

◆

Darwyn and I returned night after night to the platform. I tried my best to stay awake, wishing the light would flicker again, even just for a moment. I stared off into the darkness, longing to see it again, with Darwyn by my side. My mind wandered while Darwyn enjoyed sleeping outdoors.

The light was my only glimmer of hope. I worked myself up to a fictional reality that something big would happen from this tiny light—some change, some opportunity, some type of rescue.

Each morning, we had been returned to my bedroom.

"Lauren, the platform is not for sleeping," Ula scolded. "Why do you remain there at night?"

"This is for Darwyn," I explained in an even tone. "He has to become accustomed to living outdoors. He won't be sleeping in my bed when he is returned to the wild." I rehearsed this response over and over while out on the platform.

Ula seemed happy with my response, saying, "Well done, Lauren."

We returned to the platform each night, now without worrying about being caught. Yet, the light did not reappear, only darkness. I had the very real fear that the Invaders found it.

Maybe the light was gone forever.

I slumped to the ground upon the realization that I was just waiting for change, for a big reveal or a rescue plan. My dreams of freedom were based on a flickering light, as if that would magically change my reality. But it didn't. The light did not shine again.

Then it came to me.

Instead of the light coming to me, I thought, *maybe I need to go find it.*

CHAPTER 35

GLITCH

Escape. It was all I thought about, especially during the empty time on the platform in our living quarters. How could I escape? How would I survive on the ground? How would I find the flashing light and whatever was making it? Too many details to figure out. I could not do this alone.

I needed Milo's help. With his brilliant mind and his access to the Invaders' information, he would have to help me figure out a way, maybe even chart out an entire escape plan. We could work together, with the light as our target, our guide, our inspiration. I had no doubt that Milo could get me to the ground, and Darwyn, too. I could find the light, and then come back for the others.

Milo and I would make plans to change the course of our destiny. What did I have to lose?

"A lot actually," Milo admonished when I came right out and asked him to help me escape. "You have a lot to lose."

"What are you talking about?" I challenged. I was completely blindsided by his response. I checked on Rose and Bennett, and they were playing with Darwyn under the jacaranda trees. They didn't hear us.

"You are one of the fortunate few, believe it or not," he muttered, looking over his shoulder toward the Invaders in their usual spot on the shared platform. "They've been training you as a conduit, a bridge between us and them. You have deciphered their mental commands and taught your captors our ways. Look what you did for Rose. You even helped me to speak with the Invaders more fluidly. You have this unique ability to understand them on a mental level like no one else. These are major advancements that should not be ignored. They could help us all. And you're going to risk that to find some pointless flickering light?"

"Major advancements?" I mocked. "We don't know their ultimate plan. We could all be eradicated at a moment's notice. I haven't forgotten about the Vellatros, have you? What if nothing ever changes? Should we just let the human race go extinct?"

"Indeed, that could happen, if you anger them by trying to escape." Milo shook his head. "I like to believe that one day they'll just leave. That whatever they're doing to the planet will be finished, and they'll let us go back and start over. We just need to wait it out." Milo continued to look over his shoulder at the Invaders, clearly nervous about our conversation.

I sighed in frustration. Milo was being unrealistic. While we simply waited, they continued to fill the skies with more ships and imprison us in containments, all while babies were miraculously being born and older boys were growing up too quickly and disappearing. Everything pointed to them staying, not suddenly leaving. But I needed Milo.

"So will you help me?" I pressed.

"No," Milo said curtly. There was no hesitation in his voice.

That was it. He refused to engage with me about it any further.

It was time to leave when Ula rose and held out the ball. I meandered over to her, mopey even, while tugging on Darwyn's leash. He wasn't ready to go.

I returned to my living quarters, to the same reality—still captive, nothing more than a pet. I had believed in my heart that Milo and I could change things. I was excited for a change. But nothing had changed—no help, no plan, no opportunity, no hope, no escape. No freedom. Worse, I couldn't find the light anymore. I hit bottom . . . again. This was nothing more than self-inflicted dread arising from false possibilities, all of which I created in my head.

My anguish deepened, and my behavior reflected it. I dragged myself around the living quarters, and even the orb and my view from the window did not snap me out of it. My training sessions with Ula were strained, and the prospect of discipline or even torture could not motivate me. But the discipline didn't happen, and Jun was not summoned against me.

Unexpectedly, Ula brought in some of my favorite comforts—sweet-smelling flowers next to my bed, the rare treat of chocolate—as if these small acts of kindness could ease my misery. I surmised that she may have even vaporized my sleeping quarters with whatever it was that they used in the hangars. My restless sleep was calmed, and our all-nighters on the platform dwindled.

I tried to find some comfort in the abilities I learned through training, to focus my mind on what I had—the safety, provisions, and a panoramic view of the lush, transformed Earth. On its face, the Invaders truly did save it.

These comforts were a curse, though, tempting me to set aside any thought of what I truly wanted—to escape. Even so, comfort ushered in complacency. Matthew would have been ashamed of me, and Shai would have been openly critical of me. Mom may have been accepting of it, given how she had changed.

I began to embrace that nothing would ever change for me or any other human. Thoughts of escape began to fade as I went about my daily routines—training Darwyn, savoring the time outdoors, and returning to exploration through my orb.

With Darwyn resisting any time spent inside the vessel, I began to bring the orb outdoors. Ula did not object. Yet again, I was surprised by her willingness to accommodate me.

One evening, as Darwyn took in the night air, I observed nocturnal animals through the orb. Glowing eyes appeared in the hologram. The orb adjusted to night vision and identified the animals that scurried into and out of my view: sugar gliders, servals, a fennec fox family, even a red panda. As the panda disappeared, the orb scanned another creature, too dark and quick for me to see.

"This is a roaming panther," the orb stated, before cutting off abruptly.

Never had it provided such limited information on an animal it had scanned. The viewer glitched, throwing curvy, luminous green lines across the screen.

I lightly tapped it, thinking that I could recalibrate it like a television with poor reception, but the screen went black. The orb then declared something entirely new: "Unidentified heat source."

That was it. No further information was provided.

With the green lines gone, I leaned in closer, curious. What could have stumped the orb in such a manner? Through the viewer, I saw a faint, dark shadow—the outline of an animal that stood upright.

Its legs and arms moved just like a human . . . running.

A running human.

It can't be, I thought, my heart in my throat. *It isn't possible.*

I stepped away from the orb, afraid to lead myself back into the pit of despair, as I had done over the light. I told myself that what I saw was not real, that it was just a glitch. *It had to be a glitch.* But Darwyn was alert and quietly growling.

Something *was* out there. But I saw nothing. Just the dark.

Whatever was happening—a glitch, an unidentified heat source, a shadowy figure, or perhaps all three—I had to tell Milo about it.

◆

"Lauren, what are you doing?" Ula asked.

"I'd like to take this to the others to see," I answered, pushing the orb toward the transport ball.

"This is not for them," Ula said. "It shall not leave here. We are to go now."

Milo was the first one I saw, wheeling over toward us on the shared platform.

"I tried to bring my orb to you today to check it out," I said to Milo.

Just as I mentioned it, Milo pointed to the Invaders. Ula was rising. She waved her long, skinny finger at me.

"After all this time, I'm still freaked out when I see their body parts," I said to Milo, ignoring Ula's admonition of me.

"Yes, awkward." Milo laughed. "Darwyn has gotten massive, Lauren. He has to be 150 pounds now."

"I know," I responded with my head down, afraid to let my concern show. "I'm sure it's almost time for him to leave. I don't know what I'll do without him."

"You tamed him more than I thought was possible," Milo

added kindly, perhaps trying to make up for being so short with me last time.

I glanced at Ula, but she was involved with the other Invaders—the ones with the terrified girls who never left their side. Ula had a faint redness about her, which I understood meant she was not pleased about something. Maybe she was finally addressing the distress of the two girls.

There could not be a better time to tell Milo.

I said in a quiet voice, "I saw a glitch last night in my orb. Then I saw something new. Not an animal. Something . . . like us." I resisted telling Milo directly that I saw a human form. I could not risk the Invaders overhearing.

He didn't respond.

"What if this is somehow connected to the . . . you know?" I asked, pressing the issue.

"The orb's scanner could be dangerous to that." Milo paused.

I glanced at him, puzzled.

"Look, the orb is from them and of them. *Their* technology. It is my belief that the orb transmits the information captured by it, like the animals you have been observing, back to them. That's what I've learned from peeling back the layers of their labyrinth of codes," Milo explained.

Milo paused again, careful about the Invaders overhearing us.

"You must not use the orb at night anymore, not with that glitch," he asserted under his breath. "If it is . . . what we hope it could be, then you run the risk of destroying it with your curiosity. It could cost us everything we are planning."

"*We* are planning?" I asked.

"Yes. That glitch you experienced . . . it is *everything*. It is the confirmation that I needed to justify putting you in extreme danger."

"You mean . . . ?"

His glare was hard, but a spark lit up his eyes. "This will take some time, Lauren. Be patient with me. We must ensure you will survive so you can connect with the light."

The light! This meant he was willing to help with the escape.

"But it's absurd, isn't it?" I lowered my voice. "Thinking anyone is out there, I mean. There was no surviving . . . that." Though I secretly wished for the real possibility of survivors.

I held my breath for his answer. If I had Milo on my side, *that* would be everything.

"Well," he said with a conspiratorial smile, "all the animals on the ground are surviving and flourishing beautifully, aren't they?"

CHAPTER 36

A LOT TO LOSE

I tried to be patient as Milo worked on a plan for my escape. He was the all-knowing one, the one with access to the Invaders' secrets, the one connected to their code. He knew more than anyone else I had ever known. I was relying on him to figure out how I could leave a doorless room, pass through an impenetrable barrier, open an exit that only the Invaders controlled, and find a way to the ground.

All I had to do was wait.

Time passed. I waited some more.

Still, he had nothing for me. I was growing impatient.

Milo had begged me not to use the orb at night, but I continued to use it by day when I was outside on the platform with Darwyn. As time went on, I saw larger and larger birds flying by, and the height of the vessel seemed to be no challenge to them. These were not ordinary birds.

"*Argentavis magnificens*," the orb announced one afternoon. "One of the largest winged birds ever to have existed, with a wingspan ranging between sixteen and twenty-four feet. It weighs approximately 150 pounds and has few predators due to its largesse and flight abilities. Disease and old age are the main causes of mortality. Flying attributes consist mainly of soaring and utilizing thermal updrafts, such as those from the nearby mountain range."

I suddenly had a ridiculous idea. These creatures were large enough to hold me.

"Darwyn, what if I just jump on one?" Darwyn looked back at me as if he was listening.

On the orb, I watched it soar from afar, assessing the angles required to make this work. It was coming my way, toward the platform. I shoved my tangled hair away from my face and imagined myself landing on the bird. It could be my only chance—getting it wrong was not an option.

I ran toward the edge, just in time to catch its magnificent wings flap beside me and then into a glide along the side of the platform. I followed along, sprinting to keep pace, watching for my opportunity as it soared just within my reach. My heart was pounding. This could be it. I could be gone.

From behind me, the orb continued: "*Argentavis magnificens* became extinct years ago, suspected to be caused by a change in their climate."

I stopped and fell to my knees on the platform. I heard so much about climate change, nearly every day in school. I was reminded about just how bad we were to the Earth, and why the Invaders came here in the first place. What if the Invaders were helping after all? What if things were better off this way for all of us, for the animals, for the planet?

The last big gust of wind hit my face as the massive bird flapped its majestic wings, veering away from the platform. My chance was gone.

I wasn't brave enough to do it anyway. Plus, I would never have gotten past the platform's barrier.

I slumped over, and Darwyn slinked under my limp arm and nuzzled against me.

Even if Milo did devise a plan, would I be brave enough? I doubted it.

I doubted myself.

I gave Darwyn a squeeze and thought of my brother. He never seemed to doubt himself, not even when facing a quarterback bully twice his size. When we first arrived at the containments with absolutely no chance of escape, Matthew never gave up. After I was chosen by the Invaders, every time I returned to the hangars, he was still plotting a way to rescue everyone. He even wanted to use my position inside the vessel, thinking I had some sort of advantage living up here.

Yet, I had done nothing with it.

Shai and Rose both had tried to do something. They were much braver than me. Shai refused to give up her freedom without a fight. How did I ever think I was the one helping them? I let them endure suffering at the hands of the Invaders while I did nothing, more worried about my own well-being and delighting in the rewards for my obedience.

Matthew said we had to do whatever we could do to shift the balance of power. It was my time to try. Complacency was no longer acceptable. I had to do something.

But first, I had to temper my thoughts, soothe my racing heart, and ease my breathing before Ula sensed this change in me. Was she nearby? I thought about their secret chamber, where they mysteriously retreated for hours and forbade me from coming close. I began questioning everything about it.

What was in that forbidden area anyway?

Why couldn't I go there?

Where did it lead to?

Was it a way out?

There was only one way to answer my questions—and it meant I would have to break Ula's trust.

———◆———

A few days passed before I built up the courage to try. I convinced myself this was the only way—the only plan. I wasn't waiting on Milo anymore.

Jun had not been around for as long as I could remember, and the doulesthe always disappeared when Ula did. I never saw them eat, rest, or sleep, or anything else humans had to do to stay alive— but surely they had to, something. I watched and observed, noting that whenever they retired to the forbidden area, everything was quiet until they reemerged hours later. That was it, the time to go. And the right moment would only be when Darwyn was asleep. I could not risk him following me into the forbidden area, their chamber. I would find a way to go through.

That was my plan.

I watched and waited, peering out from behind the wall of my quarters, until one evening I saw Ula retreat behind the barrier that originated with the wave of her hand. When Darwyn finally fell asleep by my side in front of the window, I slipped out from under his paws and darted across the room.

Standing up close to the wall for the first time, I realized this section was not solid, as I originally thought. Tiny particles swirled sporadically in a spiral, then came together as a circle, as if it were breathing. The longer I stood there and stared, the more the particles made sense. The circular configuration formed and held for only a short time before reverting to chaos. I counted a pattern, which repeated every few seconds.

As I was counting, I questioned why I was standing there, risking everything—Ula's trust, ever seeing Mom and Matthew again, maybe even their lives and my life. But the next time the spiral began to coalesce, I stopped thinking. I just breathed deeply and thrust one hand through the particle wall.

I felt no pain.

I was not burned.

I did not seem to be injured at all.

My hand still felt attached and totally fine, though I could no longer see it. This was the door, the way through the wall—nothing more than simple timing, I told myself.

I thrust my other hand through and fell into the other side, landing on my hands and knees. I pulled the rest of me through. I couldn't hesitate, not knowing what would happen to my lower half when the particles returned to chaos.

Once through, my hands were shaking and my chest pounded under the uncertainty of it all.

I slowly looked around the dimly lit room.

The light was cast by two gigantic spherical tubes, like glowing eggs, suspended in the middle of the room. They were within range of me. Before I could get closer, electrical currents discharged into the tubes every few seconds, crackling noises followed. Each bolt of lightning jolted and illuminated the eggs.

That was when I saw them: Ula and Jun. Floating within the

eggs, their oval-shaped bodies glowed. The electrical energy entered their wrists and the flats of their feet, transmitting up through their spiny arms and legs, which extended to each side of the egg. The light coursed throughout their bodies, just as blood coursed through ours.

Their bodies were much smaller in proportion to their arms and legs, and their torsos jerked and contorted each time the lightning cracked. I wondered if it was painful for them. In between the electrical bolts, however, the whole egg chamber glowed peacefully. I was momentarily mesmerized by the glow and how the two bodies were united with the energy.

This was why I was forbidden from this area. This was their *weakness*.

I blinked, and reality came flooding back. Admiring their rejuvenation system was not my purpose here. The Invaders were immobilized and unaware of me. I had to take advantage of this moment. It was my chance to escape—perhaps my only chance.

The Invaders had not been in here for long before I entered. I knew I had enough time to carefully make my way out.

I slowly rose to my feet and began to creep along the walls of the room, looking for the spinning particles that would signal another doorway. I knew how it worked now. All I had to do was find the right spot—the portal leading out of this room and on to the next stage of my escape, whatever that might be.

As I inched along looking for a way out, I had to pass the daunting, electrified eggs, which held my captors. Just as I took another step closing in on them, a small bolt redirected from the eggs and zapped toward me, attracted to the brand on my arm. A tingling ran all the way down to my fingers and up to the base of my neck. That was the last thing I could remember.

All went dark.

I didn't know how long I was out before my eyes blinked open again. My meticulous calculations as to how long I had in here were lost. I worried that my only chance to escape was drastically dwindling. But I could not move. My arms and legs felt like cinder blocks at the bottom of water. As I struggled to move, I was on the verge of panicking about their whereabouts. Until I saw the eggs, just outside my reach, still suspended in the air with Jun and Ula glowing inside.

I pushed with everything I had just to lift a finger. I could tap. I wiggled my toes. My legs began to pounce and feeling came back into my body. I flipped over on my stomach and began pulling my limp body across the ground. How much time did I have before they awoke? I could only keep going and hope for the best.

Scanning the wall again ahead of me, I found it at last: the swirling particles, shifting from spiral to circle and back again. It was time. All I had to do was watch the pattern for a few repetitions, and then step through the portal—if I was fast enough. My legs began to bend and hold the weight under me. I knew I could not hesitate another moment.

Suddenly, I heard a noise on the other side of the wall. A loud whimper.

Darwyn.

He was looking for me. For the first time, my dire wolf had awakened to find himself alone.

The whimper surged to a robust howl, his loudest one yet. My chest pounded. I eyed the eggs, wondering if the sound would disrupt their peace.

The electrical pulses halted.

The room darkened.

The eggs opened, releasing a blistering hot golden glow.

I held my hand up to protect my face.

Behind my hand I saw Ula floating right toward me, her small, rounded body exposed and glowing red. The electrical volts still jolted through the veins of her lanky arms and legs. In her anger, she must have forgotten that she was naked before me. She hovered over my head just as her robe encased her frame like a shield of armor.

She peered down at me, unamused.

Tears fell down my face, just as I started sprinting toward the only way out, to the portal. But the swirling particles had stopped, returning the wall to solid form.

"Lauren, stop. There is no escape from here." Her voice enraged, echoing throughout the room. "Your privileges are gone."

My branded arm started to burn, and I was slammed to the floor. I couldn't move . . . couldn't see . . . couldn't breathe . . . couldn't run away . . . couldn't get out.

She lifted my limp body from the ground. While suspended in the air, I was swiftly transported back to my living quarters. Just as I was dropped there, the barrier returned, separating me from their quarters.

Distressing howls came from behind the walls. Darwyn was gone.

The orb was gone.

The outdoor platform was gone.

There would be no further visits with Matthew and Mom.

I would no longer be part of the animal revival program.

And soon, no doubt, I would be violently punished.

Milo had been right. I had a lot to lose.

CHAPTER 37

SCARE TACTICS

My branded arm seethed like it was on fire after being struck by the eggs' lightning. I did not care. There was nothing left for me. I lost everything. I closed my eyes in defeat as I listened to my skin crackle.

His presence was unforgettable: Jun had come. Nothing would deter him this time.

He never spoke to me like Ula did. I heard him summon me in my mind.

I refused to move.

I sensed him again, directing me to the barrier.

I ignored him, as if I had a choice. I didn't.

I rose without control, forced out of my bed and onto my feet. I slumped, refusing to put any weight on my legs. This tactic worked before, and I had no intention of cooperating by walking to them. This was no deterrent for them. My branded arm, still oozing, shot into the air, dragging me across the ground and down the stairs, while the rest of me followed along.

I was dropped before them. When he lifted his hand, I knew what would follow.

Slicing pain plunged into my already damaged arm. I felt thick, blazing liquid flowing down my arm from an open gash in my flesh. This time he had gone to his most extreme, leaving a visible wound as evidence of his torture. I crumbled under the pain and fell to the ground, nearly vomiting. I swallowed it instead. I screamed. I had never screamed from his punishment before.

The bluish hue about him was unmistakable. He seemed eager to dispense my punishment. He plunged his hand again. I shrieked in pain.

Ula faded in the background. I could feel her—anguished, disappointed, distressed. This was not what she wanted. But I attempted to escape. She had no choice except to let it happen. I sensed all of this about her without any transmission from her. This meant that we had an intertwined connection, not needing directed communication. Our communication had deepened throughout our training, our quiet time before the windows, and the interactions we shared together with the animals. In a sense, the connection was inevitable. Despite my resistance and disobedience, our connection had not been broken.

Jun struck me again. As he twirled his fingers, my limb contorted and swelled until I felt it might snap from my shoulder.

Through tear-flooded eyes, I searched for Ula.

She raised her hand, and the punishment stopped. She had finally helped me.

Jun left, with a reddened glow about him.

With the transport ball in her hand, she motioned me to come to her. I could not move from the pain. With a swift movement of her hand, I gently rose from the ground, with her amber light surrounding me and dulling my pain.

I was confused and frightened. Where could she be taking me? I had just tried to escape. I knew she would not reward me with a visit to the platform to see the others or to the hangars to see Mom and Matthew. Certainly, Jun wouldn't allow it.

I pressed against the glass, bracing myself for anything. We traveled upward, in the direction of the nursery. The chance of a reunion with Darwyn overwhelmed my heart. Instead of stopping there, though, we continued upward to a new level and stopped before a tall, unfamiliar door. It slid open to reveal an area filled with monitors, floor to floor and wall to wall—a viewing room. At the front, silhouetted by the monitors, was Jun.

He was surrounded by other Invaders with golden-rimmed robes. Behind them stood another row of Invaders, wearing simple white or gray robes. The other Invaders stood at attention, awaiting Jun's directions. When he pointed across the room, several of them hurried over, exaggerated in their deference. I sensed their yearning for Jun's approval, just as the Invaders on the platform sought Ula's. It reminded me of a term my dad once used when he was criticizing my teacher—*sycophant*.

Milo had spoken about the hierarchy in their system, and he suspected that Jun and Ula may have been the supreme leaders among the Invaders while on Earth. He surmised that we were on a substation of sorts. From my observations and more of what I could sense, Milo was right again.

As we entered, Jun flashed Ula an angry red glow, but she merely waved her hand, dismissing him, and continued into the room. Jun may have been at the top, but so was Ula.

Moving toward the monitors, Ula motioned me to watch as she stopped at each section. After only a few seconds, I wished she had never shown me any of it.

They were videos of Earth. I was watching a whole planet

surveillance system—and Jun was the commander over it all. The first section showed Earth before the invasion: people walking down the street, in shops and restaurants, appearing to enjoy the day and one another. The smiles on their faces, unlike any expression I'd seen in a very long time, reminded me of how things once were. Seeing these videos led me to believe that we were watched, maybe even studied, by them before they came.

In the next section of monitors the storm appeared, and the chaos unfolded. People ran scared in the streets, fleeing unknown terrors, as those around them simply disappeared. The screens showed the same disturbance happening all throughout the world, but I hardly needed to watch it. I lived it. I remembered it vividly.

Why show me these videos? To remind me that there was no escaping the Invaders? I already knew that. They had infiltrated all of humanity—with ease. There was no hope for my kind to return to the way things once were. Once she was sure I had gotten the message, Ula moved on.

The next wall of monitors displayed various images of the regrown Earth—vast areas of land, with buildings replaced by mounds of rubble, and varying degrees of tree growth overtaking the piles of rocks and cement. It was an homage to the elimination of human civilization.

But there . . . in one video . . . it had zoomed in on a human figure attempting to hide among the rubble. Was this happening right now? Was it possible that someone was living outside of the containments?

It was a girl about my age, peeking over each shoulder and panting as she scurried behind a dusty pile of broken cement, covered with overgrown vines. Her black hair matched her black jumpsuit, which had supplies and gadgets hanging all over it. Covering her chest was a hardened shield. She was on the ground, and she looked prepared and organized, like she belonged out there.

But *they* saw her too. They knew where she was, and she was wholly unaware that they were watching her.

"*Run!*" I yelled.

All the noise in the room went silent, and the Invaders turned to jeer at me. Ula waved her hand, shutting my mouth with an invisible, tight muzzle, rendering my lips unmovable. A quiet tear fell down my cheek under the pain and humiliation of being muzzled like a dog, and the monitor went dark. I feared what might come next for that brave girl.

Ula shifted my transport ball to the next section, where the monitors showed circling Vellatros in various containments, swiftly hauling humans to the ceiling. I did not need videos to remember the chilling screams or the looks of terror from the people below, watching it all unfold. I remember that feeling, evoked every time the Vellatros came and then left with a human. I knew what that meant: They were never seen again. By the looks on the faces in the videos, they knew as well.

But in the middle of the monitors on this wall was the largest screen of all, displaying each Vellatros abduction from a new perspective—it was of what happened next. Those abducted and dangling from the tattered capes of the Vellatros traveled unconscious through the sky over crystal-clear turquoise waters, which approached the rim of an island so tropical and lush it looked like the postcard for a vacation destination. As the video followed the Vellatros continuing inland, it became clear that the vast middle of the island was barren and desolate, a desert where the sun's scorching heat radiated along the ground, with little more than dirt and rocks for shelter. It was there—the island's desert core—where the poor souls were dropped. Onto an island in the middle of the ocean, with no escape.

This harsh environment was in stark contrast with the extraordinary regrowth that I could see right outside the windows of the vessel. And just as we arrived in the hangar on that first day, those taken to this godforsaken island arrived with nothing for survival: no shelter, no food, nothing but the detested olive-green uniform.

As the number of humans dropped onto the island by the Vellatros grew, the other Invaders in the video room began to surround Ula and me. Jun stood right beside my transport ball. I sank as low as I could go in the transport ball to try to disappear from their view, while my heart pounded under the fear of being surrounded by the Invaders. But I was in a see-through ball, watching as the Invaders took turns inspecting my movements.

Their attention turned from me to the screens. Seemingly, the Invaders' entertainment had begun.

On full display were the humans abandoned on the island, left unconscious while their skin started to show signs of slow peeling under the scorching hot sun. Other humans emerged from behind rocks and out of holes in the ground, creeping like animals, closing in on the new arrivals. Those that had emerged and somehow survived in these elements were disheveled, despondent, and appeared detached from any semblance of humanity. They were large, some of the largest of men. Through their tattered clothing were protruding muscles, veins popping out and coursing through their skin. Their skin was rugged and covered with an unusual film. Their eyes were bloodshot, and they growled through their open mouths, frothing even.

While I was terrified about what these survivors intended to do with the new arrivals, I felt a sudden rise of excitement surrounding

me . . . an excitement coming from the Invaders. My worry deepened. I turned away from the screen and caught the eye of one of the
Invaders standing beside Ula. It raised its pointy finger back toward
the screen for me to continue watching.

I turned quickly away from that Invader's gaze, finding the
newly arrived humans regaining consciousness with the hordes of
zombie-like humans closing in on them. They tried running away,
only to be pulled down into large holes or cave openings. Their
chilling shrieks were soon drowned out by howls, seemingly thrilled
about the catch. The new arrivals never had a chance; not even one
returned to the surface. This appeared to be the Invaders' version
of a criminal justice system—and people, before the invasion, had
thought *ours* was unjust.

I covered my eyes and cowered inside the transport ball, horrified at what I had just watched. Ula taped on the transport ball for
my attention as she moved us away from the Invaders delighting
in watching the criminal island massacre. Ula had one final set of
videos to show me.

The screens showed girls and young women, some my age, some
a little older, in large containments with a softer, more welcoming
environment than the cold steel of the hangars I had known. The
rooms were large, with comfortable-looking beds, rocking recliners,
and buffets of familiar foods from home. *This doesn't look so bad*, I
thought, until I noticed a common element about each of them in
the room—they were pregnant. I remembered Mom's warning: The
women had been separated from men far too long for natural conception. Maybe Mom was among them, helping them.

Another screen on this wall displayed heavily pregnant women
reclining on white-sheeted gurneys in a sterile room, surrounded
only by Invaders. These women were giving birth, but the process

seemed calm, even blissful. No turmoil or strain, no screaming in pain as they pushed. Being one with the experience of childbirth. Each baby arrived with ease, dropping delicately into the hands of an Invader, who then placed the child on the chest of its loving mother.

I almost smiled at the beauty of it all.

But as the mothers rolled out of the room on their gurneys, I noticed each one of them tightening their swaddle around the babies, clinching so tightly I was concerned the newborns would be smothered. The looks of desperation on the mothers' faces were startling and rather confusing to me.

I soon found out why. The babies were lifted through their mothers' scrambling arms by a familiar invisible force—and I knew there was no fighting it. Whenever the force summoned us, we moved, willfully or not. These mothers were as helpless as I had long been, but their agony went deeper. As each baby was pried from its mothers' grasp, the women were yanked back against the table, straps surrounded their ankles and wrists.

"My baby!" screamed the dozens of women on these screens, continuing their hopeless struggle. "Give me my baby!" The anguish on the mother's faces was bitterly painful to watch.

The Invaders did not listen to them, instead taking the babies back to the comfortable room filled with Invaders, while each of the imprisoned mothers was rolled toward a wall of equipment. Their beds angled upward as tubes were attached to their chests, filling bottles with extracted milk for the babies they likely would never see again.

The anguish, fear, and sheer terror each one of them felt . . . that I felt for them . . . it was all so very real.

"You must understand," Ula said quietly. "Your age is proper for this room." It was a warning, and I had no doubt that Jun would take pleasure in sending me there.

I vomited into the transport ball, narrowly missing my feet.

My chin was lifted by her invisible force. "It disrupts my peace, pains my soul," Ula uttered softly. I wiped my mouth, astounded that she acknowledged the suffering.

Jun must have mandated me to view these utterly distressing videos to strike fear in me, to prevent another escape attempt. But he had failed to realize something: Things had changed.

I had changed.

I survived his beatings, and I would survive the next one. I would work harder to escape. My resolve grew stronger. There was nothing he could do to stop it. And the more he pushed me, the greater would be my fervor and my drive. The time of comfort and complacency was over.

I would never stop . . . until I could be free.

CHAPTER 38

DISCOVERY

Back in my bedroom, I replayed all the horrific images over and over in my mind. I thought of all those people in the videos. None of it made sense. If the Invaders were here to preserve Earth's resources, to rebuild our planet and restore its original beauty, why had they converted a deserted island into a commune for the living dead? Why were they breeding a new generation of human children in a captive society, highly controlled and sterile, without passion or emotion? If their motives were pure, why would they commit these atrocities and ignore the collective suffering of the humans of Earth?

Tears soaked my pillow, and I buried my face into it to muffle my cries, not wanting them to hear my distress, nor show them my weakness. But I could not just lie there defeated. No one was coming to help me. And *I* was the closest to the supreme leaders.

I sat up to collect myself, wiping away my tears. But without

Ula's amber light, like I had in the transport ball, the immense pain from Jun's beating came rushing back, with my arm throbbing. Tears streamed down my face again from the pain—just moving hurt. Focusing on the light on the ground—my target—I closed my eyes and breathed deeply. The wound would have to be dealt with before I would confront Ula, no matter what the consequences were.

The brand on my shoulder was damaged, a bloody gash slit open by Jun's brutal punishment against me. With my other hand I squeezed as chunks of pus and blood slowly flowed down my arm. I gulped, swallowing the intense pain.

I felt something strange. Something hard was burrowed under my skin, like a metal marble. Tracing what remained of the brand with my fingers, I felt a tiny ball move against another one, clinking together beneath the flesh.

What's under there?

I poked at the area and felt it again—things were moving around under my skin. Something sharp was needed. Reaching for my backpack, I pushed aside my old clothes and found my journal and pens. I plunged a pen straight into the wound quickly, before I could think about it. My eyes rolled to the back of my head, and I grabbed on the bed to stabilize myself under the pain. As blood dripped down my arm, I inhaled a few large gulps of air, trying to calm myself and avoid transmitting my distress to Ula.

I had to go deeper. I had not yet reached whatever was in there. With the pen, I searched for the hard objects, slicing until the muscle and skin released one of them. I dropped it into my free hand for inspection: a small, hardened black pellet.

I stared at it for a long time. How did it get there? Was it implanted in the hangar long ago, when we were branded? Did all the prisoners have them? Could this be how they controlled us? I thought of Milo and wondered if I'd ever see him again. Maybe he would know what it was, how it got there—and what we could do about it.

The others had to come out, but I had nearly fainted to get to this one. With my shaking hand I again jammed the pen into my pulsating arm, excavating the remaining pellets. In the end, I pulled out five in total and swirled them around in my blood-soaked hand. Only then did I think of the consequences.

They were going to know. Jun could no longer fling me around like a rag doll, which he seemingly so enjoyed.

What had I done?

I disobeyed them again.

I wiped my hands and wrapped my arm with my old shirt to stop the bleeding, wondering how I was going to hide this from them. The only way to avoid detection and further punishment was if I excelled at Jun's training, even without being controlled by him. I would have to become the most compliant human in captivity.

While lost in my planning, I did not realize that the doulesthe was standing beside my bed. It was the first time the servant had ever breached my pod. Recoiling, I slid my hand under the blankets to hide the pellets. I stared at it, intensely, unsure of what it would do to me.

The servant pointed to my arm, and I realized there was no need to feel threatened by it. After all, it was only a couple of feet tall.

It held its hands above my arm and began rubbing them together. A warm, amber glow—just like Ula's—grew between them, while the servant brought it closer to my wounded arm. The warming light infused the injury, and the bleeding subsided, replaced by a tingling, tugging feeling as the strands of my skin began to regrow. Long strings of skin intertwined, covering the exposed muscle and blood vessels. The wound was closing as the doulesthe wove new skin around it.

Overwhelmed by the intensity of this healing process, I drifted in and out of consciousness. When I awoke, the pellets were still in my hand, under the blankets.

The doulesthe was gone.

———◆———

It was nighttime, but without Darwyn near me, I couldn't sleep. Every time I shut my eyes, the terrible images from the videos kept replaying in all their disturbing detail. I swirled my pellets in one hand, clutched my stuffed kitty in my other arm, and stared at the ceiling, thinking.

I knew too much now. I felt so guilty enjoying the comfort of my bed, while atrocities were taking place on the Earth's surface. I thought that being imprisoned in the containments was the worst of what was happening to people, but I was wrong.

After a while I got out of bed, pushed the pellets inside my shoe, and wandered down to where my living space met theirs. No one seemed to be around—neither the Invaders nor the servant. Maybe they were in the forbidden chamber room, recharging.

All was quiet, empty, and dark, with the only light in the vessel coming from the stars above. With the barrier having been taken down, I had the chance to get back to the training area, which Ula set up for me the first time she welcomed me into their quarters. My smaller chair, next to her much larger one, with some soft blankets and pillows for my comfort nearby. Darwyn loved sleeping with his legs in the air on his back in those blankets. So much had changed since that first silent moment in front of the windows with Ula.

For so long, that view had been all I had to hope for. Now there was more. The human suffering I witnessed on those videos ran deep. I was resolved to find the light.

And suddenly it was there—far off in the darkness and low to the ground, but there all the same. That was no star.

It flickered.

It flickered again.

The light, I felt it calling out to me.

I was desperate and searching for hope, and hope had appeared just when I needed it most. Maybe it was irrational to build up a flicker of light as something of such import, holding it out to be my solution to the suffering, to save the humans, and to save me. But it was all I had to go on, so it would have to be enough.

It was there, it was really there. The light.

CHAPTER 39

THE PLAN

W hen I awoke, still in my chair in front of the window, I found
Ula and Jun hovering over me. Jun only came when he
wanted to discipline me.

My whole body tensed, and I didn't move. I was convinced that
the pellets were how Jun controlled my body and delivered my punishment. To make this work, I would have to wait until Jun directed
me. He was in control. He was the master.

I remembered Ula's teachings: *Be calm, clear-minded.* I focused
on the memory of the golden light she had extended toward me,
hoping it would allow me to transcend my hesitation and finally
connect with Jun. I had to watch my fear dissolve. I had to dis-
pel the terror of his beatings. I had no choice. Only by accepting
him—calmly, willingly, peacefully—could I avoid punishment. And
only by avoiding his attempts to punish me could I keep them from
learning that I had removed the pellets.

I obeyed his every command, without hesitation or resistance. There was no need to punish me, and he left without utilizing my arm. I averted an additional beating—and even better, any detection that the pellets were removed, at least for now.

Fully submitting to him was humiliating and revolting, but I vowed it would be the last time. My compliance with their commands would be no longer, if I could avoid it. I would not have to listen to or follow them again, if my plan came together.

Once he left, I released my shoulders and shook out my arms to release any hold he had over me. I had done my best. Had it been enough?

"Jun was pleased with your compliance," Ula said.

I just stared at her and remitted a feeling of discontent and of betrayal.

"This was of your doing, not mine," she reprimanded. "You will be permitted to join the others today." Before I could respond, the glass transport ball quickly surrounded me, as if she wanted to go before Jun changed his mind.

On the platform, the other Invaders surrounded Ula, vying for her attention, just as the Invaders in the video room had surrounded Jun. As I was released on the grass, I saw Milo wave from a distance and start wheeling his chair toward me. I moved toward him as fast as I could. Ula's attention was something I could do without.

"I saw it again. I saw the . . . shooting star," I said, hoping he would get the hint. "It's not often that I get to see one, but it's still out there."

Milo didn't pick up on my reference. He had his own topics to discuss. "Where have you been? Are you okay?" he asked earnestly while looking around to see if any of the Invaders were nearby. "You acted without me, didn't you?" Milo knew that when Rose and I were absent from these visits, we were likely being punished. Milo and Bennett never missed a visit, though.

I blurted it all out as quickly as possible—how I thought I found a way out, how the Invaders seemed to recharge themselves in the egg-like chambers, how the silver energy entered them and ran through their veins, how they had forced me to watch all the videos of people suffering, how they were breeding stolen children, and letting the Vellatros carry people to their ultimate death.

"But the important thing is that while they're recharging, they're incapacitated," I insisted. "Milo, they were *incapacitated*."

"A weakness, hmm?" Milo muttered, taking a deep breath in. He seemed to be trying to compute something in his mind. "But then . . . how did you get caught?"

I tried to hold back the tears. "Darwyn howled . . . then they woke up."

Milo paused. "And where's Darwyn now?"

"He's gone. Back to the nursery, I think." Despite my efforts, my eyes welled up. "It's all my fault. You were right—I lost it all."

Milo reached his hand toward mine and grabbed it delicately.

I glanced at his hand and then at his face. His cheeks had turned a soft red.

He moved quickly to retract his hand toward his wheelchair, but I caught his wrist first. Though I wanted to thank him for his kindness, I held his hand for a far more important reason.

"Milo," I whispered, "I need to show you something."

I pulled his hand toward me, not caring if he blushed again. There was no point getting distracted. Instead, I gently rolled the pellets from my other hand into his.

His eyes widened as he closed his hand and pulled it back to his lap, calmly asking, "What am I holding?"

"Some sort of pellets. They're from my arm," I said quietly. "From under my skin . . . my brand. I think it's how they're able to control us."

Milo's mouth was open, but no words came out.

I wanted to roll up my uniform sleeve and expose my scarred arm, but it was too risky with the Invaders nearby. "The servant helped to heal me."

He seemed almost equally astonished by this. "Since when does the servant interact with you? Why would it do that?"

I shook my head. "I don't know why it helped me. The doulesthe usually just follows Ula around when she is there and keeps to itself otherwise. I don't think it came from the same place as Ula and Jun, but it used the same amber glow that Ula uses."

"I've long suspected that the servants are from another planet— maybe one that the Invaders conquered before coming to Earth. But the similar glow is unexpected, rendering the real possibility that it was harvested from the doulesthe by them."

"At first I thought it spied on me, but now I don't know," I admitted.

Milo nodded. "If it were to spy on you, I assume it would be under duress, just like us. It may have just been an act of kindness . . . or it sees something about you needing to be helped. We must find out more before we decide to trust it."

I could hear the pellets lightly rattling in his hand. He was swirling them around, as I had.

"I've seen nothing about these pellets in their database. They even broadened my access recently, but there is nothing about . . . this," he finally said. "Can I keep them?"

I furrowed my brow, concerned. "That's dangerous," I replied. "For both of us."

"I want to run diagnostics on them. Maybe I can get some answers," he explained. "I'll keep them safe, undetected."

I nodded, placing my trust in Milo, but I had to tell him one last thing. "When I moved past their electrical chamber, I was zapped by a bolt of energy. It seemed drawn to my brand . . . their recharge energy was attracted to these pellets. It knocked me out. I thought you should know before you examine them."

"I'll keep it in mind," Milo reassured me, "and do my best to figure out what it means."

That was all I could ask of him. "But we need to hurry with the plan," I insisted. "I failed on my own. I need you on this."

"After all that they just put you through, you want to try again?" Milo challenged me. "Things seem to be getting better for you, not worse. Think of the ramifications, Lauren. Is it worth losing everything all over again, for an attempt that's likely to fail?"

I thought about it for a moment. I already had been allowed to return to the park. Maybe next, I would get back the orb, see Mom and Matthew again, or even be brought back into the animal revival program. I just couldn't stay in that vessel any longer, humiliated and broken, without at least trying to escape properly. And I feared that I might not survive another beating by Jun, like Shai.

"Well, I found these chambers; this is crucial. It's an opening that I didn't have before," I pressed. "We can capitalize on this opportunity, somehow . . . find another exit."

Milo did not look convinced.

"Milo, you don't understand. There are these videos. People are seriously suffering. I've seen it."

"I know what you are talking about," Milo added. "I've seen them, too."

"How long have you known about this?"

"Long enough," Milo firmly replied and turned away from my judgmental stare.

I couldn't fault him. We'd both been coerced into silence by our own comforts and false sense of safety. Neither of us wanted to disrupt what the Invaders had given us. But we had to do something about it.

"Milo, she was upset by it, too . . . by the videos . . . my beating . . . what's happening to our people." I paused and nodded over to Ula's direction to ensure Milo knew who I was talking about. "*She* told me so. I think it'll be different for me next time, with another attempt."

"Of all the captors, I guess yours—or at least her—seem to be the most forgiving," Milo responded.

"Maybe even spared from death, if I were recaptured," I said with a half-smile.

Milo nodded slowly. "Oh, and about that shooting star . . . did you make a wish?" He grinned.

So he understood my reference. "I did," I responded. "It's amazing . . . and I *have* to find it."

◆

As our plans solidified, my ability to block Ula from my mind grew deeper and stronger, until I created a mental blockade that she could not penetrate. I compartmentalized my anxious feelings behind this impenetrable wall in my brain. While I never could have imagined that this capability was possible, I practiced and perfected it. I had to; it was a matter of survival.

Still, I was nervous until Milo gave me the pellets back a few days later, when we met again on the platform. When he slipped them into my hand I wrapped my fingers around them, relieved that I had gotten back a part of me.

"Also, you'll need this." Milo dropped a larger black pellet in my hand.

This one was not from my arm. "Why is it so much bigger than the others?"

Milo explained that he recreated the physical elements from the materials from my arm pellets with other materials he had access to in his quarters. I didn't fully understand, but as he further explained, fusing the pellets together had created a stronger electrical output in line with the larger size. The Invaders did not realize just how dangerous it was to share advanced technological information with someone of Milo's intelligence, any more than they realized that training me in mental manipulation could come back to haunt them. They assumed they were superior to humans in every way, so they underestimated us.

"Your instincts were right," he confirmed. "These pellets communicate with the Invaders' networks. I have completely reconfigured this one to identify and disable one of those invisible doors in your quarters, so you don't count spirals, or whatever, to get through them. I anticipate this to act like a master key for you."

"But this key will only provide a temporary disabling, allowing you a limited time to go undetected," he warned. "I suspect that when your Invaders retreat into the forbidden area to recharge and the servant is nowhere around, that's the *only* time that you can use this."

We had a plan for getting out of my room, but we still had to figure out how to get me to the ground. Milo searched the database for a weakness in the Invaders' transportation system—a way for me to transport to the ground. He had not yet cracked it.

Milo considered all aspects of this escape, including my survival should I make it to the ground. He tracked weather patterns and animal migration, both of which had changed drastically since our normal lives on Earth. We had to wait for the right time, although fortunately the climate for us was less harsh and unpredictable than in other parts of the world. As for the animals, I already was familiar with those that had long occupied the region: woodland creatures like bears, wolves, and so on. I knew from the orb that I should expect to encounter some very different species, too. Until I could adapt to life on the surface, I would need to rely mostly on camouflage, with the overgrowth of foliage working in my favor.

"I've been tracking the animals. They're working in a pattern and are seasonal. Remember, we learned about migration in school. That's still happening," Milo explained, implying that we had to wait for the right time. Our indirect communications did not prompt any suspicion by Ula or Milo's Invader. Either we got too good at hiding our plotting, or our captors had become too trusting of us. It proved to be working either way.

"These are all good thoughts, Milo," I remarked. "But I need to get *there* before worrying about any of this." Slightly irritated, I snapped at him. I didn't want to wait any longer trying to figure out all these details, which would be meaningless if I couldn't get to the ground.

At this point, the orb had not been returned. There was no longer the de-extinction program for me. I had not visited Mom and Matthew again. All I had to focus on was escaping, and Milo didn't have this figured out for me yet.

Milo looked at me thoughtfully. "You had a puppy before Darwyn, right?"

"Yes, Thor." My shoulders slumped. I missed them both.

"And how did you potty train him?" Milo asked.

I didn't know where Milo was going with this, but I indulged him. "Baby gates."

"Exactly." Milo exclaimed. "You put up a fence to keep him where he needed to be."

"In the kitchen, mostly, so if he had an accident, it was on the tile and easy to clean."

"And then slowly you moved the gates, right?"

Milo was right. We moved the gated enclosure toward the sliding door, onto the patio, and finally out on the grass, showing Thor where to go. "It got so bad that the puppy wouldn't go potty unless I was out there watching him. What a doofus." I smiled at the memory.

"But it was possible for the dog to jump over the gates as he grew, right?"

"I guess. But he didn't."

"That's what's going on." Milo clapped, as if he had just solved our problem. "He could have escaped the gates, but he never did . . . because he didn't realize he could."

I turned my head sideways. "What?" I wasn't following him.

"It's like the dog with the large stick in his mouth that tries to get through the door. If he goes straight, headfirst, the stick goes across the door frame and prevents the dog from getting inside." Milo went on. "But if he would just turn his head to the side, so the stick was vertical—voilà! He isn't stuck!"

"Because he's a dog, though, he doesn't figure it out?" I hesitantly uttered, squinting at Milo. Suddenly, it clicked—or I thought it did. Milo was saying that the Invader's barriers could be outsmarted or penetrated if we just looked at the problem correctly. We were preventing *ourselves* from getting out because we weren't looking at it from the right perspective. We needed to figure out how to turn that metaphorical stick or jump over the gates.

"And do you have any idea how the dog might figure out how to get through the doorway?" I asked.

"I think I do," Milo replied, with a great big smile.

CHAPTER 40

ALMOST THERE

"It's time, Milo," I commanded. It was my final visit to the platform—or so I hoped.

"I know," Milo replied, looking away. I suspected that he felt the same way I did. Sad about losing a good friend if the escape was successful, and worried about losing each other if it wasn't.

"We have it all planned out, now. I'll be okay," I assured him. While I outwardly sounded confident to Milo, that was far from what I was feeling inside. Ever since we finalized the plans, my stomach had been twisted, and I was constantly nauseous. But my training sessions with Ula had calmed me while also allowing me to practice suppressing my feelings around her. It seemed she did not suspect a thing.

I had to say my last goodbye to Rose and Bennett, even if they were unaware of it. I gave them each an extra squeeze.

"What's that for?" Rose asked.

"Just been missing you on my last few visits here," I said. "Take care of Milo until I see you again, okay?"

"He's my buddy. I always do," Bennett drawled. He reached out to scratch his back, but I grabbed both of his hands and just held them for a moment. He squirmed at the start and tried to pull away, but then his hands went limp. He wouldn't realize what I'd done for him until after I was gone, but I hoped he could find some comfort in the healing.

"Lauren," Milo said, "this will be the only chance you have."

This was not another spontaneous escape attempt like my failed one in the forbidden area. Milo's plan was as close to foolproof as possible.

I had a chance.

Milo had risked a lot to create the pellet device, which would disable the power source briefly so I could pry open the heavy doors in Ula and Jun's living quarters. And by infiltrating the Invaders' database, he finally discovered a passage to the ground. I still couldn't quite grasp how it was all connected, but I understood the concepts Milo had explained to me.

His theory was as complex as it was simple: that alien technology could be emitting augmented reality feeds to alter our view of the world around us—hiding what *really* connected the Invaders' vessel to the Earth's surface. Milo believed the Invaders were using this on a massive scale to conceal what was happening around the vessel and the surrounding area.

"I never thought of AR before," I admitted.

Milo went on. He explained that on the ground, a massive system of portals and transportation corridors allowed the Invaders to move swiftly or disappear before us as if into thin air. In reality, they were moving in or out of certain image feeds and into their fast-track

corridors, like the glass-and-steel tubes surrounding the main vessel. He compared it to how humans had been able to direct video
feeds of one area from various vantage points by using numerous
flying drones. But humans' AR tech was profoundly antiquated in
comparison. He surmised that the Invaders' technology emitted
from the vessel itself, with additional reflective bays erected throughout the Earth to transmit the reality they wanted us to see.

"The way their tech is manipulated, it suggests an air of mystique
with the façade of superiority. This way, their headquarters are protected from infiltration based on the appearance of an unattainable
target," Milo added.

"Pull back the curtain—the AR curtain—and you expose the
wizard." I tried to simplify his theory.

Milo nodded. "Precisely."

He went on to explain that the Invaders used these portals and
transportation corridors to resupply and rearrange containments on
the ground all around the world, as if by magic. And Milo suspected
that the Invaders were not doing all this alone, but with the support
of a whole workforce operating in the shadows, unbeknownst to
any humans, all hidden by their AR—a possible workforce of the
doulesthe.

"The most important aspect about all of this alien technology is
that while it might hide from our view what connects the vessel to
the ground, it's still there." Milo leaned in closer. "It still exists. You
just need to find it."

"Okay, but if it's hidden, how do *I* find it?" I asked.

"Let's continue to track this through. You recall when they first
arrived, the Invaders created the worldwide blackout, instantaneously neutralizing computers, communication, military forces,
and entire governments all around the world. That's the only

explanation because we never even heard rescue sirens. It was silent, dark, and all of us were instantaneously captured."

"Yes, I remember, every detail," I responded. "I had nightmares about them in the hangars . . . until those nightmares were replaced with other nightmares."

"I know how they did it," Milo revealed. Through an enormous outpouring of power, he went on to explain, they created the purple dome around the entire Earth, their AR projection coupled with a counteractive neutralizing force, which escaped his understanding. But continuing the necessary level of energy to cover the Earth would have required a massive power source far beyond nuclear or anything else within human means—and theirs.

"If they continued covering the entire Earth it would have destroyed everything, and quite possibly themselves. Destroying the Earth runs counter to what they claim to be doing here, supposedly saving the Earth from us humans," Milo said. "The over-surging of this power could have made it possible for people in certain regions to avoid capture."

I was left shocked at the fact that Milo acknowledged there could be survivors.

If Milo was right, the Invaders had quickly corralled humans into colony-like containments to operate their projections in smaller regions. For the same reason, the humans were forced to sleep and were limited outside while the technology recharged. Effectively, the aliens created the reality under their control.

From the videos I saw with Ula, it appeared that our vessel was the largest one, but as smaller vessels continued to arrive, they scattered around the world. Applying Milo's theory, these smaller vessels, consisting of the same metallic and glass reflective materials as the main vessel, powered these projections wherever humans had been imprisoned in containments.

"We discovered another weakness." Milo's excitement grew. "I suspect there exist pockets where their vessels' projections do not provide altered coverage—where the AR doesn't skew our reality." As we learned, the Invaders' strength was not impenetrable, as it seemed for so long. The need to recharge in their egg chambers was one area of weakness. The limited reach of the projection feeds was another.

Milo's theory made sense. There was a way out of the vessel, and I just needed to find it. "It's hidden in plain sight," he promised. "If you can just figure out how to see it, you can get out."

That was the escape plan. And at the pivotal moment, I needed to stay calm and see things in a different way. I would escape the Invaders by using the skills I learned from Ula, and her alien training. Once on the ground, I would search for the flashing light—for survivors . . . for the elusive figure that glitched the orb.

Milo's hand was shaking as he shoved a compass in my hand. "I've had this with me since the invasion. I stuffed it in my pockets as we were trying to escape."

"I thought you said that you were never in the Scouts."

"I wasn't. My parents never allowed it. They thought it was below our family and a waste of my time. They even complained to the librarian when I took home survivalist books, claiming the books encouraged doomsday tendencies, conspiracy theories even. I guess, after all of this, they were right. None of it helped when *they* came. Do you know how to read one?"

I knelt next to his chair and grabbed his hand. The shaking stopped—I almost mastered this technique by now—but I did not release his hand right away. He seemed to know the calm was coming from me. His eyes were teary, and so were mine. He put his other hand over mine and squeezed.

"I spent a couple years in the Adventurers' Club," I confessed, nodding. "I know how to start a fire, make shelter, scavenge for food, all of that." At least I used to know all those things.

I paused, not sure what to say next. I wanted Milo to understand how important he was to me. I could not have done the planning or any of this without him.

"Thank you." I rose from the ground and hugged him tightly. He hugged me even tighter. Then I pulled away, grabbing his shoulders, and looked firmly into his eyes. "I'll be okay."

"I believe in you, Lauren, but it will not be easy." He gulped. "And dealing with all of this is going to be tough, too, without you." I knew that must have been a big share for him.

I jogged over to Ula and the transport ball, hiding Milo's compass in my hand, still running through the plan in my mind.

When we arrived back in their living quarters, I started up to my bedroom, but Ula called me back. "Lauren."

I stopped on the bottom step, trying not to panic. What if I hadn't managed to block my thoughts after all? What if she sensed my apprehension? Did she know what I was planning?

I breathed in and out, trying to temper my emotions, and slowly turned away from the stairs. Peering around the wall from my pod into their quarters, I squeaked out, "Yes?" She was peering directly into my room. I gulped.

"We have been pleased with your obedience," Ula explained, fixing her round black eyes on me. "You may choose another youngling to help raise and prepare for release. We will go to the animal program when you arise in the early light outside." She turned and glided across the room to where Jun was waiting. Together, they crossed into the forbidden area.

Milo had been right . . . again. I just earned back my place in the animal nursery and in Ula's good graces. I was wholly compliant with Jun's commands, while my training with Ula was bringing me closer and closer to transcendence—even if I was not exactly sure what she meant by that.

Yet here I was, about to embark on a suicide mission, with the goal of finding a silly light that projected a false sense of hope. If I stayed, maybe I really could help Earth and all the animals. What cause was more noble than that?

Why was *I* the person who needed to do more? I pondered this question as I walked back up the stairs. Escape and retaliation were what Matthew and Shai wanted—but maybe not necessarily what I wanted. And Milo would be so relieved if he saw me return to the platform.

Or would he be disappointed?

Ula and Jun were in the forbidden area, and the doulesthe was nowhere to be found. It would soon be time.

The silence in the vessel became deafening.

I sensed none of them nearby. I was alone.

I had to do this.

I grabbed my backpack and threw in Milo's compass, along with my kitty, my journal and pens, and the tattered old clothes from home. Memories of the day the Invaders first arrived rushed back, but I pushed them away and clutched Milo's reconfigured pellet in my hand.

My backpack was beside me, packed and ready to go. I sat on my bed shifting the pellet between my sweaty hands, occasionally wiping it dry. My knees started to bounce as I wavered. Stay or go?

I started downstairs, telling myself that I would just check things out—to confirm that I was indeed alone.

The large room was lit only by the light of the moon and the stars. All was silent.

I quietly hurried to the wall where I passed with Ula in the transport ball, opposite the forbidden area. Aside from the rustling of my backpack against my hips with each step, the room remained absolutely quiet.

I stood before the wall where the door should be, panting with fear.

I convinced myself: *Just try it.* Maybe the pellet wouldn't even work.

I rolled Milo's reconfigured pellet forward to hold it by my fingertips. The door frame lit up immediately, with miniscule lights flashing like a rebooted computer. I jumped back in surprise. This was something I never saw before, not even with Ula. What had Milo done? What if one of them saw the lights? If I was not successful, would they let me live? If I was able to escape, what would I find? Would I be able to survive on the ground?

But I had no time to indulge these swirling worries, because an opening suddenly appeared within the lighted frame. There was enough room for me to slide through.

Go! Just go!

I darted through the doorway.

I was in the corridor, the one I had been in with Ula. But this time there was no transport ball. Underneath my feet, the flooring was thin, almost nonexistent, and strong winds blew up from the dark void—an unexpected change from my previous times in the corridor. I held on to the wall and lifted the pellet to the door, allowing the energy source to trigger it to shut.

With another gust of wind, I lost my grip and fell downward through the corridor.

My stomach dropped, just as it had when I was inside the transport ball. But the drop had never lasted this long when I traveled with Ula. I fell past several floors of the vessel already, moving too far and too fast. I needed to grab onto something that would stop my fall.

Just below my toes, I saw light: the multicolored passageway I had seen the first time the hangar ceiling opened, with the Invaders traveling through. My feet had nearly touched down when I whooshed sideways along the passage, floating swiftly just above the swirling floor.

I nearly panicked, knowing that I couldn't be discovered in here. But I had no control as my body continued swiftly floating along the moving floor. I had to choose an exit point—and fast.

Various openings seemed to offer the possibility to exit, but I was afraid. The floor was moving rapidly, and the exits were small. It seemed impossible—until I remembered what Milo had said about looking at things differently, like the dog with the big stick in its mouth. I had to see things in my own way.

Ula had simply exited with ease, despite the speed of the moving floor. At the next exit, I stopped thinking and jumped.

I landed in an interior hallway, where I took a moment to collect my thoughts: I had landed. It was dark. It was quiet. That meant no Invader was around. And I was no longer getting blasted by winds.

This was all good, I reassured myself, but I needed to be quick, and I had to be strategic. Otherwise, this would all be for nothing.

The interior presented two options. In one direction were faint blinking lights that led to a rounded corner, and I could not see beyond the bend. The other way led to a similar rounded corner, but a bright light shone from there. A window to the outside? It had turned daytime.

A tall silhouette appeared at the lighter corner. My heart skipped, and my head began to ache at the thought of encountering an

Invader. Ula and Jun were sensitive to my emotions. What if they all were? After all, I sensed the other Invaders' emotions in the video room. I had to temper my thoughts, soothe my racing heart, and ease my breathing.

The Invader's silhouette grew bigger. It was coming closer. I had to move. The dim corridor was my only choice.

Moving quickly beneath metallic pipes, on narrow beams, with the blinking lights reflecting off the walls around me, I reached the end of the corridor and found myself in front of a blue energy transport, just like the one Ula had used to travel up to the animal nursery and the video room.

This was it. This was their method of transport. But I did not want to travel up to the higher levels, swarming with Invaders. I needed to go down, to reach the ground.

It was time to test Milo's theory about the Invaders' skewed reality. Milo was convinced that I would discover the hidden trigger, if I just focused on the way that Ula taught me and looked at it in that mindset.

Standing before the blue energy transport, I thought of all Ula taught me. All of it had been the ideal training . . . but replicating that energy and intensity in my present challenging circumstances and worried about another Invader showing up, was complicated—likely impossible.

What if Milo had overestimated my abilities?

I had to try.

I breathed.

I calmed.

I closed my eyes.

Time stopped. I felt transported to the great window, as if I had never left. Overlooking the beauty of Earth with Ula's golden glow, growing and expanding toward me—enveloping me completely. I opened my eyes.

All around me, as I stood in that dim corridor, was that same glow. No window. No tranquil view. No Ula. But the glow came nonetheless, and it came from me.

Before me appeared something new: Several bright buttons lit up on the wall next to the transport. How could I have overlooked them? But I knew I hadn't. They simply were not there before. I had tapped into that transcendent power she spoke of and that which she had taught me.

My arm felt like it was a hundred pounds as I lifted it toward the buttons. With a trembling finger, I reached toward them. This could change everything, and I had no idea what would happen if it worked. I had to be courageous, just as Matthew had been on that bus for me. I had to do this for him—for all of them.

I pushed a button. The stream of blue energy circled around within the transport, but I had no way of knowing what that could mean. Whatever might happen, I had no choice.

The transport opened, and I jumped in.

When the transport closed again, I searched for something to grasp and waited for it to move.

Nothing happened.

Go down!

It didn't move.

Another Invader could come along and find me at any moment.

Milo's pellet.

I held the pellet above my head, hoping to trigger a response.

Two columns of lights appeared on the transport door, and it began to move.

The transport started upward.

No, no, no . . . not up!

I threw myself against the lighted columns and pushed one button after the next—every single button—while still holding Milo's pellet above my head.

"Down!" I yelled. "Not up! Go down!"

The transport stopped . . . delayed in suspension . . . went up several floors and then dropped. My body flailed along, and my stomach dropped.

The transport continued to fall for what seemed like forever.

Then it stopped. No jolt, no thud, but a smooth landing—so smooth, I suspected the transport had not actually hit the ground at all. The column of lights switched off.

My mind raced. If I wasn't on the ground, where could I be? And how would I get out?

Refusing to panic any more, I calmly pushed on the door . . . and it opened.

It can't be that easy, I thought.

But it was.

The door had opened.

A cool breeze struck my cheeks. The air was crisp, and it was the sweetest air I had ever tasted.

Looking out, I saw that it was dusk, and the colors were spectacular: blue sky being replaced by orange and pink hues of the falling sun. I remembered sunsets like these. A radiance shone in the distance, joining the chaotic sky—the light from a faraway hangar.

A single tear fell down my cheek.

The transport did not go all the way down, but the ground was just below me.

It was a drop, but I made it.

I was free.

ACKNOWLEDGMENTS

To Lauren and Matthew, thank you for not groaning every time (just most of the time) I bounced ideas off you while creating this story. Maybe you'll want to read the full book one day.

To Paula, thank you for reading every version of this story and being my biggest supporter. To Laura and to my family, thank you for all your support and encouragement.

Thank you to everyone else that helped and supported to get this story ready to share.

ABOUT THE AUTHOR

After more than two decades crafting persuasive narratives of her clients' stories for court, L. Galuppo ventured into the world of creative writing with her debut novel, *Eco Reign*. This fresh and gripping take on the alien invasion genre plunges readers into a unique and unsettling world where the focus shifts from human resistance to the harrowing journey of a teenage girl who becomes an alien's pet. While the aliens claim to have come to save Earth from humanity, their true motives are far more complex and sinister. When not weaving intricate plots about otherworldly invasions, L. Galuppo enjoys time with her family, friends, and pets, finding inspiration in the everyday moments of life.